Outdoor Stories

by J. Allan Dunn

Off-Trail Publications
Elkhorn, California

Front cover art by C. Reiter from
Short Stories, March 25, 1939

OUTDOOR STORIES
Copyright © 2011, Off-Trail Publications
ISBN-10: 1-935031-15-5
ISBN-13: 978-1-935031-15-4

OFF-TRAIL PUBLICATIONS
Elkhorn, California
offtrail@redshift.com

Printed in the United States of America
First printing: March 2011

CONTENTS

— — *Outdoor Stories* — —

J. ALLAN DUNN
1872-1941

That Which Is Not Indoors
By John Locke

J. ALLAN DUNN WAS ONE OF THE MOST PROLIFIC ADVENTURE WRITERS IN THE PULPS. An Englishman, born in 1872, he came to the United States at the age of 21, and never returned to his homeland.

He dabbled in the arts for many years, but struggled to find a successful niche. He wrote intermittently: stories, poems, newspaper articles, even vaudeville plays. Nothing gained him traction. He lacked a firm sense of direction. Finally, in 1913, he moved from San Francisco to New York on a do-or-die mission to establish himself as a professional writer. He was 42 years old, an advanced age, in 1913, for a man to be finding himself.

He sold a story to the *Saturday Evening Post*, "Tamatau of Totulu." It was a South Seas tale, of the type he'd been intending to write for a good many years. It appeared in the January 3, 1914 issue. The *Post's* editor, George Horace Lorimer, gave him encouragement and advice. Suddenly, Dunn's purpose became clear to him.

He appeared in *Adventure* for the first time in the October 1914 issue with "The Greenstone Mask," a 42-page adventure set in the South Seas and New Zealand. Editor Arthur Sullivant Hoffman must have loved the story. It received the cover illustration and led off the issue. Dunn was top-billed over Edgar Wallace, Talbot Mundy, and other well-known authors. Not bad for a writer with a thin record of publication and no following. Sullivant anticipated reader curiosity in *Adventure's* back-of-the-magazine column, *The Camp-Fire*: "After reading 'The Greenstone Mask' you'll want to know something about Allan Dunn."

Dunn would occasionally pop up in tonier magazines like the *Post* or *Collier's*, but it was to be the pulps that gave him his biggest stage. The rough-paper fiction magazines were on the rise when Dunn discovered them; Dunn's ability to weave solid prose, his innate sense of drama, and his knowledge of the world's adventure spots, made him an excellent candidate to help fill the industry's growing need for content. From that first appearance in *Adventure* through his death in 1941, Dunn would publish over twelve-hundred pulp stories. Many of them were lead novels and serials, the kind of stories that would find second life in newspaper serialization and book reprints. His main genres were adventure and western, but he wrote detective stories as well.

Dunn would write nearly eighty stories for *Adventure*, the majority from 1915-28. Some of his lead novels took up almost half the weighty magazine's length. But considering the entirety of his 27-year career in the pulps, *Adventure*, published by Ridgway, does not constitute the centerpiece of his legacy. At heart, Dunn was a Street & Smith man. Although he frequently appeared in pulps published by Munsey, Popular Publications, Standard Magazines (Thrilling), Doubleday, and others, fully 58% of his appearances were for Street & Smith, a company that cultivated regular contributors. (By comparison, his second best market was Munsey, mostly *Argosy* and *Detective Fiction Weekly*, which received about 15% of his career output.) His first Street & Smith appearance was in the November 30, 1914 *Top-Notch*; his last was in the August 30, 1941 *Wild West Weekly*, that issue hitting the newsstands several months after Dunn's death in March. *Wild West Weekly* had been his main market in the second half of his career. He appeared an astonishing 471 times, often twice in an issue. About 400 of the stories were split between two character series. The Whistlin' Kid, bylined by Emery Jackson, appeared 240 times; Bud Jones of the Texas Rangers, under Dunn's name, appeared 164 times.

Of course, appearances, which count 10-page stories, 100-page novels, and serial installments as equal units of measure, only give an approximation. The numbers are not currently available to factor in page-counts, or the most accurate measure of volume, word-counts, which pulp writers were typically paid by. However, a good guess from the available numbers is that the 58% figure would actually rise, owing to the fact that Street & Smith, as Dunn's major market, received most of his longer works.

Street & Smith's *Outdoor Stories* was an odd title. It lasted a mere thirteen issues, from September 1927 to September 1928. The company was known for its consistent publishing record, reliably producing long-running pulps like *Detective Story*, *Love Story*, *Western Story*, *The Popular Magazine*, *Top-Notch*, etc. Street & Smith magazines were institutions on America's newsstands. That record began to shift a bit with *Outdoor Stories*, the first of a series of perhaps experimental titles that were to be short in lifespan. We should note that other publishers started to experiment promiscuously in this period. The pulp field was shifting from general magazines that appealed to the broadest possible audience to specialized titles that were aimed at niche interests.

The history of *Outdoor Stories* is intertwined with another Street & Smith pulp, *Complete Story Magazine*. *Complete* started its life as *People's Magazine*, which debuted in July 1906, one of the company's earliest pulps. The final issue of *People's* was dated 2nd August 1924. It was converted to *Complete Story*, as part of an overhaul. The new title assured readers—some of whom minded—that the pulp would run no serials, as *People's* had, with the frustrating To Be Continued where The End was expected to appear. It also reduced in length from 192 to 144 pages, and in price from 20¢ to 15¢. *Complete* otherwise continued the editorial policy of *People's*, including its twice-a-month publication schedule. *Complete*, like *People's*, was genre nonspecific, but generally male in emphasis with adventure, western, and mystery stories.

The overhaul had been ushered through by the editor of *People's*, A.L. Sessions. He also edited *Sport Story Magazine* (another twice-a-month pulp) and *Sea Stories*, which meant that he, and his assistants, were getting out three titles and five issues every month, which was perhaps too much. In mid-1926, *Complete* was reduced to a monthly, renamed *Complete Stories*, and passed over to the editor of *Ainslee's*, Kenneth P. Littauer. Littauer soon left the company, ending up as fiction editor of *Collier's*. *Complete* then fell into the hands of staffer Edmund C. Richards, the third editor in less than a year. A few months later, Richards launched *Outdoor Stories*. He only ran one blurb for *Outdoor* in the writers' magazines:

> We are in the market for short-stories of 5000 to 8000 words; novelettes of 15,000 to 25,000 words, and good verse (not doggerel). Stories should be of the out-of-door variety, with plenty of action and human interest. Animal stories are desired. Our rate of payment is from 1 to 2 cents a word on acceptance. [*The Author & Journalist*, September 1927]

A richer description was included in the November 1927 *News Trade Bulletin*, Street & Smith's trade journal for news dealers:

> Like most of the Street & Smith magazines [*Outdoor Stories*] has a name which exactly suits it. In this publication appear only stories of the outdoors.
>
> It does not make any difference where in "outdoors" the action is laid, nor what kind of a story it may be. One thing is positive, however, and that is that no stories of indoor sports appear in this publication.
>
> For example, a single number may contain a Western story, a story of an exceptionally intelligent animal, such as a dog or horse, another may be laid in the wilds of Mexico. There may be a story of adventure on the high seas, a North Woods story, and then a long, broad jump to Africa, and so on.
>
> There is a big field for a magazine like *Outdoor Stories*, especially during the coming winter season, when so many men will be housed up, who practically live outdoors during the rest of the year.

The main rationale for creating the magazine was probably that Street & Smith lacked a pure adventure title. *Complete Stories* included mystery fiction and miscellaneous material; likewise *The Popular Magazine*. *Top-*

Notch was aimed at a younger audience, and included a lot of sports fiction. The rest of the Street & Smith titles—*Western Story*, *Detective Story*, etc.— were narrowly focused. It seems logical, then, that a pure adventure title that conformed to the product line would have been titled *Adventure Story Magazine*. But the word "adventure" may have been considered problematic. Ridgway's *Adventure*, established in 1910, was the marquee title in the genre, and at the time *Outdoor Stories* was created, no other publisher had poached "adventure" for a title. For instance, Fiction House went with *Action Stories*, and Clayton with *Ace-High Magazine*, both coming on the market in September 1921. It wasn't until Clayton introduced *Air Adventures* in October 1928, and then renamed *The Danger Trail* to *Adventure Trails* in January 1929, that the ban, if it existed, was lifted. Thereafter, "adventure" was used in any number of titles. It probably wasn't fear of trademark infringement that made the publishers reluctant; more likely, observance of professional courtesy. But when the pulps began to specialize in the late '20s, such niceties became increasingly unrealistic. "Adventure" is too basic a word.

And who was this *Outdoor Stories* editor? Edmund Clark Richards was born in Massillon, Ohio, just west of Canton, on January 25, 1876. His parents were Horace M. (*b.* 1849) and Emma Paul (*b.* 1856) Richards. They were married on March 25, 1873. Like his father before him, Horace was an Ohio native, and a blacksmith. Emma was an Ohioan, too; she kept the house. Edmund had one sibling, an older brother Warren, born in 1874, his name borrowed from Horace's father. Warren became a lumberjack and remained close to home.

After leaving high school, Edmund studied for the priesthood at St. Mary's Seminary, Cincinnati, the third-oldest Catholic seminary in the United States. It was a five-year program at the time. He was ordained in June 1899 at St. Mary's Church in Columbus, the first person from his immediate family to receive higher education.

He became rector of the Crooksville and Moxahala parishes in 1900, in the area just southwest of Zanesville, Ohio. He resided in Moxahala. He broke ground for a new church in Crooksville in 1901, which was completed that year. A priest's house was added in 1902, and became Richards' residence. In February 1906, he was appointed rector of St. John's Church in Logan, some twenty miles away. The man he replaced moved to a church in nearby Lancaster. All locations are within a narrow sector extending fifty miles east of Columbus, suggesting that parish priests tended to stay within a relatively confined area of the diocese.

Still, Richards has a record of travel, including an extended visit to New York City in 1906, and trips to Europe in 1910 and 1913. He published a critical article in the April 1911 *American Ecclesiastical Review*, "Architecture and the Church in the United States," which contained "a plea for better church architecture, by showing the intimate dependence of architecture on the ideas of religion." He railed against the "churches of modern commercialism," "monstrosities in stone and stucco." The article leaves the impression that Richards visited historic churches on his 1910 trip, e.g. "[The priest] has looked perhaps with awe upon the church at Amiens; stood in rapturous attention before the portals of Rheims, or felt his very heart leap up when he first beheld the splendor and the glory of Notre Dame de Paris"; "No one who is not familiar with the English Catholic churches can have any idea of their exquisite charm."

In 1907, Richards arranged for a marble high alter to be installed in St. John's. The alter has engraved upon it the images of his patron, St. Edmund, and St. John the Evangelist; as well as Richards' initials. During his ten years at St. John's, Richards also had installed tiled sanctuary floors, and he beautified the grounds.

In 1916, Richards resigned from the pastorate at Logan, requested to be deposed from the priesthood, and was put on suspension for six months, no doubt to give him time to reconsider. Nevertheless, the deposition was granted on December 15. We don't know the reason for his request, but there's an obvious conflict between his interest in the wider world and the restrictions of life in small-town Ohio.

Richards' draft registration, dated September 12, 1918, indicates that he was living in Manhattan. He listed his occupation as Roman priest, employed by the Bishop of Columbus in "special literary work." Since he had already left the priesthood, and Ohio, we interpret those statements as concealment of the fact that he was working as a freelance writer, and essentially unemployed. At 43 years old, he would not have been a candidate for soldiering. He was unmarried, and appears to have remained so his entire life.

The 1920 U.S. Census recorded him in January; he was still living in Manhattan, and employed as a magazine editor. Presumably, this was with Street & Smith. From October 1922 to February 1923, he placed four nonfiction pieces in *Western Story* under the name E. Clark Richards, all concerning the materials created by Indians, pottery, blankets, etc. He had two further articles in *Detective Story*, in 1923 and '24, under the name Edmund Richards. These articles almost certainly indicate his employment with Street & Smith. He has no other known publications in the pulps.

In June 1926, Richard Merrifield, son of author Izola Forrester, was hired by Charles Agnew MacLean as assistant editor for *The Popular Magazine*. MacLean had been *The Popular's* chief editor since 1905, the year Merrifield was born. In letters to his mother, Merrifield offered insights into his coworkers; quotes are available in the Izola Forrester Family Papers wiki (www3.iffp.com).

Merrifield complained that MacLean and Richards distracted him with their endless intellectual arguments. Merrifield eventually warmed to the older Richards, though, and they became friends; he included Richards in "Dick's Immortals," as he called his inner circle. In a 1928 letter, Merrifield described his officemate:

> My friend, Edmund C. Richards, editor of *Complete Stories*, told an odd story yesterday. Mind, he was brought up a Catholic in Rome, and learned his Latin and Greek and theology in a seminary. When he was my age he broke out of it and dashed to Paris and became the libertine. He lived the life of an English country gentleman for many years and cultivated his garden and collected antiques. Has read widely, and is a philosopher and follower of Santayana. Now he's an editor. He dresses beautifully, and has a theatrical, booming voice. Likes the women much, but despises the lure of the flesh and longs for the intellectual life pure and simple. Has thick black hair in pompadour, and a strong, clean-shaven face that is now a little flabby around the gills. He is forty-seven, I think—perhaps more. Anyway, he is delightful, and I like to hear his broad, deep English accent.

Richards actually turned fifty-three in 1928. Merrifield was off on another point, as well. Richards would have been Merrifield's age in 1899, the year he was ordained; the break-out dash to Paris must refer to Richards' 1910 trip, when he would have visited the churches. Presumably, the phrase "brought up a Catholic in Rome" means "brought up a Roman Catholic," and not that he spent time in Rome as a child. The "life of an English country gentleman" no doubt refers to Richards' years in Logan. Merrifield's colorful description is an example of how little of the real man emerges from the dry biographical data of names, dates, and titles; this brief passage is far superior in giving an impression of Richards, and it stitches his varied experiences together as the life of a single person.

As noted, Richards became editor of *Complete Stories*; this would have been several months into 1927. His previous assignments with the company aren't known, but each Street & Smith editor had up to three assistants to help with the tremendous number of submissions that came in. It's likely Richards had been an assistant on *Complete*, and probably *The Popular*, and that his turn for promotion to full editor had simply come due. *Outdoor Stories* was added to his responsibilities later in 1927, giving him two magazines a month to publish. In the late summer of 1928, three simultaneous changes were made to Richards' lineup. *Outdoor Stories* was dropped, replaced immediately by a WWI pulp, *Over the Top*, which shared its title, a reference to climbing out of the trenches to enter battle, with the bestselling Arthur Guy Empey novel of 1917. Great War fiction was all the rage in the pulps in the late '20s; Street & Smith was reaching forth for their slice of the pie. The third change was the return of *Complete Stories* to bimonthly publication. The net result was that Richards now had three issues a month to get out. In the space of a year-and-a-half, he'd gone from one to two, then three issues, which certainly suggests that he was proving himself a valuable man to the company.

Over the Top did a bit better than *Outdoor*, lasting twenty-one issues to *Outdoor's* thirteen. The last issue of *Over the Top* was dated June 1930. It was immediately replaced by *High Spot Magazine*, an adventure pulp aimed at juveniles. Richards put it rather bluntly in a solicitation blurb in *Writer's Digest*: "It is intended to appeal to readers with a lower I.Q. than those who read *Complete Stories*." That's a frustrated intellectual's view of the pulps. Richards may have regretted his choice of words because a month later, in *Writers' Markets & Methods*, he described *High Spot's* aims in more charitable language: "When I call it a juvenile I call it that advisedly, as it is a juvenile in the sense that *Action Stories* and other Fiction House magazines are juveniles. You don't 'write down' to hit it by any means, as it is for young folks of from anywhere from sixteen to sixty if you get what I mean." Other blurbs described the desired content: "*High Spot Magazine* is devoted to gripping stories of action and mystery, and embracing the whole world of man-adventure"; "[*High Spot*] is in need of novelettes of twenty to thirty thousand words, with speed and action, but with characters other than cowboys. For example, they may be truck drivers, oil drillers, or construction workers." But for all its editorial craftsmanship, *High Spot* only lasted ten issues.

Complete continued to motor along at two issues a month, but all three of Richards' "experimental" titles had failed. During the remainder of his tenure with Street & Smith, *Complete* would be his only advertised responsibility. The pulp underwent small variations. In 1931, *The Popular* was merged with *Complete*, with the resulting magazine named *The Popular Complete Stories*. It didn't mean much; it was just a way of killing *The Popular* while trying to guide its dwindling readership over to *Complete*. The title reverted back to *Complete Stories* after eight months. In 1934, only nineteen issues of *Complete* were published, down from the full complement of twenty-four; by the May 1935 issue it was a permanent monthly, renamed *Street & Smith's Complete Magazine* through the January 1936 issue. Having his responsibilities reduced to one issue a month may have left Richards feeling the job eroding under his feet. Indeed, Street & Smith would undergo a major contraction of their pulp line in late '37, an indication that many of their lesser titles had circulations too low to compete on the increasingly crowded newsstands. *Complete Stories* would be one of the victims. But Richards wasn't around for the coup de grâce. He left Street & Smith in the summer of '36, precise reasons unknown. Hazlett Kessler presided over *Complete* until its demise. Richards joined the Jacques Chambrun literary agency, whose main claim to fame would be in handling *Peyton Place* (1956). The agency also handled western author Louis L'Amour through the '40s and '50s. We don't know how long Richards stayed with the firm.

Richards began to publish on the side. No doubt, after spending many long years in the pulp ghetto, he yearned to publish the intellectual matter of which he was capable. Of course, wanting to be published, deserving to be published, and actually getting published, are three chambers of Hell whose doors don't necessarily connect. So it's not surprising to find a spotty record of accomplishment during this period. His first known piece is "The Challenge of John Steinbeck" in the Summer 1937 *North American Review*, an early piece of Steinbeck criticism that continues to be referenced. The remainder of his publications consist of ten book reviews that appeared in the *New York Times* from 1939-44. All were of intellectual or scholarly works, usually history.

No one grows up wanting to be an editor; it's a role that many unfulfilled would-be writers stumble into. And that's what the arc of Richards' life suggests: a penetrating intelligence, a desire to write that never found focus—as Dunn had—and a job as a pulp editor that probably started out, in his intentions, as stopgap employment, but lasted over sixteen years.

The trail runs mostly cold after 1944. In 1950, Richards appears to have gone on an around-the-world trip. A long-treasured dream to be indulged in his retirement, perhaps. He died on December 19, 1954.

He leaves an unusual legacy. He may be the only person to ever change careers from the priesthood to pulp magazine editing.

And now to return to J. Allan Dunn and *Outdoor Stories*. . . .

Since he was one of Street & Smith's biggest authors, popular in the adventure field, and had three stories in the magazine, he and *Outdoor Stories* must have been an instant match, right? It makes sense, but the payment records for the three stories, in the Street & Smith Archives at Syracuse University Library, tell a different story. "The Lagoon at Mareva," from the January 1928 *Outdoor* was received on April 17, 1925. "New Guinea Gold," from the July 1928 issue, was received on June 18, 1926. From about mid-1924 through mid-1926, at least 90% of Dunn's output was going to *Complete Story*, with the remaining miscellaneous material shared amongst *Adventure, Short Stories, Argosy*, etc. No other Street & Smith title published Dunn stories in this period, so we can safely conclude that "Lagoon" and "New Guinea Gold" were originally written for *Complete*. Both are quality stories, and they'd been paid for, so why were they set aside? The answer is to be found in the June 1925 and January 1926 issues of *The Author & Journalist*. Both issues ran a plea from *Complete Story* editors, warning of their overstock on long stories. This certainly applies to "New Guinea Gold" at 45,000 words; but "Lagoon," at 13,000 words, is only a short. Here we find that Dunn was probably a victim of his own prolificacy. During this period, he was in virtually every issue of *Complete*, sometimes with two stories. In that case, the second story was published under the byline of Joseph Montague. The February 25, 1925 issue is a case in point. It had a 57-page Dunn story leading off the issue, and a 28-page Montague story buried in the back. Dunn's 85 pages of content constituted over half of the 144-page issue's length. "Lagoon" may have been set aside because editor Sessions, wanting more variety, didn't want a third Dunn story in any one issue. The magazine couldn't keep up with Dunn; in fact, he may have been the contributor most responsible for the oversupply problem. The problem was exacerbated when editorship passed to Littauer, and publication dropped to a monthly. That's the end of Dunn's prolific period with *Complete*. From that point forward, he is seldom found in the magazine, meaning he probably never developed a strong relationship with either Littauer or Richards. Instead, he leaped over to Street & Smith's new pulp, *Wild West Weekly*. Its editor, Ronald Oliphant, became the primary recipient of Dunn's bounty, publishing his many stories from the first issue (August 13, 1927) forward.

When Richards took over *Complete*, he would have inherited the unpublished inventory; perhaps this was part of the inspiration for launching *Outdoor*, to use up good material that had already been purchased. It would have lessened the risk of the experiment. The other Dunn story reprinted herein, "Rama, the Rogue," *was* written specifically for *Outdoor Stories*. It was received on April 20, 1928, published in the August 1928 issue, and the subject of the cover illustration. It was an action story and an animal story, exactly what Richards had called for in his sole solicitation blurb.

Dunn received 2¢ a word for both "Lagoon" and "New Guinea Gold," receiving $250 and $980, respectively. By 1928, his rate had risen to 2½¢, and he received $525 for "Rama."

Richards, despite his gardening prowess, would probably not have been considered an outdoorsman; *Outdoor Stories* was just an assignment, unrelated to his personal interests. Dunn, on the other hand, was quite the sportsman, and the stories published in *Outdoor* reflect this. He was an avid sailor, his passion cultivated during five years he spent in Honolulu at the start of the century. During his many years in the New York area, he sailed with friends on Long Island Sound. This interest propels "The Lagoon at Mareva," and many other sea stories he wrote in his career. Dunn also enjoyed hunting, which is reflected in "Rama, the Rogue." "Rama" displays a measure of compassion for wildlife, though, so we shouldn't think of Dunn as a wanton big-game killer. Plugging a grouse was more his speed. All three of the stories show Dunn at his best, offering well-written, well-researched, and entertaining adventure fiction. Nowhere is this more true than in "New Guinea Gold" (or, as Dunn submitted it, "The Covered Trail"). It's an epic tale of friendship and revenge, reflecting a broad range of Dunn's interests and passions. It exhibits a wide-ranging knowledge of foreign places—people, flora, and fauna—the stuff that made Dunn a legend within New York's Explorers Club.

Why did *Outdoor* fail? Perhaps because *"Outdoor Stories"* was a colorless, indistinct title, not overly suggestive of the magazine's contents. It would be about the same as if a detective magazine were called *Indoor Stories*, a literal description for the most part, but not much of an inducement to the customer. Perhaps if Street & Smith had been bold enough to call it *Adventure Story Magazine*, the outcome would have been better.

Outdoor Stories

THE LAGOON AT MAREVA
By J. Allan Dunn

I

THE DOCTOR OF THE *MIOWERA*, ashore at Papeete, was drinking a rum punch with the chief engineer at the Cercle Bougainville—the club where all the copra and pearl buyers congregate. The doctor was speaking.

"If one were inclined toward the theory of Lombroso," he remarked, "there would be little trouble in cataloguing that chap with the ginger-colored hair."

"I dinna ken your Lombroso," said the chief. "He sounds like a dago, an' I hav'na much confidence in the judgment of dagoes. They're too easy excited. But I wad be inclined ta say that the mon ye speak of is about two pairts rogue, two scoundrel an' one bully. I dinna like the looks o' him. The lad that's wi' him is in bad company."

"Lombroso would agree with you about his looks," the doctor went on. "The theory I speak of was advanced by an Italian scholar who believed that there is a criminal type—a creature brought into the world predestined to crime—to be surely recognized by certain physical and moral traits. This man has most of them—a heavy jaw and a prognathous or outthrust chin; long, large, projecting ears; a skull that lacks symmetry; a rectilinear nose; strong wrinkles on his face, and eyes that lack ordinary, human softness—glassy and feline."

"Ye've used some jaw-breakin' wor-r-ds, but I follow your drift. When he glanced at us as we cam' in, I noticed his e'en glarin'—pale, chiny blue, wi' no mair expression than marbles."

"He shows other characteristics. He uses his left hand for his glass, but he is not awkward with his right. Ambidexterity is one of the peculiarities marked by Lombroso. Also, abundance of hair on the head, though usually a scanty beard. Large cheek bones. Unusual width of the extended arms and, with them, an extraordinary, apelike agility that, so far, our ginger-haired friend has not displayed. Also, frequent gesticulation, which he invariably uses.

"It is the general consensus of opinion that Lombroso jumped at his conclusions too hastily—that bad blood through inheritance, consequently weakened fibers and abnormal formation of tissues may well produce a type that is susceptible to the more or less criminal impulses that are resident in the best of us, but that environment has much, if not everything, to do with the outcome."

"Ah! I' that case," said the chief, "I should be verra inclined to think that he was bor-r-n i' a jail an' brought up i' a reformatory. I'm wi' your Lombroso this far—that there are some men who wull never be drooned. He has a hangdog look to me, though the lad wi' him doesna appear to ha' discovered it. An', by the same token, the young un is no fule. He likely lacks experience but, if his jaw doesna stick oot as far as the other's, it's nane the less a good fightin' jaw, an' the lad has a bonny look. I'm thinkin' he's no gudgeon to a pike. Shall we be off, sin' oor glasses are empty, though 'tis unco' hot outside?"

"I'll prescribe another punch," said the doctor.

Before they had finished the cool drinks the pair they had been observing got up and went out together, the elder talking freely, with many movements of his hands and long arms to emphasize his arguments, the younger listening attentively and every now and then asking a question.

Outside, they were joined by a third, a black-bearded white man, whose skin was tanned as dark as a native's. The ginger-haired one pointed to a none-too-smart schooner lying with many others at the sea wall of the harbor. They walked toward it, went aboard and vanished into the cabin.

A Tahitian acquaintance of the doctor came to the table, sat down and ordered a third round. The medico asked him if he had noticed the men who had left—if he knew anything of them.

"I know 'Bully' Burr. The young chap with him arrived on the last steamer. Burr has got him in tow for some purpose that will probably serve as an initiation into the gentle art of losing his money. Burr's here with the rest of the pearling fleet, waiting to start for Mareva in the Tuamotus—or the Paumotus, as they now call 'em. The *rahui*—that's the closed season— comes off the lagoon at Mareva next week."

"Pearler, is he?" broke in the doctor.

"He calls himself that. He's got the name of a poacher and a pirate. Takes shell out of season or steals it. You might call him a hijacker. He hasn't been caught at it yet, but he's got a bad name. He and his partner, or mate, 'Black' Johnson, are a precious pair of scoundrels, to my mind. Young Denison has been warned against them, but you can't do much in that line with a lad who's keen to go after pearls.

"Denison's got some money and he wants to buy in. Not enough to get a schooner of his own, I imagine, and there are none for sale, anyway. Then he knows nothing about the practical end of it. Burr's probably broke. He spends his money like a buccaneer. He'll take in Denison, more ways than one, but Denison will have to buy his experience, like most of us. The school of the South Seas is one of hard knocks. Those who get their degrees, and come by them honestly, turn out to be worth while.

"Denison's a nice kid, but a bit headstrong, which is all right at his age. He'll come through none the worse, I imagine, unless Burr gybes the schooner on him some day and knocks him overboard. But he hasn't committed murder yet, to my knowledge.

"The government has its eye on him. He's sailing close to the limit, and, if the law ever grips him, he'll have short shrift. That bird will wind up on Noumea in the penal colony, if he's lucky. If not, he'll swing. He looks like the rascal he is, but he's a good talker and full of tales to fire a youngster that's adventurous. If Denison buys in with him, he'll get his fill of adventure—of sorts."

II

ROGER DENISON, TWENTY-FIVE, SIX FEET TALL on the naked feet that trod the wet planks of the *Akua*—the schooner in which he was now a third owner— buoyant with vitality and the novelty of his surroundings, confident in his ability to look out for himself, had no misgivings as the *Akua* slipped through the narrow, treacherous pass in the barrier reef of Papeete harbor. Favored by a wafting breeze, the ship met the waves of the open sea, heading with the rest of the fleet for the Pearl Islands of the Tuamotu Archipelago.

The *Akua* was plainly not the slowest of the schooners that started for the great lottery to be held in the lagoon of Mareva Atoll. She lacked paint and she was infested with cockroaches. She reeked of former cargoes of copra, shell and sharks' fin. Her main cabin was disorderly, her tiny staterooms were musty cubicles, sadly in need of a scrubbing, of clean blankets and bedding. But her lines were curves of speed and beauty, her canvas was new and her rigging good—thanks to the money of the new partner, whose cash had also supplied the provisions and certain demijohns of liquor, besides paying the overdue wages of her crew.

The salt breeze blew strong and sweet and hummed through her gear.

There were rainbows about her prow, and the swash of the surge, as the peacock-blue sea divided at her bows and closed in at her stern, was music in his ears.

It was late afternoon when they sailed. The sky was sulphur-colored behind the fantastic mount of Moorea. Here and there it showed openings of blue, deeper than the richest sapphire, revealing infinite space. The lagoon, unruffled within the barrier reef, lay like a lake of fluid gold, in sharp contrast to the wind-clawed sea, colored like ripened Concord grapes, reflecting the sunset on its rippling crests.

An island in the lagoon was a gem of olivine, set in the yellow water. On the slopes of the mountain, the ridges and cliffs assumed mysterious shapes in the shadow that was the dragging cloak of departing day. The land wind cleft the shoreward palms, and the spray on the reef was like gray smoke.

The sulphur sky glowed and faded to pale green. The short tropic twilight melted. The peak was indigo against purple, with lights twinkling faintly along the shore in wan imitation of the stars. The already high moon took on the color of beaten gold. Blows like a drum saluted the bows of the *Akua* in a roll of welcome. The schooner shifted her course, heeling, the sheets hauled by the chanting native crew, cat-footed, naked save for breechclouts. The savor of supper cooking came from the galley. The cabin twilight was illumined.

"Time for a snifter," called Burr, his head out of the slide. Denison roused himself from his reverie—a dream of gleaming pearls probed from rough-coated shells, of Fortune beckoning beyond the ocean's rim—and went below.

He took his measure of gin dashed with bitters and a squirt of lime, marveled at the half tumblers poured down the throats of Burr and Johnson and fell to with gusto on the meal of fresh fish, taro tops and sweet potatoes, followed by a soggy pie of canned apples. It all tasted like a feast to him. The world was his oyster. He might lack a sword to open it, but there were other methods, and he was certain that he would find within a pearl of great price.

Burr, telling of coral beaches and grass villages under the palms, of golden-skinned girls with flowers in their dusky hair, of sea monsters and lagoons that held fortunes for the adventurous, was a modern Ulysses, rough and ready, but good, jovial company. He was learned in the ways of the sea and therefore to be envied and respected. Johnson, the black-bearded mate, taciturn, performing prodigies of knife shoveling and loud mastication, was a good fellow.

Denison would rather have gone on deck when they settled down to more gin and a worn deck of cards. "Cutthroat poker," they called it, but it was life, and the loss of thirty dollars did not vex him. Were there not pearls in

Mareva Lagoon to be brought up by the native divers who had thronged there to be hired as experts? He almost fell asleep over his last hand, which he lost, and went on deck to sleep on a mat, not so easy a matter as he had imagined, with the schooner veering as the breeze changed.

But the harping of the wind in the rigging, the hoarse orders of Johnson, the native chants of the sailors as they hauled in or out, served as a lullaby. He slept until the beams of the rising sun levered open his eyelids, where he lay on the slanting deck, and awakened him to a sparkling sea that ran in faceted pyramids to the clear horizon. Flying fish planed in frantic endeavor to dodge the hunting school of hungry dolphins, and the reef points slatted on the stiffly hollowed sails.

He got a grinning boy to fling a bucket of water over him half a dozen times, drawn fresh and hissing from overside in a canvas pail, making his firm body tingle from head to foot. A Tahitian quartermaster was at the wheel, his brown skin gleaming as the muscles rippled under the skin. The odor of coffee came from the galley. There was no sight of land, only the challenging mystery of the open sea. Burr came on deck in his pajama pants, his long arms a-swing, frowsy and yawning, conning the course and the sails.

He rapped out an order, and a native came running with a young coconut and a square bottle. Burr poured a generous slug of the liquor into the cool milk of the nut and drank it noisily, then winked at Denison.

"Try a Tuamotu eye-opener," he said, but Denison shook his head.

"You'll come to it," said Burr with a grin. "Try a hooker in your coffee."

The mate slept through their breakfast and came on deck later to take the wheel under an azure sky and broiling sun. Denison found the deck burning his feet and put on his sneakers. Johnson let him take the wheel, at Burr's suggestion, and he felt the tug of the canvas wings and the lurch of the hull set against his strength, as, with the water for fulcrum, he levered the schooner to its course, mastery invigorating him.

"We've passed most of 'em," said Burr. "The *Akua* don't look so good, but she's got the heels of any of 'em. Nothin' like havin' a fast ship. Comes in handy lots of times. We'll paint her up when we git back. Her bottom's clean, anyway—copper-sheathed. You see the first to land git the pick of the divers.

"There's some knows the different lagoons like so many books, some knows pearl oysters by the look of 'em, some as can stay down half again as long as the rest, some who can go down twice as often. An' there's a few have got all them advantages rolled inter one. You can afford to pay them extra, an' they're bid fer quick."

He did not add the fact that most of these expert divers knew him too well and were none too keen to work for him. While he was engaged upon an apparently legitimate enterprise this trip, Burr never overlooked chances because they might not be entirely according to the general conception of honesty. Cheating divers out of their pay and percentages was the same thing to him as cheating at cards—a pastime, pleasant and profitable.

That afternoon they overhauled a barkentine, hull down to leeward, and Burr chuckled.

"That's the concession ship," he told Denison. "She started half a day ahead of us. Carries the folks thet run the amusements. You'll find Mareva all fixed up like a fair. Everything, from hot dogs to a movie film—toy balloons, roundabouts, chuck games an' pin alleys. Two 'Johnny Darms' aboard of her, to keep the peace. It's a great sight, son."

On toward evening, a sail was sighted ahead of them, gradually heightening on the horizon. Johnson was in charge of the deck at the time and sent a native named Kopeke to call the skipper. Kopeke was a sort of quartermaster, taking spells at the wheel and even occasional charge of the deck. He had a cheery face, intelligent and nearly always smiling. His beach English was quite intelligible, and he had showed Denison several little tricks about steering, in a manner that was friendly and unobtrusive.

Denison liked him from the start, wondering a little that the man was not more of a favorite. He came from Mareva, he said, and knew the island reefs and currents, though he did not claim to be an expert diver. He was working his passage back, it seemed, at which Denison wondered a little. A hand as useful as he ought to command wages over and above his board. He resolved to put in a word for the man or to give him something out of his own pocket.

Kopeke seemed to be in awe, or fear, of Burr and, in lesser degree, of Johnson. Denison heard the skipper bellow at him for disturbing his nap. Soon he emerged, scowling, Kopeke coming almost cringingly behind him. But Burr's mood changed when he saw the sail and took a second look at it through the glasses that hung at the head of the companionway.

"It's the *Wikiwiki*, all right," he said to Johnson. "Claims to be the best boat of the fleet," he said. "We'll beat 'em in, with a little good luck, eh, Johnson? Trim that beggar's comb a bit. Too blamed cocky about his boat, is Logan."

He rubbed his hands, his good humor restored.

They played poker again that night, and Denison lost twenty-odd dollars. He did not have many left now, but there was his third share of the profits of the trip. He had been lucky to get established so soon, he fancied. His share had cost him twenty-five hundred dollars, practically all he had brought from the States, a slender inheritance from his father.

But it would not do to play away all his end at poker with men who seemed able to win from him consistently. It was true that his luck might turn, but he sensed that the skipper and his mate regarded him as a tenderfoot in cards. Two or three times he had seen looks passed between them that smacked of covert amusement. He noticed also that if he won at all, it was usually on his own deal, but he did not lay any stress on that.

At six bells he announced himself as out of spare cash. He had rather expected the suggestion that he should play on credit against his lay of the profits and generously credited the pair with a virtue they did not possess when they made no such proposition. That Burr did not care to play for a share he had no intention of passing over never occurred to him.

He went on deck and found Kopeke at the wheel. He asked for it and fancied Kopeke handed it over a little reluctantly. Kopeke gave the course, southeast by east, with a wind that was strong and almost due aft, so that main and fore were out wing and wing, the schooner running before the breeze, the moon halfway down over the starboard quarter.

Denison's seamanship had been confined to bay sailing off San Francisco, and to an occasional run down the coast to Monterey and San Diego. He had not done much night sailing, and he found it none too easy to keep the *Akua* on her course. Daytimes he had the flag at the peak to watch against danger of a gybe. Now it was different. The big seas came sliding up aft, gleaming brilliantly, lifting the schooner like a cork on their great shoulders. Twice Kopeke, hovering near, caught at the spokes, as the vessel swung, and the wind threatened to get back of the mainsail, before Denison could check her.

"Suppose she go along all the same gybe, capitani he plenty mad," said Kopeke.

Burr and Johnson were playing cribbage now. He could hear their voices counting the crib, the occasional jeers of Burr, who seemed to be winning, the inarticulate growls of Johnson and the clink of bottle and glass.

Kopeke touched him on the shoulder.

"We catchum *Wikiwiki* soon," he said, pointing to port.

Denison craned to look around the mainsail and caught a glimpse of the schooner they had been pursuing, her sails silver in the moonlight. To his surprise she carried a reef in her main.

"Maybe sail tear," said Kopeke. "She too fast, that *Wikiwiki*." He seemed to make an excuse for the other craft. The *Akua*, gliding up a wave, lurched. A gust brought the boom of the mainsail slightly inboard, and Kopeke hastily clutched at the wheel.

"Better I take," he said. Denison, vexed at his lack of skill, relinquished the spokes. He meant to acquire skill in seamanship, though his position was nominally that of supercargo, the duties of which office he had also to learn. He had a book of navigation in his cabin, and he had hoped to get Burr to show him how to take a sight and work out position, but the skipper had not produced a sextant, He was sailing by dead reckoning, sure of his course, of the impossibility of missing the eighty-odd isles of the archipelago.

There was a bellow, as the skipper came up the companionway, cursing at Kopeke. Kopeke shrank as if from an expected blow.

"My fault, skipper," said Denison. "I had the wheel. I was looking at the *Wikiwiki*. She's abeam."

Burr stepped forward, standing just abaft the mainmast. He came back with more complacency.

"You better let the wheel alone nights, especially with a follerin' wind," he said. "We want to beat that beggar Logan so bad he'll quit braggin'."

"He's got a reef in his mainsail."

Burr glared at him for a moment, his eyes glittering in the moonlight.

"If he's afraid of his sticks in a capful of wind, so much the better fer us," he said.

Denison was inclined to accept Kopeke's explanation as the more reliable. He did not think that Burr believed what he said. It was a little thing, a straw that showed which way the breeze blew. For the first time, a doubt of Burr's sportsmanship entered his mind. The skipper was intent only upon the business end of things, he reflected, and let it pass.

Well after midnight he awoke to gaze at a galaxy of stars, flaming in a sky of ebony. The breeze had failed, and the *Akua* was rolling. Burr and Johnson were quarreling in the cabin. There came the crash of glasses and a curse.

"Call me a cheat, will ye? Why, you dirty swab, I'll make a steak out of your face."

"No, you won't. An' you'll call *me* no names. A fine license you got to talk about fiddlin' cards. Why—"

Denison's mat lay between the low wall of the cabin house and the rail. He raised himself on one elbow to peer through the opened skylight. He saw Burr rise and strike at Johnson, who dodged the blow. There was the gleam of a knife in the mate's hand. Then Burr's long arm shot across the board like an ape's, gripping Johnson's wrist, twisting it until the blade fell to the ground and the mate's face twitched with pain. That was Burr's left arm and hand. A blunt revolver appeared in his right, shoved under Johnson's nose.

"Pull steel on me, will you? I'll feed you a bullet, you—"

Hate and fear were in the bulging eyes of the mate. The gleam of yellow teeth showed in his black beard, through a slime of foam. Baffled murder was in his heart. Burr thrust the gun forward until it fairly rattled against the other's teeth.

"You know where I can send *you*, my bucko," said the skipper. "I've got the goods on you. And I've got them planted where they'll be dug up and shown in the right quarter if anything happens to me, foul or fair. I'm insurance for your neck, 'Black Tom.' Think of that before you pull a knife on me again. Now then, did you shift those cards—or didn't you? If you want to talk again this side of hell, speak up."

Burr's voice was filled with desperate purpose. It held Denison in a sort of paralysis at this sudden stripping off of bluff good-fellowship from the two who were his partners, who held his money. Burr had the whip hand of the mate by knowledge and evidence of some crime that would hang him—that was clear. It was also plain that he would not flinch at murder in his fury.

He could see the flesh back of thumb and forefinger bulge on the skipper's hand, as he squeezed the pistol to the pull. He saw the ugly hammer lifting slowly. Johnson saw it, too.

"Damn you—yes, I cheated!" he gasped.

"Then I win," said Burr and lowered the gun, sweeping the stakes up with his left palm. "Take the deck, mister, I'm turning in."

Denison lay down again on his mat, his heart beating fast. It was not fear that bothered him so much as the knowledge that he was unarmed, partnered with desperate men who had cheated him at cards and doubtless meant to cheat him out of his share in the ship and her profits. He would have to go carefully until he perfected plans for his own protection.

His jaw tightened with the determination not to be tricked. Probably they despised him, and he might use that to advantage as a cloak for timely action. But he was, beyond doubt, in peril. He did not believe either of them would hesitate to kill and then throw his victim to the sharks. All he had was in this venture, and he did not intend to be done out of it.

He saw the mate's face, plain in the lowering moon, emerging from the hood of the companionway, evil as a thwarted devil's.

Johnson glanced at the binnacle, cursed Kopeke for being off his course, which he was not, and walked to the rail, stooping to look down closely at Denison, who feigned sleep.

He had sought adventure. It looked as if he had run afoul of it.

III

IT WAS THE AFTERNOON OF THE THIRD DAY when the palms of the first of the Tuamotu atolls showed like pins stuck into the blue velvet of the sea. The islands seemed to wade toward them, rising out of the water, showing a faint fringe of green that was based at last by a white fringe of foam. The sea lost its brilliant blue and became marbled in green and brown, where the mushroom corals reared close to the surface, almost awash. The foresail and staysail were furled and, under jib and main, they cautiously skirted through the shallows that, beset with currents, gave the atolls the name of the Dangerous Archipelago and put insurance premiums up.

With Kopeke at the crosstrees, Burr himself at the wheel, they wove a hazardous way between the fairy islets. The wind was their friend, the current their enemy, as they glided through the twisting channels, guided by the clear call of Kopeke from aloft.

It was fine navigation, with the hiss of creaming surf about them, with now and then the crash of breakers cascading on a reef within a biscuit's toss. Burr's face was grim, his eyes anxious, as he barked his orders in response to Kopeke's hails and the mate echoed, with the native crew jumping to obey, trimming sail, and twice fending the too close-hauled schooner off from the coral fangs.

The sun was close to the horizon when Kopeke at last called out, triumphantly, "Mareva! Mareva!" and, twisting his legs about the main halyards, came sliding down to the deck. Burr puffed out his lips in relief and turned over the wheel. From now on Kopeke knew his way as well as the keeper of a maze. He gripped the spokes with confidence, his bare legs compassed out, his splay feet gripping the deck.

The dusk came sifting down. Lights showed ashore. A red and green beacon eyed out. In the last of the twilight, Denison caught a flutter of flags, a line of wooden shacks, and then the men jumped to the sheets, laying the canvas almost flat, as Kopeke spun the wheel. The schooner shot into what seemed the middle of a maelstrom of spouting, roaring waters, rearing hills and fountains of spume through which she hurtled.

Then, suddenly, she was in a quiet harborage, an oval lake that seemed miles long in the nightfall, set about with rustling palms. The chain rattled out, as the canvas sank to the boom. The *Akua* glided in a little way and stopped gently, nosing at her cable.

Theirs was the first arrival of the fleet from Papeete, although there were already other craft in the lagoon, coming from different places. Not all the concessionaires were with the barkentine, and Denison found, when he went ashore, that the flags he had seen were part of their display. Tents had been erected in the choice places along a strip of wide, white sand, which would ultimately be the midway of the little island carnival. A portable engine chugged away, supplying storage batteries for the lights that swung in festoons of red and green and blue and amber over the attractions.

Burr and Johnson went off directly to the house of the island head man, a half-white ancient named Parker, who welcomed them, if not with effusion, at least with a grunt at sight of the demijohn they bore.

Denison walked along the outer shore line. He discovered that Mareva was an irregular oval of small islets, or sections of an inner reef, linked together and presenting at low tide a fairly continuous line of land. There coconuts, pandanus, wild oranges and bananas grew. The lagoon, he estimated, roughly, was about three miles long and about a mile wide.

He found another opening to the lagoon, besides the one through which they had entered, and discovered that there was an outer, sunken reef that broke the first fury of the sea. Between this rampart and the circling reef that was also the land itself, there was a moat of comparatively calm water. Thus the waves broke only lightly upon the coral blocks of the seaward beach, while the two main entrances and the smaller, shallower breaks acted as sluices. Ultimately, he imagined, the whole lagoon might become choked with coral growth and the atoll become an islet proper, instead of an annular reef.

Under the moon the lagoon seemed milky, opalescent, reflecting the stars dully, lacking the transparency he had expected. He fancied that this might be a condition of the tide, then laid it to shallowness, as he saw certain places toward the far end that were clear and dark, holding the shadows of the palms like a drowned, inverted forest.

Here was the great pool of the lottery in which he hoped to find a prize. Now to that chance was added the uncertainty of his being able to get his share. The vision of the quarrel in the cabin was a little dulled, but, when he tried to argue with himself that there was no danger so long as he kept his head, that Burr and Johnson would not dare openly to rob him, there came up the grim suggestion that "dead men tell no tales," that the agreement between them had never been recorded and that his copy of it was in his own pocket.

Johnson's face emerging from the cabin in baffled hatred, the click of the automatic's muzzle against the mate's teeth—these were memories clear enough to be sinister. They had used him for a "sucker," needing money to buy new sails, to replenish their stores and pay back wages—if indeed they had paid them and not kept the money for themselves.

Not every one was going to get pearls. There might be universal disappointment—even with the shell. It took five years to grow good shell from spat. Seven years meant triple values. Mareva had been closed for eight. There would be plenty of shell, but would it be worm-eaten, or would the little red crabs have spoiled the crop?

Pearls were always a gamble. In a lagoon like this, after so long a *rahui*, the most inexpert diver might chance upon the grand prize, though of course the experts, using their water glasses, noting the bottom conditions and the growth of certain weeds, would bring up the greater average.

If the *Akua's* outfit were lucky beyond the ordinary, if they secured gems of any value, Denison was now fairly certain that they would try to do him out of his share, perhaps by cheating, perhaps with subtlety. A big value would make them greedy, a small one discontented, unwilling to divide. He imagined that they might openly attempt to cheat him in such manner that he must resent it or prove himself the laughable gull.

If he started to quarrel, that might be the end of him. The ferocious, astounding agility of Burr in his lightning attack against the knife was not calculated to improve the nerve of an unarmed man. It was one against two. However much Johnson might hate Burr, that latter scoundrel had been clever enough to protect himself by insuring that Johnson would be denounced upon his death, and the two would undoubtedly make common cause against their young partner.

Walking under the stars, with the palms rustling overhead, land crabs scuttling over the sand and the steady pound of waves in his ears, the feeling of being a stranger in a strange land was intensified. Out here every man was for himself. It was the frontier of the sea. He had to figure his own battle. To acknowledge himself gulled would mean that he would be laughed at. And he had been warned against Burr in Papeete, more than once.

The gendarmes—the two Johnny Darms whom Burr had spoken of contemptuously—would not act on his assumption that his partners were going to carry out a swindle. He must wait.

Denison was an older man, in looks and thought, when he came back from that stroll. His jaw was firmly set, and his eyes shone with determination. Burr might be a wizard with a weapon, but he had done some shooting himself at various times. Some way or another he must try to get hold of a gun. He had a fixed desire to show that he was to be reckoned with on even terms.

He had only seven dollars left, five of which he meant to give to Kopeke. But he was no longer uneasy; nervousness had left him, and he was grimly determined not to be defrauded. At least he was forewarned—this time by his own observation—of the kind of men with whom he had identified himself. He resolved to watch closely for the first sign of trouble, then to make the first move and make it a decisive one. They were quite capable of sailing away and leaving him on Mareva. But there was slight danger of that as long as the pearling season was on.

He had come ashore with Burr and Johnson, and the boat was still moored to the inner shore by a rope fastened to a slab of coral. Song—or what was intended for it—was coming from Parker's shack, where crude revelry was in full swing. He heard Burr's voice leading.

> "A-rovin'—a-rovin'; rovin' has been my ruin.
> So fare you well, my black-eyed belle,
> I'll never see you more!"

And then came the raucous chorus of a dozen men, masters and mates of the vessels that had come direct from other lagoons on which there was no *rahui*, tempted by the opening of Mareva.

Denison felt a sudden revulsion toward them. This was life, all right, but he had glimpsed its seamy side. He could not get away from that howling, even aboard the boat, and he imagined that it would be kept up all night long. The voices were drunken. As long as the liquor lasted, they would make a night of it, and he did not doubt but what there was plenty. Burr and Johnson would come aboard boisterously and turn out surlily.

The *rahui* was not to be declared officially off until the day after to-morrow.

To-morrow there would be more visiting, more drinking, the start of the carnival. No liquor was allowed to be sold under the law, but every schooner brought plenty, and there was always palm toddy, fermented concoctions of oranges or the root of the ti plant to be had.

He had not noticed any mosquitoes. Fresh water was scarce on Mareva; visitors depended on their own supply for cooking and washing, using coconuts for drinking. So there was lack of breeding grounds for the insects, he supposed. This immunity made him determined to sleep ashore. He walked again up the beach, this time on the lagoon side, where the yelling of the "rovers" was only a faint echo. He dug a hollow for his hip in the sand of a pandanus grove and turned in as he was.

He slept heavily and late, awakening to discover the lower lagoon lined with craft, moored or mooring. The barkentine was in, and boats were already passing between it and the shore, with Barker's puttering launch towing two rafts on which were stowed the paraphernalia of the concessionaires.

The *Akua's* boat was gone, and he saw it trailing at the stern of the schooner. There was smoke coming from the galley stovepipe, and it quickened his appetite. He had paid for that grub. So for a quarter he hired a native to take him off in a canoe. The American coin was familiar currency to the smiling Tuamotuan.

Kopeke was on deck, cleaning the brass rails that guarded the glass of the cabin skylights, using an old rag and liquid metal polish. Denison was surprised to see him, having understood that Kopeke's unpaid duty ended with their arrival at Mareva, but he took the occasion to give him the five dollars, a gold piece he had brought with him from California. Kopeke's delight was only curbed by his fear of awakening the skipper and the mate, who, he explained, were still asleep.

"You staying on board?" Denison asked him. Kopeke's face clouded.

"Lele while, mebbe. Suppose capitani he want."

"But you're not going back with us?"

Kopeke shook his head.

"I get along of too much trouble at Papeete one time," he said. "One time I find a girl along that place. She born along on Amanu, all same Tuamotu. She like me—I like her, plenty much. One Tahiti man, he try too hard make that girl like him. That no good, so one time he try to kill me. By golly for damn, I too quick for that Tahiti fella.

"I take his knife this place"—he showed Denison a scar near his left elbow where he had warded off the blow—"same time I make my knife eat his flesh—drink his blood. By golly, too much blood he come. Capitani hide me when police look for me to hang me. All same that man go dead. I not see that girl again. Not so much good. She tell police. So capitani bring me back to Mareva. That plenty good, only too much he get mad sometime'."

Denison remembered now that Kopeke had not appeared on deck until the *Akua* was at sea. He imagined there was truth in the story, but wondered whether Burr had not colored it somewhat to suit his own purposes. It seemed a favorite device with the skipper to "get something" on his associates and hold it over them to his own advantage.

"Aren't you afraid of the gendarmes who are on the barkentine?" he asked.

Kopeke shook his head.

"Capitani speak he fix them all right," he said.

Denison had heard tales of the bribing of lesser French colonial officials, but he doubted whether Burr's influence could fix things for a murderer. He asked the name of the girl and the jealous lover, resolved to look up the affair when he returned to Papeete, to ease Kopeke's mind if the "too much blood he come" had been only a superficial wound. Kopeke had not been the attacker, according to his own story.

"Everything all right now," Kopeke grinned. "I got one girl here on Mareva. Before I go, she speak she no like me. Now I come back, she like me too much. I still like. Bimeby I tell her that, mebbe so. Not too quick."

The roar of Burr sounded in the cabin below, calling for his eye opener. Kopeke diligently bent to his work, the talk went out of him, and Denison went to stand at the rail and watch the last of the arrivals until breakfast.

A sloop came nosing in, one headsail on a stubby sprit, and a short club on the foot of the jib and a single sheet for ease in tacking. It was a weather-beaten craft of some eight tons, its sail patched in many places, worse off by far for need of paint than the *Akua*. It sailed sluggishly for the look of its lines, which were good enough, suggesting that it would have been the better for a haul-out on a beach or marine railroad with a cleaning-off of the marine growth of weed and shells that tropic waters foster.

There was a small cockpit, with most of the deck room covered by a trunk-cabin top. At first Denison thought there was a boy at the wheel, and he waved his hand in cheery greeting as the sloop went close by. An old man, gray-bearded, gaunt of body, bronzed of skin, with a red nose like a lobster's claw, stood in the bows, ready to lower sail and send over the patent anchor, as soon as the mooring was picked out from what the fleet had left of convenient holding ground.

Then he saw that the slender, upright figure at the wheel was that of a girl, wearing a middy blouse and duck pants. Her cropped hair was dark brown, revealing glints of copper in the sun. She had a broad forehead and an oval face, tanned a true bronze. Vivid red lips gave strong contrast. But it was her gray eyes gazing up at him, after a swift gauging of the course ahead, that held him with their haunting wistfulness.

They looked at him directly, searchingly, and with a first suggestion of scorn that melted as she saw his embarrassment at his mistake. Denison realized instantly that here was the sort of girl—for all the shabby boat and her darned clothing—who held herself aloof from that pearling crowd, armoring herself in pride against attempts at familiarity that, beyond doubt, must come her way.

This he read in her eyes, and more. There is something about the thoroughbred in gameness, in carriage, in every line, that is instantly recognizable. What she read in his own eyes was enigmatic, but a slow flush appeared beneath her tan, and then she suddenly smiled.

It was not a face that often smiled, he fancied, remembering the ancient mariner in the bows with his telltale nose and the tangled beard and untrimmed hair, but it suddenly broke into charming contour, a dimple in either cheek, a flash of small white teeth. He grinned in return, and then the sloop glided past on the flood and left him gasping.

Even in Tahiti, white girls were scarce. To find one, like this, on a remote atoll, left him as astounded as if he had picked up a shell at sea margin and found a perfect pearl within the gnarled exterior.

Burr came on deck, gross in his rumpled, soiled pajamas, his eyes red with drinking, heavy with sleep. He stumbled over the bottle of metal polish, and the fluid ran over his foot, fiery with acid.

"What the hell!" He broke off his curses to aim a vicious blow at the cowering Kopeke, who managed to dodge but could not evade the catlike agility of the man, who seemed to break from sluggishness with a dynamic burst of energy that was startling.

One long arm snaked out and caught the native's left arm above the wrist. The same instant the other arm was pinioned. Kopeke twisted about with both wrists held now in the grasp of one great hand. The skipper frogged him to the rail and caught up a length of rope used for becketing the wheel. With this he beat Kopeke about the head and shoulders, the stout line raising welts, until the writhing Tuamotuan broke loose and crouched on his haunches, his arms wrapped about his head.

Denison stepped in front, his eyes flaming.

"Get out of my road!" shouted Burr. "I'll teach the clumsy cur to litter up the deck. I'll pickle his hide for him."

"You've done enough," said Denison. Burr had no gun, and the younger man was white-hot at the unnecessary cruelty. Kopeke's eyelid had been cut, and blood dripped from it on the deck. His brown skin showed purpling welts that crisscrossed on his face.

"Why, damn you!" said Burr in a fury. "What in hell do you mean? I'm runnin' this schooner, you young cub. Interfere with discipline, will you? For two pins I'd give you a taste of the same medicine."

Burr's pale-blue eyes glared with an anger that suggested insanity. His enormous jaw stuck out, exposing his stained lower teeth with the gross lower lip drawn down.

"Try it," said Denison coolly. His right arm was bent, the elbow back a little, his fist clenched. That projecting jaw was tempting him as a target. His eyes measured the distance. Burr's apish arms were a-swing, the rope end dangling.

"That isn't discipline," said Denison. "That's sheer brutality."

Burr snarled, spat at him and swung the rope in a lightning blow. It curled stingingly about Denison's instant guard, and then he lifted on his toes and swayed forward as his fist shot to the angle of the jaw.

Burr's jaws, open for more invective, closed like a sprung trap with the jar of the beautifully timed and distanced blow. His eyes rolled upward, and the light went out of them, so that they looked like the eyes of a dead fish. His knees gave way at the same time, and he pitched forward, stretched full length, his cheek hard against the deck planks, a trickle of blood from a bitten tongue.

Kopeke stood horrified, yet gazing at Denison as if he looked at a god. Two of the crew came hurrying aft. Denison examined his knuckles. They had stood the impact. Not for nothing had he been accounted tough game among the heavyweights of the division overseas.

The mate came lurching up the companionway, staring stupidly from Denison to the skipper.

"Who did that?" he asked.

"I'll give you two guesses," said Denison evenly. The glow of battle was still on him. He was not yet counting possible costs.

Burr groaned, rolled his eyes and sat up, supported by his hands, spitting out blood. He saw the rope end first, and then his gaze traveled up Denison's well-poised figure.

"By golly!" he said thickly. "I didn't think you had it in ye. We'll even up some other time, mister. You caught me half soused."

"You struck me with the rope, Burr," retorted Denison. "If you don't want to call it evens, suit yourself."

Johnson was looking from one to the other, speculatively, licking his coarse lips, a half smile in his eyes. The mighty had fallen.

Burr got to his feet, wobbly about the legs, and glared at Kopeke.

"You don't want to forget there's two Johnny Darms here," he said. "A word to them, you brown scum—" Kopeke shrank back, terrified.

"If the gendarmes wanted him for anything, they'd have been looking for him soon enough," said Denison. "I think you're running a bluff, Burr."

"The hell you do!" For a moment they measured glances, and then Burr turned away.

"I'd cut along on shore, if I were you, Kopeke," advised Denison. "And don't worry about the Johnny Darms."

Kopeke gave him a look of doglike devotion, but shook his head.

"Too much I am afraid along of him," he said. "I stay."

"I'll see he doesn't mistreat you," Denison told him. He did not know much about the native character, but it was clear that Kopeke was more scared of Burr than confident of his new champion, for all the feat he had performed. But he was grateful enough.

"Capitani say he get even along of you. All same you watch out. Me too, I get even with you, 'nother kind of way. But I too much 'fraid I go along Noumea. That no good place to go. Capitani he too damn smart."

The half-blood cook announced breakfast, and Denison went down. Burr was in his cabin. Johnson gave Denison a grin of greeting, with a half glance toward the closed door of the stateroom, but said nothing. The grin was eloquent enough.

Burr came out before the meal was well started, dressed in shore-going ducks.

"I reckon we'll call it even, Denison," he said. "You got me right, but I could lick you just the same in a rough and tumble. I give you credit for a wallop. I'm eatin' soft food this mornin'."

He offered his hand, and Denison took it from policy. The skipper's manner was bluff, but there was malice in his cold, blue eyes. He called for gin and filled up half a cup of hot coffee with the liquor.

"You didn't sleep on board last night," he said.

"It was quieter where I bunked," answered Denison, He meant to continue sleeping ashore while the diving was on.

"We did hit it up a bit. It'll be noisier ter-night."

An hour later the three of them landed in the same boat, amicably enough.

"Nothin' doin' till ter-morrer," said Burr, "except to hire divers. You can't help much there, Denison."

Denison, nodding, saw the mate thrust his tongue in his cheek. He seemed to have gained respect from the mate, if not an ally. The two went off together, and Denison strolled up the rapidly growing midway, where the concessions were being swiftly assembled. There was a merry-go-round with a wheezy calliope; stands where one threw at pins, tossed hoops or rolled balls for prizes of dolls, cheap, gaudy prints, blankets, tinware, and lamps. There was a bowling alley; a platform for dancing with another steam orchestrion; booths where waffles and "hot dogs" were to be sold—the essence of a third-rate fair.

Native men and women, the latter in cheap gowns, the men in holiday ducks, though a few wore the scantier native garb, strolled up and down, ready to patronize. Some had already bought canes and balloons; some munched hot dogs. At the end of the street, a tent bore a banner, scrolled in red, "Movies To-night," Two nearly derelict automobiles carried shouting fares up and down a half-mile strip of sand, coining a harvest.

Now and then a skipper stopped a native and haggled with him for diving, but few bargains appeared to be struck. It was too early in the day. Denison saw a shrewd-eyed Chinaman and guessed him a pearl buyer. It was a garish scene in the atoll setting, filled with novelty. At night, when the strings of colored electrics and the flaring gasoline torches were lighted, it would be even more interesting.

The two gendarmes strutted importantly in their uniforms with the cocked hats and short swords of authority. Drinking was plainly going on, but they paid no attention. There were no sales evident. In some of the shacks there was noisy talk and laughter, where the traders, the pearlers and the buyers were strengthening acquaintance—the clink of glasses, the blare of an accordion.

Denison was frankly looking for the girl. He wanted to learn more about her, to know her. But he saw nothing of her, though he was sure he had seen her rowing the ancient mariner—who he guessed was her father and was sure was an old scalawag—ashore. That such a rose should bloom in such surroundings did not trouble him. He did not get that far. Youth called to youth.

Close to noon, returning toward the landing, he saw a crowd in the middle of the street and, pressing through, beheld the girl. With her was her father, reeling drunk, clutching a bottle in one hand and offering it to one and all with tipsy generosity, unaware that he was pouring out its contents on the ground with every hospitable gesture.

The girl stood beside him, her eyes hurt but her head up, trying to get him away. Denison fancied this was not the first time, or the twentieth, that she had to do the same thing. He did not see just what he could do, and he purposely did not do more than glance at her. The man caught sight of him and lurched toward him.

"Havva li'l' tip wi' me," he said. "You're a stranger—a Johnny Newcome. These fellers think I ain't good enough. Think I'm an old beach bum, but we'll show 'em, me an' my gal, Mary. We'll show 'em yet!"

Denison hesitated, wondering whether he could draw him away from the jeering mob. The girl's eyes caught his pleadingly, with a message to leave them alone, a pitiful blend of pride and shame that touched him, to the quick. Her father tried to thrust the bottle at him, and it fell from his hand to the sand, unbroken but with the dregs draining from it into a little puddle.

The man stooped to pick it up, staggered and fell, while the crowd laughed. He shook an angry fist at them and picked up the bottle, tilting it and looking at it in owlish dismay.

"Empty!" he muttered. "Gotta git some more." The girl tried to get him to his feet, but he shook her off, and, as she tried again, Denison took his other arm and hauled him to a stand.

"You come along with me, old-timer," he said. "Let's get away from this outfit."

"You're my frien'," he said. "To hell with them! Let's go git some more gin."

The crowd tried to block the way, but Denison brushed the nearest aside, none too gently, and got clear. With the girl on the other side, he led the old man between two of the booths, through scrub pandanus, to the sea beach. The drunkard helped to solve the problem of what to do with him by stating that he wanted a "li'l' nap." His feet dragged until Denison eased him down on the sand in the shade of some palms and made a hummock of sand for a pillow. Denison spoke to the girl.

"He'll likely sleep for a while now," he said. "You'll be hungry. Can I get you something—bring it here?"

She shook her head mutely. Then, as he lingered, she said:

"Please go and leave me with him. I thank you for what you have done. You have been—kind." Her lower lip quivered, and she caught at it with her white teeth for an instant. "I know how to handle him. Please—please go."

He bowed and left her. From the thicket he looked back and saw her fanning her father with the dried and fallen leaf of a palm.

"Poor kid," he said to himself. Then: "Poor Mary."

On his way again to the landing, a tall man stepped up to him.

"You did the decent thing just now," he said. "I came up as you took him off. He's an old boozer with a mighty nice girl. He ought to be keelhauled, and, if he came up drowned, it wouldn't be much loss. I'm Weller of the *Wikiwiki*. Glad to see you aboard some time. I reckon you're a newcomer?"

"My name is Denison, Mr. Weller. I'd be glad to come. I bought a third share in the *Akua*." He spoke automatically and flushed as he saw the face of Weller harden, his eyes grow cold.

"Ah!" he said crisply. "Then I may have been mistaken." And, with a curt nod, he turned away, leaving Denison standing like a fool, burning with unmerited shame.

IV

PARKER'S DECREPIT MOTOR BOAT TOWED A SCORE OF CANOES, whaleboats, and cutters out into the windless lagoon, each casting off at their appointed spot, the string having been arranged in proper order. It was slack tide, and the released craft drifted over their places unmoored. They had drawn lots for position, and a fresh drawing would take place every other day. Over this the gendarmes had presided.

Every boat had its glass-bottomed boxes, an iron-hooped net, with a smaller one for the diver to wear about his neck for bringing up his oysters, a pair of plain-glass spectacles to wear under the surface and food that included young nuts for drinking. The sun was well up as they made ready for the plunge, the pellucid surface unruffled. In every boat but one there sat one or two native divers, stripped to loin cloths.

The exception was the small dinghy belonging to the sloop. The ancient mariner had the oars, the girl sat in the stern in a bathing suit of faded red.

With Burr, Johnson and Denison there was a diver whose red-shot eyes proclaimed his long service at the game. He was about fifty, deep of chest, but with varicose veins standing out on his legs, the result of many immersions. He was the only one who would dive for them, Denison gathered, and he was partly drunk.

The sloop dinghy took its place not far from them and, as the girl stood up, her figure caught Burr's eye before she sat down on the gunwale, taking long breaths, her feet in the water. He leaned forward eagerly.

"Hell's fire, but she's a little beauty!" he said. "It's all of twelve fathom where they are. I'm damned if she ain't goin' down."

"Old man Murray's stepdaughter," said Johnson, and Denison's heart gave a quickened beat. The old reprobate was not her father. There was none of his blood in her. He might have known it. "Reckon he spends so much fer booze she has to do the divin'. She's a proud bit."

"She could be tamed," said Burr. Denison bit his lip. A row would not mend matters, and now their own diver, having located his patch of shell, was ready to go over. Burr and Johnson watched him as he sank down with arms erect for a dozen feet and then turned over and swam down, clutching at the coral of the bottom, scooping away with one empty shell at the live ones, tearing them loose from their anchorage.

Denison watched the girl slide into the water with barely a ripple. He was too far away to see her under the surface, but he held his breath with her as he waited for her to reappear, thinking of the hazards below. There were no sharks, but there were great eels that sometimes attacked the men. There might be giant squid.

There was the heavy pressure of the water, always a menace—it was almost an agony of apprehension that he waited for her to come up, glancing now and then at the second hand of his wrist watch, traveling with what seemed a lagging pace. One minute—two—passed, and then he saw her head break water, saw her rise to her slim waist, gracefully.

She hailed her stepfather and swam toward the dinghy, where she clung for a moment before she came in handily over the stern, emptying her net. Her stepfather pried open the shells, seeking through the gills, kneading the boneless mass and throwing the shells petulantly overside as they proved empty of treasure.

"Look at the blighter chuckin' shell away," said Johnson. "It's pearls or nothin' with him. Much he cares for the workin' end of it. Let's see what we got?"

Denison watched the girl go down ten times, and then, after the expostulation of the bearded man, they rowed away to their sloop. The rest of the boats stayed on the lagoon and, in two hours, the girl came out again. By this time there were two small pearls and a baroque in the *Akua's* boat, and Burr was furious at the tippling diver who proclaimed that he was through for the day.

"We're over a good patch," said Burr. "On'y got ter-morrer to clean up. Keep yore mouths shut, all of you, an' mebbe we kin swap to keep the place. Cripes, they got somethin' good in the dinghy! Look at the old man!"

Murray was gazing raptly at something he held in the palm of his hand. He glanced around cautiously before he handed it to his daughter.

"It's on'y a baroque, Mary," he exclaimed hoarsely, "but it'll buy a bottle."

"Lyin' like a thief," commented Burr. "I'll bet it's a good un."

"The gal's tucked it away," exclaimed Johnson in a greedy whisper. "See him crabbin' at her."

She had put something in a little bag of soft leather that was tied about her neck with a thong and, to stop her stepfather's grumbling, she slipped overside again, though she had not "taken her wind."

"She's a wise li'l' bird," said Burr. "Knows he'd trade it off to Ching Loo fer next to nothin' if he chucked in a case of booze. I'd like to see it. Now then, Pohia, are you goin' over again or not? Take a drink."

Pohia took the drink and went down, but he remained only a moment. When he came up, he was gasping like a landed fish, his eyes crimson, distended. Violent cramps seized him as he crawled on board, and he lay panting, his breathing spasmodic.

"He's done for the day," said Burr disgustedly. "Mebbe we'd better show what we got an' git us some diver thet ain't bin lucky."

It was the custom to give a fifth of the value of the catch as bonus to a successful diver. Boats that were lucky could command the better men who, in many cases, would hire out for more than a day at a time in the beginning. It was largely luck, this lottery, and superstition ruled.

Denison watched Pohia, helped to massage him, aghast at the thought of what might happen to the plucky girl, the only woman to dive at Mareva. If only he had not been such a fool as to buy in with Burr. He might have made a deal with Murray and used the money to hire divers. Now he had two dollars in cash and a doubtful third share with a pair of crooks whe, as they talked over their luck, the good indication for better returns, plainly left him out of the reckoning.

That night when the pair went ashore, he stayed aboard, knowing that the girl was still on the sloop. He told Kopeke to send him off a shore canoe if he could get a native to leave the first night of the carnival. The big fair was now in full swing with the discordant blare of music, shouts and laughter under the strings of lights that seemed so strange beneath the quiet stars over the palmy atoll.

At length a small outriggered craft came off. In it was Kopeke.

"I take you," he said. "Where you like to go?"

Denison told him and caught a sympathetic flash of dark eyes. They paddled for the sloop, but, before they reached it, the trailing dinghy was drawn in and old Murray got into it. Denison heard the girl's clear voice.

"I wish you wouldn't go, father."

"You ain't got no respect fer me," he said. "Want me to stay away from all the fun? You goin' to gimme that pearl?"

"I am not. You know why."

"Then gimme the money you got. I know you got some. Hand it over. Ef you don't, I'll git so blind drunk you'll have ter come ashore an' git me. I kin get tick on that pearl when I tell the chink about it."

Denison motioned to Kopeke, who checked their craft, and they floated motionless on the star-spangled water in the loom of a schooner's side.

"It's no use your talking about it, father. I'm going to take it back to Papeete and get a decent price for it. It's going to send mother back to the coast, to a hospital. There may be enough to buy back the place."

Denison felt like an eavesdropper as he realized what the phrases meant and pictured the girl's mother, tied by some evil chance to this Murray, who was little better than a drunken beach comber.

"You ought to be ashamed of yourself," the girl's clear voice went on, low but carrying distinctly over the sounding board of the water. "It's what we've hoped for—our only chance come true at last."

"Now don't pick on me, Mary. I've done my best. You're right. Gimme the money, an' I'll keep my mouth shut. There's a good gal. I promise."

There was the chink of silver, and the dinghy drew away, Murray sculling eagerly for the shore—and liquor.

After a while Denison motioned to Kopeke to paddle on. He felt that he could not stay away. He could see the girl seated in the cockpit, staring at the land. Then he heard a sigh, and he gestured to Kopeke to turn back. But the girl heard the light plash of the paddle and looked toward them.

"Good evening, Miss Murray," said Denison. "You're not ashore?"

That was a silly speech, he told himself, but it brought an answer.

"I did not care to go. I am not lonely." Denison took his courage in his hands.

"I am," he said boldly. "May I come aboard?"

She seemed to be studying him through the gloom.

"Yes; for a little while."

The ebb was beginning to make when Denison went ashore. He had arranged for a bed in a shack run by a woman who made a business of serving meals for the traders. It was well away from the carnival street; it was clean and the charges moderate. Aside from his two dollars, there would be his share from the sale of the pearls they had found, which he was determined to see he got as promptly as they were sold. He had talked this matter over with Burr, and the latter had assured him, a little too glibly, that he would turn over in the morning a third of the money he expected to get from their haul.

For a while he wandered in the carnival street, watching the amused crowd, mostly natives, like so many grown-up children. The traders had gathered together in various groups of their own at different shacks, to discuss the finds of the day. The amusements soon palled on him, and he went on to his lodging place, finding it empty but the door open. He turned in on one of the cots, listening for a while to the muffled noise of the carnival.

His thoughts returned to the girl. If he had said he was lonely, it had soon developed that she was infinitely more so. Seated together in the cockpit, they had forgotten the shouting crowd ashore, the patient Kopeke who had made the canoe fast to a cleat and curled up in the bows of the sloop; smoking the cigarettes he had bought with part of his five-dollar trove.

Denison and the girl, youth with youth, had been drawn together. She had told her pitiful story, simple enough. Of the little ranch they had once held, of the death of her father and the coming of the bearded stranger, who had been the father's friend, shortly after his death.

There was money in his purse from a lucky find of shell. He told glamorous tales, finally married the widow and took them down to the wondrous South Sea fairyland, where his true nature crept out gradually. She told of the illness of her mother, her homesickness, the delinquency of Murray and the resolve of the desperate girl to retrieve their shattered fortunes and return to California. Now they could do this.

She had shown him the pearl she had brought up, a gem of perfect symmetry, gleaming with faint fire in the light of Denison's match. It was worth perhaps five thousand dollars, perhaps twice that amount, if it matched another pearl in some big dealer's store.

So Denison had told his story, and still youth had called to youth, until, when he rose to go, they had come together naturally as children, but still man and maid, and he had kissed her.

"I didn't mean to let you do that," she said. And then he had kissed her again.

Denison was smiling as he fell asleep. His own problem was still unsolved, but he meant to stay the season out. Somehow he was sure that luck would be with him to force a sale of his share and go back to California—with her. The drunken Murray was still an encumbrance, but they had not spoken of him. Youth hurdles obstacles that lie in the path of romance.

V

HE WOKE TO FIND THE ROOM STILL EMPTY; woke to the sound of shouting that was not that of carnival, but excited, turbulent, threatening. A presentiment of evil was upon him, and he could not shake it off. He dressed rapidly and went back toward the darkened street of the fair. The electrics were out, but some gasoline flares still flamed. There was a throng of excited people, of natives scantily dressed, of stern-faced whites and, among them, the two gendarmes, questioning. Denison pushed forward. Weller of the *Wikiwiki* was there, eying him coldly. He turned to the next man.

"What's up?" he asked. The man, well primed with liquor, voluble and excited, faced him.

"They found the body of old Murray with a knife through his heart, back of the chink's hut," he said. "The old man got a big pearl yesterday. He was braggin' about it, the fool. Some one's done him in. They've got the chink, but he swears he ain't done it. Would anyway. Says Murray promised to sell it to him, but said his gal had got it. The chink give him some money to bind the promise—and some booze, of course. The old fool got drunk an' went round tellin' how he was rich an' was goin' back to Californy on a ranch.

"Some one thought he had the pearl an' done him in. Murder, that's what it is, matey."

"How about his daughter?" Denison's tone brought the man to momentary sobriety with its imperative demand.

"Ah! What about 'er, matey? Thet's what. She ain't aboard her sloop. What's more, they's another boat missin'—the *Akua*. Thet chap Burr—he's in this mess, I say. He's a bad un, he is. I bet he an' his mate Johnson an' thet greeny they got in with 'em 'as done in the old man an', when they found 'e didn't 'ave the pearl, like 'e told the chink, they grabbed the gal an' lit out on the ebb. An' them two froggies stand askin' questions. Git out an' chase 'em, I say. There's been too much talk."

There was a close grasp on Denison's arm. One gendarme held him, the other in front of him. Weller stood by.

"You talk French?" he asked Denison. "If you don't, I'll talk for you. They want to know where your partners are? And where you've been? You know this man Murray has been murdered and his daughter taken?"

"I can talk enough French," said Denison. "I've just heard the sloop has gone. I've been asleep at Mrs. Burton's. You can ask her," he added as he caught sight of her on the edge of the crowd. "My cot's been slept in. As to my partners, I know they're a pair of scoundrels, with Burr the worse of the two. I know they saw Murray and his daughter looking at a pearl she had brought up. I was on the sloop last night after he had gone ashore, and she showed it to me.

"They took my money because I was a greenhorn, but I've nothing in common with them. What's the use of talking? You've got a fast boat. Why don't you go after them? You can hold me if you want to. But for Heaven's sake don't waste time, with that girl in Burr's power. He's got the pearl, and he's got her, Weller. Let the gendarmes fuss if they want to, but get after them."

Weller's face had changed. He spoke rapidly to the gendarmes.

"I was mistaken twice, I fancy," he said. "But they've got away, Denison. Murray's been dead for all of two hours. On the ebb, with no moon, they'll be long out of sight. I believe you're clear of all this, but—"

"You must, if you've got any sense," cried Denison. "That doesn't stop you from *trying*, does it? You've mended your mainsail. I saw your men working on it. That's the only reason we beat you in on the way down. Why don't you all go after him?"

"There are about two men on Mareva who'd try to get by the reefs by starlight. One of them's Kopeke, and he's gone—with them, I reckon. As for another, if there is one, we can't find him. And then we don't know which way they've headed."

There was a break in the crowd. A native pushed through, water dripping from him. Kopeke! He looked around and saw Denison in the grasp of the gendarmes.

"Captaini, he make me go with him," he said excitedly. "He tell me I hang if I no go. They take the white woman. Capitani, he hold gun along my head—he say he shoot, suppose I no go through the reef. I too much afraid. But I remember you, Denisoni—you kind to me. You in love along white woman. I go through reef, but I know one more outside, not too far, but too far for white man to swim. So I get ready.

"They go below. Girl, she run in capitani cabin, lock door. He stay below.

Jonisoni, he very drunk. I run boat on reef. Tide no good. No can get off. I jump. No care for shark. You good to me, Denisoni. You knock capitani down when he beat me. So I swim to Mareva. *Akua* on reef."

Weller jumped to action, silencing the jabbering gendarmes, bidding them come along with him.

"You too, of course, Denison. Kopeke will take us there. The ebb's nearly over, but we can make it."

There was a volunteer crew that he had to thrust back. As it was, the deck of the *Wikiwiki* was crowded, when the schooner, with Kopeke at the wheel, shot through the gap and threaded the dangerous mazes of the coral.

It seemed hours to Denison before they sighted the dull shape of the *Akua*, her bow lifted on the shoal. Light showed through her skylight, as the *Wikiwiki* shot up into the wind. Quickly both whaleboats were lowered. Denison had a gun now, and he clutched its butt as he sat in the stern, while the native rowers bent the stout oars and raced through the glowing sea. They found the native crew huddled in the bows, quiescent, frightened, and they boarded. A shape staggered toward them with a muffled exclamation, and Weller felled Johnson with a hard blow that sent him sprawling into the scuppers.

Below Denison heard pounding on a door, the half-drunken voice of Burr, the splintering of wood.

The skipper was attacking the door of his cabin with an ax.

He turned, as Denison leaped the last steps of the companionway, his face suffused with rage, his eyes maniacal. He flung the ax at Denison, and the keen edge grazed his shoulder as he stooped, firing at the same instant with Burr, who had whipped out the revolver from his belt and leveled it.

There was a cry from the girl inside the stateroom, and then shot upon shot, the smell of powder gas, flashes from the muzzles. Denison felt the sear of a bullet on his scalp, the shock of another in his shoulder, a third on his side, and was barely conscious of men springing down into the cabin.

When he came to, he was on cushions, the girl bending over him anxiously, helping Weller with a bandage that was being wound about his bare arm.

"He's come round," said Weller. "Where's that gin, one of you?"

The harsh liquor choked but revived him, as he managed to swallow some and felt its hot strength.

"Steady, son," said Weller. "You're all right. One through the shoulder and a rib broken. They'll mend. You got him."

"I got Burr?" Then he caught sight of a body on the floor, shrouded with the checkered tablecloth.

"Between the eyes and through the heart. He won't need hanging now. Good shooting and good riddance. Here, you fellows, clear out of this. You're cluttering up the cabin. Get up on deck. All he needs is the doctor—that's me—and a nurse."

The cabin emptied. Denison rallied his senses to look into the eyes of Mary Murray.

"We'll take you back aboard the *Wikiwiki* in a few minutes, Denison," said Weller. "Then you can go aboard your own schooner, if you want to. I reckon it's yours. Johnson's told a lot of stuff in a fit of delirium tremens that'll put him where he won't bother you. I don't believe there's any claim against the *Akua*. They kept that clear. And you've got something coming to you—a good deal, maybe. If you'll promise not to get too excited I'll leave you in the charge of your nurse for a little while. I'd lie down if I were you."

Denison saw the legs of Weller ascending and heard the slide close. Then the light of the swinging lamp was eclipsed.

Mary Murray was bending over him, stooping down. He heard a smothered sob, he felt the splash of a tear on his face and then the touch of her lips on his.

After all, his real adventuring had just begun.

OUTDOOR STORIES

| Vol. II | JULY, 1928 | No. 5 |

NEW GUINEA GOLD
By J. Allan Dunn

I

Two Ways to Adventure

PORT MORESBY IS THE SEAT OF GOVERNMENT IN NEW GUINEA. It lies upon a narrow neck of land, with the harbor on one hand and the sea on the other. For nine months of the year there is little or no rain, and the ground gapes under the broiling sun, the dampness of the air and the never-ceasing wind. In the wet season of the southeast monsoon, from December to March, it is a melancholy spot indeed, without formal roads, with the houses of the whites scattered along rough paths across the grass and waste land. There are not many of these houses, the residents being only the government officials, the staffs of two trading stores and a few people interested in the mines and plantations of the interior. The lieutenant governor lives a mile out, but the government buildings, hospital and prison are in the town. The two hotels are little to boast about.

In one of them, two Americans, Jack Somers and his pal, Ned Mitchell, sat listening to the steady downpour, looking out through a dirty window at the gusts of wind-blown rain. They were consuming their last package of tobacco and ruminating over the harsh words their landlord had just bestowed upon them. The unpainted wooden house boasted a few bedrooms, but actually it was little more than a drinking and gambling saloon, frequented by dirty and drunken men.

Yet the town was the threshold of adventure. Back in the bush of the great island lay treasure; there was gold in the rivers and up in the saw-tooth ranges where cannibals and pigmies lived in the crudest savagery. Pearls in many places, where streams made lagoons between the mangroves and the reef. Silver, osmiridium, manganese, copper, coal and petroleum. Above all, to the true adventurer, there was scenery unsurpassed in the world, wild peoples and vast territories untrodden by the feet of white men.

It was the lure of gold that had brought the two there, after an unsuccessful and somewhat amateurish attempt at pearling on Thursday Island, which lies off the northeast tip of Australia not very far across the Torres Straits from Port Moresby itself.

If it had been much farther they would never have arrived. The trip landed them almost penniless as it was, to find that prospecting in New Guinea was not a simple matter to those unacquainted with native ways and short of cash.

"Twenty-eight shillings and four pence, Jack," announced Ned, tossing the coins on the grimy counterpane of their broken-springed bed. "In other words seven bucks—and thirty-two owing the buckaroo who runs this shebang, which we vacate this evening before supper, unless we shell out. There isn't a job. We've come, we've seen and we're whipped. They may chuck us in jail if they think our baggage isn't worth the bill—and they'll appraise it themselves."

"We'd eat, anyway."

"They feed 'em yams. Jail's full of natives with the itch."

"Monsoon's nearly over. Things may liven up after the rains. It's the last week in February. They blow out by the first week in March. And—in the meantime? Are we downhearted?"

Ned frowned.

"I'm not far from it, buddy. We've offered ourselves in every capacity known to a white man. The natives do all the rough work for a penny an hour, when the prisoners are not on the job. There are no houses to be built, no odd jobs of electric installation, we haven't got anything to sell and, if we tried, the storekeepers would call up the lieutenant governor and give us the bum's rush. They won't let us dig, a beggar would starve to death, there are no ships in the harbor that want assistant navigators or pursers or even able seamen. The place is a dump. The town of the unburied dead. The gambling games are crooked. I wish I was a carefree mosquito. I would be a first-class bloodsucker and I'd start in on the pirate who owns this miserable hotel."

Somers had been sucking his pipe in silence.

"There's a schooner arrived this morning," he said. "I heard them talking about it in the barroom. Some one said it belonged to what they call a 'Yank.' Meaning an American, one of a despised and benighted race who got in wrong by once mentioning that they had something to do with the winning of the late war. This weather reminds me of the trenches, Ned. Same old rain. Only the slum was better than the mess they dish out here. Canned rag, black tea, moldy bread and waxy potatoes."

"You'll be missing it to-night, old scout. Also your little white bed with its pleasant little population. I need fumigating—or debugging. The chap who told me he wanted his radio fixed couldn't get a battery so I lost *that* job. Any more 'baccy?"

Jack tossed him the package.

"If we show any money at the store they'll spill it to His Nibs downstairs and they'll send a patrol of native M.P.'s to frisk us. I suppose we owe it to the brute, but sixteen simoleons per week for what he calls board and room is sheer robbery. He charges the locals two quid. Some difference."

The two had chummed since the signing of the armistice had left them not only jobless but affected with a post-war adventure complex. This was not yet sated, despite luck that had oftener been ill than good. Both had taken it philosophically, enjoying the experience, seeing the world and paying their way in many strange fashions. They had run launches and boilers, oiled in engine rooms, acted as stewards, supercargoes, stevedores, as second mate and quartermaster, as hotel clerks and peddlers of Yankee notions. They had gone hungry and many a time been broke. They had quested on hopes more or less forlorn, but still the rainbow of fortune shimmered against the horizon and still they hoped to find the pot of gold at its foot.

Somers had been top sergeant in the company where Mitchell had once climbed to the rank of corporal and lost it the next week for a too ardent search after *vin rouge* and other excitement. Somers could have had his commission had he not been in too great a hurry to volunteer. They had seen their share of service, got their share of shrapnel and a whiff or so of gas for full measure. Somers had a *Croix de Guerre* for conspicuous gallantry and Mitchell should have had one. Mitchell had ducked high school and Somers had worked two arduous years through college when the war stopped his higher education. The world was now the university for both of them and they were learning fast, cementing also a genuine friendship which, with Mitchell, was augmented by a profound respect—never indicated on the surface—for his pal's superior learning.

Port Moresby was the first place that had seen them fairly stumped. In Mitchell's estimation it served them right for coming to such a place.

But there they were, and twenty-five dollars to the bad. They had discovered that the "rainy season" in New Guinea was well named, practically prohibiting exploration. Also, the gold fields near Port Moresby had been found to be patchy and were played out. There was gold enough in Papua, but it lay up rivers that ran through dense jungles and deep ravines. Men had gone there after the precious metal and most of them had left their heads behind them to grin in native clubhouses, while their bodies had undoubtedly served as "long pig." For two white men to start off alone without a train of bearers was worse than folly, and natives had to be fed and paid.

Their one chance to get out of the situation seemed to lie with the skipper of the Yankee schooner that had been reported in. That might give them a retreat if they could work their passage. His crew was certain in these waters to be native, but he might be able to use them aft—or he might not.

They were still discussing the matter, none too keen to go out and run the gantlet of the landlord's looks, request for his bill and possible abuse. He had gone nearly to the limit the last time they had talked with him. Somers had barely got Mitchell away without an attempt to "knock his block off."

The rain had let up, for a wonder. Through a rift that quickly closed again they could see the misty tops of the Astrolabe Range which were only as foothills to the high, hidden mountains beyond. But in that swift glimpse they saw a sharp peak clothed with verdure, save for one naked fang of rock. And the sun was shining on it, back of the vapors that invested Port Moresby. A shimmer of emerald, of topaz and hyacinth; with hints of sapphire in the shadows; a flash of gleaming opal set in turquoise.

"See that, Ned?" asked Somers. "Or was I dreaming? Was that the sun shining back there in the mountains?"

"Looked like it to me. I haven't had a shot of liquor to-day. But it looked a long way off."

"It means that the monsoon will soon be over. In a day or so. Port Moresby is always wrapped in a fog blanket after every other place, they say. Great country back in there, old son. I'd give five years off my life to get into it."

There came a knock at the door. The two looked at it questioningly.

"Notice to move on," said Mitchell. "The old bandit is goin' to tell us the room is rented. Well, we're packed, if they let us take the stuff out."

Somers took the pipe out of his lips.

"Come in," he called.

But it was not the heavy-jowled face and paunchy figure of the landlord that appeared. Instead there entered a tall, spare man in white ducks, mostly hidden beneath a ship's slicker. He wore a captain's visored cap on his head, which he removed as he came in, his eyes surveying them keenly. They were peculiar eyes which, at a second glance, revealed themselves of different colors, one gray and one hazel; eyes that were baffling in their actual expression. The man was burned by sun and wind to the color of Spanish leather. He wore a mustache and goatee that were black, streaked with gray. His forehead seemed abnormally high through baldness that left two aggressive tufts of hair which, with his aggressive eyebrows, gave him the appearance of a somewhat battered Mephistopheles, though there was no mistaking the vigor of the man in the flash of his eyes and the quick movements of his lean, upright body.

"Somers and Mitchell. Am I right, gents?"

An American beyond question. They guessed at his identity as he revealed himself.

"The land shark that runs this boarding house told me I'd find you in. I heard about you down at the wharf. Told me you were Americans. I'm skipper and owner of the schooner that came in this morning. The *Molly*, registered out of San Francisco. Name's Chance. Samuel Chance. I've knocked about New Guinea, off and on for ten years. Pearls, birds of paradise, and bugs. Last is my hobby. I'm by way of being an entomologist, an amateur one, and I've found some rare specimens—made money on 'em, too.

"Now then, I've got a trip in view. Been waiting for the rainy season to get over. It's breaking up. You'd never guess it at Port Moresby, but up the coast she's clearing. It's an inland trip. Start from Yule Island and leave the *Molly* there. Up through the Mekeo country by way of the Angabunga River, through the Lapeka District. Don't suppose you know those names but it's the beginning of the hill country—Kuni folk. Work my way up the mountains to the Mafulu villages. No one knows much about them. I'll have to take natives, with one or two of my own boys, but mostly natives. My men wouldn't make good bearers through the bush—don't know the lingo, couldn't get supplies, and you can't pack enough, anyway. The carriers eat themselves out of their loads in a week. I want a white man along. My mate's all right, but he's a squarehead and he can't handle interior tribesmen. Got no tact. I'd go alone, leave him to look after the schooner—as I will anyhow—but I've got to have some one to bring up my rear, keep awake when I have to sleep.

"It's a dangerous trip. There are cannibals up there. They don't like white men. They don't even like 'em to eat, though a white skull is a big trophy. The going's hard. It's even betting we won't come back. They drum ahead all the time and you've got to put the fear of yourself and your *mana* into their hearts. They tell me you've seen something of this part of the world. You're young and husky. I can't use both of you—can't afford it. I'll pay a thousand dollars for the trip. Hope to make it in three months—may take six. Extra hundred a month for every one over the three. Pay five hundred now, in advance. What d'ye say?"

His unmated eyes shone shrewdly as he surveyed the two younger men. Their own eyes were glowing, though the mention of the fact that he only could use one of them dampened their ardor.

"You're chums," he went on. "You can get all the Moresby gossip an hour after you come ashore. I understand you're a bit up against it. I've been that way myself. You had tough luck over Thursday Island way. All right. I can get the one who stays behind a job. Hundred a month, on a sisal plantation, five miles out. Friend of mine runs it. Wants a super. Got a Britisher now and wants some one to talk his own language nights. He'll make it ten dollars more if you can play pinochle. Know you don't like to split, but it's only for a few months. Give you both a stake to go on with. Sorry I can't use both of you. Needn't settle it now. Talk it over. Come down to the schooner for chow tonight. I can give you some good Scotch and a real cigar. Got a chink cook. He's coming with me on the trip. Best man I've got.

"Look here"—he pulled out a fat wallet bulging with British notes. "No offense between Americans. That pound keeper who thinks he runs this dirty dump has got you chalked up. Told me you were broke. Said I could get you cheap. Regular bounder. Take a couple of five-pound notes. Nothing to do with the job. A loan. How about it?"

"That's mighty decent of you," said Somers, "but I don't think we'll take it, unless one of us comes with you. We'll worry through if we don't take you up. But," he added, anxious not to seem churlish, "we'll be down for that meal, not to mention the Scotch and cigars, with bells on. And we'll make up our minds in the meantime. We don't want to split but we're not riding too high at this minute. We appreciate your offer."

"Fine, fine! Talk it over. Glad to see you, anyway. I'll have a boat waiting at the main wharf at seven bells—five thirty. Time for a cocktail. How's that? Orange blossom. With ice. I'll bet you haven't seen ice since you landed in New Guinea. Have a cigar apiece now. I've got lots of 'em. Real Manilas, packed in tea."

He produced a cigar case of woven grass, offered it to them and took one himself. He lit a match and blew it out after he had ignited their two smokes. Then he struck a second match.

"Not superstitious, though I've had my eyes opened since I came out this way. Just the same, three off one match is no good. See you later."

He was gone. Mitchell and Somers looked at each other half unbelievingly, uncertain for the moment whether or not their visitor had been flesh and blood or the apparition of a dream. He had come so pat to their need. But the cigars were proof of his existence.

"Well," said Mitchell, "he's a live one. Too good to be true."

"The original fairy godfather. What do you think of him?"

"I don't know. He's got rummy eyes. He's a good deal of a funny face, and he offers too much money. If he was a coin, I'd bite it and ring it to make sure it was good. A thousand dollars for three months, hiking to the Mafulus or the Me-fool-yous. Hunting bugs. I'll say he's a bug specialist. Comes by it natural."

"It's ten dollars a day. Guides get that back home. He said it was dangerous work. And he offers to put up half of it in advance. That sounds pretty good to me, Ned."

Mitchell agreed, reservedly.

"Money talks, but I've got a hunch tells me there's something phony in the deal. And I hate to split up, Jack. I've got another hunch says if we do we're doing it for keeps."

"You've got the heebie-jeebies sitting here broke, looking at the rain. I'll admit the man looks like Mephisto—"

"Whoever he is! I know. The chap who showed up and turned a guy called Faust into a young buck. That's just the sort of gink this one seems to me. I remember that Mephisto. I saw the play in the films. This Faust is sitting there lookin' like Santa Claus, grouching because he's got rheumatism and hardening of the arteries and Meffy comes up through the floor in a bunch of smoke and fire and gets him to sign his soul away with a pen that fizzes when he shoves it into the ink. This Chance might be his own brother, coming in the way he did. Don't you sign anything, Jack. I won't, you can bet your life. I hope this cigar don't go off like a firecracker. If it does, it's fair warning."

He grinned as he spoke, whimsically but with a note that told Somers that there was real feeling. Jack set it down as the desire he himself experienced, to make light of the fact that here was an opportunity they could not turn down, but which meant parting.

"The chow sounds good to me, Ned," he answered. "And I said just now I'd give five years of my life to go up into the back country."

"There you are," said Mitchell. "Making an offer, just like Faust. And up jumps the devil."

But his eyes shone as he spoke, and Somers knew that he, too, was thrilled at the thought of the trip into the unknown.

"We can't turn it down, Ned. Let's match for it. Toss up the half sovereign. Heads you go, tails you stay."

"Right." Mitchell poised the little golden disk on his thumbnail, ready to flip it, but he hesitated with a curious sense of reluctance.

"I don't like his goat face," he said. "And I wish his eyes were mates."

"They aren't crossed, anyway. Flip it, Ned."

The coin spun upward. The mists had parted again, and a stray beam of sunshine caught it as it whirled toward the ceiling.

"Good omen!" cried Somers as they both rose to look at the result. The coin had fallen on the bed—reverse up.

"Tails!" said Mitchell glumly. "I stay. Don't go, Jack. Let's chuck the thing. I don't like it."

He was so much in earnest that Somers considered his suggestion soberly. There had been something about Captain Chance that he, also, had not entirely liked, though he could find no fault with the proposal save that it separated them. There came a second knock.

This time it was Grimes, the landlord, beefy, flabby, ready to bully or fawn.

"You gents made up your mind whether you're goin' to stay or not?" he asked. It was plain that he knew they had been made an offer, probable that he had been listening.

"We're staying for a while," said Somers shortly. "We'll give you your money to-night, Grimes,"

"Ah! That's quite all right, quite all right. Always glad to accommodate real gents. 'Ad quite a chat with Captain Chance, I see. He's a quaint sort of a cove, but he's got the oof. If you sign on with him he'll pay on the nail. Means wot 'e says, 'e does. I'm wishin' you luck. Anything I can do for you?"

"Yes. Get out," snapped Ned. Grimes remained unruffled but nodded at them and left.

"That fellow gets my nanny," said Ned. "I don't want his wishing me luck. I'll bet he knows something about Chance that's funny, Jack. Chance ain't regular. I know it."

"You'd have gone if it had come heads, wouldn't you?"

"I reckon so, but—"

"Then that settles it. You'll be on the sisal plantation. I'll leave the advance with you."

"No."

"What would I do with it on the trail? I'll come back with another five hundred, or more. You'll have most of yours. Enough for a stake. I'll learn a lot about the country and you'll be picking up dope. We'll be out on our own by August."

"I suppose so. I'd like to know what he's after. I'll bet it ain't bugs. I sure hate to see you go, buddy."

"Same here, old horse." They were not given to showing emotion but they had been together for a long time, through much of good luck and bad, and there was a strong bond of friendship knit between them. They gripped hands hard and then turned away to fumble, one with his pipe, the other with his shoelaces.

The watery sun was gathering strength. When they went out to go down to the schooner the rain had ceased, and the wind, for a wonder, was not howling across the promontory from the straits. The monsoon gales were breaking; the wet season was over.

A boat was waiting for them, with a native crew at the oars. A half-caste steersman touched his cap to the two visitors and told him he was second mate on board the *Molly*.

"He'd never walk back of me on a trail," whispered Ned to Jack. "Part Malay, ain't he? Lascar?"

The man had the face of a proper villain, squinting when he smiled. But Somers had seen too many natives who looked like murderers to pay much attention to features.

Going over the rail, they were met by the first mate, the "squarehead," who introduced himself as Hansen. He was a typical seaman with his racial type emphasized in his pale-blue eyes and wooden face. Somers fancied that he would be dependable enough in his regular duties but set in his ways, hardly the man for unexpected emergencies, for quick action in the bush.

"Skipper bane shaving," he said. "Will you please go below?"

The cabin of the *Molly* was well furnished. Many framed cases of beetles and butterflies covered the panels, filled with objects of strange metallic lusters and brilliant wings. Chance called from his cabin through the partly opened door.

"Be with you in a jiffy, gents. Sorry not to be ready. Had some stores to check up. Wang'll bring you a cocktail. I'm one ahead of you. We'll have another before we eat."

The table was set with white linen, polished silver and glass, which was not usual aboard a trading schooner, but betokened a liberal table and a skipper who liked to travel in comfort.

A door opened from the galley alleyway. There was a whiff of spicy curry following a bland, stout figure in spotless white. This was Wang, with a face all smiles, yellow as an old pool ball, slant of lids and lacking one eye. There was one lustrous black orb and one of dead white, like the white of a peeled egg. It was an uncanny combination. His voice was a mellow singsong.

"You likee olange blossom? Yes?"

He set down two regular cocktail glasses before them and stood back to watch them drink as if the compounding of the appetizers for their especial benefit was his chief duty and pleasure.

The drinks were iced and deliciously tinged with absinthe.

"You likee?"

"Fine, Wang. First chop."

Wang smiled and withdrew.

"Rum lot of eyes aboard this hooker," whispered Ned. "Skipper's don't match, first mate's like glass marbles, second's squint and the cook's shy one. Don't go, Jack."

Somers laughed at him but Mitchell was serious. His hunch was working and he believed in hunches. The next moment Captain Chance entered the main cabin. He greeted them breezily.

"Glad to see you aboard. Hope one of you is coming with me. Saw my friend after I left you. The sisal job's open. Like curry? Wang's a regular magician. All he does is to rub a pot and produce a meal fit for a king. Wang!" He clapped his hands and the Chinaman reappeared, bearing three more cocktails on his tray. Chance lifted his glass.

"Here's wishing the three of us luck," he said.

Jack's glance caught that of his pal. Was it only fancy, or did Chance's tone hold a hint of mockery? The setting sun was reflected from the glass of the open skylight. The iridescent wings of the great insects glowed with an eerie light, or so it seemed. Chance was waiting, glass in hand. The man was a little eccentric, that was all.

"Here's hoping," said Somers and drained his own. But Ned took his cocktail slowly and set the glass down with a thoughtful air. Then Wang appeared again.

"Cully all leady," he announced. "Velly good."

II
JUNGLE

FACING YULE ISLAND ON THE SOUTH COAST OF NEW GUINEA, not far from Port Moresby, the Angabunga River opens its mouth in a confusion of mangroves and mud banks, difficult to distinguish and hard to enter over the shallows where the mosquitoes swarm and malaria hovers. It is a harsh portal to the back country, guarded by crocodiles, infested with leeches.

The outfit was in a whaleboat. Chance, Somers, Wang, the half-caste second mate, whose name was Tefu, another of the schooner's crew who hailed from the New Hebrides and a jabbering, undersized rabble of Roro natives, four of whom were able to handle oars.

It was a truly tropical river, embanked in a jungle of mangrove and nipa palm, winding in a serpentine course that was often choked with tangled floats of water-lilies or blocked with fallen trunks. At times the mangroves were so thick that they rose like green cliffs, while their sickly smell and the rank odors of the oozy swamp all about them tainted the air.

Many colored and beautiful birds stood on the edge of the stream and on the fallen trees, or skimmed along the surface. The harsh scream of parrots and cockatoos blended with the mournful cries of wood pigeons. The heat was sweltering under the bright sun, sucking up the moisture, and the air reeked with pestilential odors. Somers found his white linen soaked with perspiration as if he had been in a vapor bath, but the spare form of Chance showed nothing similar and he seemed in perfect ease and good humor, pointing out now and then some rare butterfly, with wings as broad as the palm of a hand, flitting across the deck.

The dark skins of the natives were wet with sweat that dripped off their apelike faces, but they rowed steadily. There were many stores in the boat, piled high, carrier loads of food and gifts, the former largely consisting of rice, tinned meat, plain biscuit, sugar, jam and tea. There were rifles and side arms, picks and shovels, tent canvas and furniture, cooking and eating utensils with miscellaneous packages and boxes that were the especial property of Chance. The trade goods outweighed the rest; they were needed as cash for payments to natives for food and various services and good will. Over all this Wang presided.

At noon they went ashore at the village of Bioto. The thronging natives were curious as to their intentions. Chance spoke their dialect and one of the Roro men helped to interpret. The village chief said that though they traded with the Mekeo folk, through whose territory the expedition was to pass, they were afraid of an attack. The Mekeos were a bad lot of men, whose sorcerers were always working them up to forays.

From here the trail went overland to Oroi, which the party reached at nightfall, tired out but unable to sleep because of the virulent mosquitoes. Captain Chance dosed out quinine liberally against malaria. Their caravan was now augmented by a score of Bioto men, thirty carriers in all, to take them to the next village where they would get others. On they went, mile after sweating mile, through flat, swampy country, through thickly wooded bushland, set with gums, screw pines, bamboos, and here and there a sacred banyan and groups of sago palms. The insect life was wonderful, magnificent butterflies and beetles of every hue, but there were few flowers. Chance was thoroughly interested in the insects and Somers soon entertained no doubt of the genuineness of his hobby, though the actual reason for the expedition had not been mentioned.

Sometimes they plodded for hours along river paths hemmed in by thick, impenetrable reeds, fifteen feet in height, hiding the view but giving no protection from the sun. It was hard going, even for the natives, encumbered as they were with their loads. Chance went ahead, second in file, close behind the Bioto man who was the guide. Somers brought up the rear. If the natives were hostile they had a thousand chances to ambush the expedition, and Jack kept vigilant watch, though Chance insisted that this was friendly territory.

They still traversed occasional stretches of government roads, often merely horse tracks but sometimes fairly good. Day after day they marched on, coming to open clearings and gardens planted with yams, sugar cane, bananas, and areca nuts. In the late afternoons, they would meet men and women returning to the villages, always marked by a grove of coconut palms, the women packing heavy loads of firewood, fruit and vegetables, and staring at the white men with the frank curiosity of monkeys.

Their arrival was always the cause of fear, for they were suspected of being government agents, and the relief of finding this a false alarm meant friendliness from the chiefs, gifts of food and promises of carriers and guides,

paid for in trade currency of axes and knives, and sticks of tobacco. The
tariff was fixed on a regular basis, but it was impossible to get the natives to
go farther than from one village to the next.

The Mekeo people proved friendly enough and lacked the sinister look
of many Papuans. They were well built, though none stood over five feet
three or four. Their skins were chocolate in color, and clothing was scant but
made up for by a great deal of tattooing. Their villages were built about large
open spaces, the commodious houses having big platforms in front. In every
village there was a clubhouse where the visitors were entertained, a building
with quaint beaklike roof projections over the veranda, lodge rooms for the
secret societies, home of the bachelors, temple of the tribal cult.

Always they found their arrival anticipated, drummed ahead by great log
tympani. Chance told Somers that he was looking forward to reaching the
village of Sekeo where lived a powerful chief, named Titumi, and a yet more
powerful sorcerer called Morimori, whose influence extended far beyond the
limits of the Mekeo country. If they could get his good will, persuade him
that they were journeying with no intent to disturb the people or upset their
customs, and placate him with gifts, they would have little trouble in passing
on to the Mafulu territory. Once there they would have to be on their guard.
The Mafulus were a wild tribe who ate human flesh on every occasion, who
hated strangers and were adepts in the use of poisoned darts, blown through
bamboo tubes. Morimori had some blood relationship with these and had
given them proofs of his undoubted magic powers at one time, so that they
respected him. It had something to do with the appearance of a comet which
he had predicted and claimed to have dismissed.

"If we get in right with Morimori," said Chance, "we're O.K. Otherwise
we might as well turn back. And Titumi is jealous of him. We'll have to out-
wizard the one and bribe the other."

They reached Sekeo after nightfall and found it lit up with bonfires and
hand torches of coconut boughs. The clubhouse was screened by curtains of
coconut fronds closely interfaced. Through this the white men were led to
the presence of Titumi, who was inordinately fat, creased from neck to knee,
shining with oils, stained with ceremonial paint, decked with bracelets and
feathers, greasy and important.

To him Chance ceremoniously presented a great imitation diamond set
in a ring which had been severed near the mock stone, so that the chief was
able to set it through the septum of his nose, to his own great delight and the
admiration of his followers.

Morimori was absent, marshaling the dance that waited the arrival of the
visitors to commence. They took places on the platform, and Wang, being
treated as a white man, comported himself with great dignity, his blind eye a
source of wonder and doubt as to its magic qualities.

The open space was lit up with coconut flares, while ceremonial speech after speech was made, with compliments to the visitors and stress on the importance and valor of Titumi and his warriors. The name of Morimori appeared taboo.

Then the dance commenced. Two long rows of performers began moving in a monotonous, shuffling step alternating rhythmically with a sidewise goosestep hop. Their knees remained bent and their feet never left the ground, as they kept time to the beating of the drums and a wailing chant. The costumes were the interesting part of the performance to Somers, as he squatted for three hours while successive groups of bucks went through dances that were supposed to be different but in which he could see little change.

From head to foot the warriors were stained a shining red, with bands of other colors around their faces. Their necks, chests and backs were heavily ornamented with necklaces and pendants of shells, teeth and beads. Bright-colored leaves were stuck in the armlets, leg bands, anklets and wristlets, while each head bore a framework of cane, ten feet high, in the form of a gorgeous bonnet covered with feathers and plumes of parrots, cockatoos, birds of paradise and bower birds. From their loin bands hung tails of various materials, and now and then the dancers caught hold of these and looked like bands of dressed-up apes as they howled to the monotonous drumming.

From a pile of coconuts the singers quenched their thirst as did the departing squads of dancers. Nuts were also served on the clubhouse platform. The village was full of visitors, men and women, clustering in the shadows. The ceremony seemed interminable, but no one showed signs of weariness, and presently there was a startling enough episode.

Out of the jungle came a roaring noise and then the deep voice of a mighty drum. The ground was cleared of dancers in a twinkling. The people seemed to shrink into the shadows, and the open space was deserted.

What seemed a bush with inverted leaves came sidling out of the blackness, moving into the open, where it halted. Then it parted and out of it came a weird figure, a monstrosity that had an enormous head, with round, blank eye spaces and a pendulous trunk. It looked something like a giant squid with one tentacle; in reality it was a plaited mask of wicker that reached to the wearer's middle, below which hung a long skirt of red and yellow strips. The figure began to revolve, faster and faster, to a shrill piping that came from the tree-tops. The strips flew wide and the trunk swung out, as the thing whirled like a dervish, swifter and swifter until it suddenly collapsed, close to its brush tent, and crawled into it. As on a signal, the torches were extinguished. There was only the faint glow from almost dead cooking fires, barely serving to emphasize the black pit of the space below the observation platform.

Something began to glow there, a heap of ghastly luminosity that grew in stature until there showed the form of a man smeared with some phosphorescent material. Then began a dance that was both weird and sinister, performed in absolute silence. Somers could feel the suspense of the onlookers, hear the deep, suppressed breathing of those beside him on the platform. Morimori began to leap, higher and higher, to twist in mid-air, to caper and make little darts here and there.

Suddenly he disappeared, shrouded doubtless by his grassy tent. Torches flared up, but the space was vacant. Suddenly Morimori spoke from within the clubhouse and the chief, his voice shaking a little, bade the others enter.

There was a fire burning on a stone at the far end, but it barely lit their way down a long aisle between stalls that were the quarters of the occupants. Against the far wall Somers could see something standing that looked like a great fish, with eyes of shell that caught the fitful gleam, with rows of teeth in its open jaws—the god of the tribe. Beside it stood things like mummies, skulls that had been modeled with clay into rough likenesses of their late owners, bodies that were stuffed dummies with hands and feet of roots or boughs, chosen for their resemblance to the actual thing.

On shelves were row upon row of skulls, reaching high to the vaulted roof. And a musty smell, rank with human odors, filled the room. Again came the wizard's voice in savage jargon, sternly demanding to know the white men's purpose.

Somers thought the voice issued from the wicker, painted framework of the fish god. Chance answered, through the interpreter:

"Show us with whom we speak."

The voice came mocking. Now it sounded above them, then from the rear, ventriloquially.

"Cannot the white men see in the dark? I can see you and know your desires. I know where you travel. What you seek. Three of you go and two return. Which one stays? Can you tell me that, white men, whose wisdom is so great, whose *mana* is so strong, that you seek the wisdom of Morimori? Can you not see me? Are your eyes less strong than mine?"

"The eye of the white man gazes, Morimori."

At that instant a white ray shot out, illuminating the end of the great hall, sweeping to the roof, showing the mummies, the rows of skulls, showing the startled faces of gasping savages who huddled away from the electric beam of Chance's torch.

As it came back to the god it suddenly showed the figure of the wizard. He had chosen to reveal himself, surprised by the sudden magic of the ray. He was a horrible sight, stark naked, save for strings of teeth and necklaces formed of dried finger joints. Small preserved heads of animals swung on his chest and an apron of hair hung from a string of shell about his hips. He was smeared with yellow ocher from feet to neck, his face red, with the eye sockets blackened and his lips emphasized with the same sable pigment.

He faced the beam unblinkingly, his eyes malevolent. For the time he was out-wizarded, surprised.

Chance screwed at the base of his torch, focusing the beam so that it spotlighted the hideous figure, and advanced slowly, Somers beside him, Wang close behind. Fear reigned in the place.

"We see," said Chance, "and we are not afraid. If two return, they will come back this way bringing gifts." The interpreter's trembling voice translated.

"Death is a small thing to a white man, Morimori. Our *mana* lives in our ghosts. We fear not, even as you do not fear, and we shall speak to one another as brave and mighty men. For we can see in the dark, we can make fire from water, turn night to day."

The torch shut off. There was a sibilant whispering all about them. Somers gripped the butt of his automatic. He knew the swiftly shifting minds of these primitives, that out of fear might come a sudden frenzy of attack. But Chance had rehearsed his performance with Wang as assistant. There was a sputter and then a blaze of white light that filled the big house, as the Chinaman lit a length of magnesium ribbon and tossed it into the air, following it with the discharge of a Roman candle firework, vomiting balls of colored light that floated up toward the roof and died out in green and crimson.

"So go souls into the uttermost darkness," said Chance. "Thus we bring them back. Bring me a bowl of water, a big bowl."

There was a wait. Then the chief himself brought a calabash, as Chance once more switched on his torch. He held it so that the water was just illumined by it, held his left hand over the liquid, and muttered an incantation that brought a smile to Somers, hidden in the shadow:

> "Fee fi fo fum.
> From the darkness let them come.
> Eeny, meeny, miney mo.
> So they come and so they go."

He opened his hand. Out of the water there leaped instant hissing flames, as the pellets of metallic sodium ignited. It was almost child's play but wonderfully effective.

"I will show you more marvels, later, Morimori," Chance went on through his native medium, "but these things are for wizards and shall be shown alone."

This was a sop, a promise of secret knowledge, a deference to Morimori's position, shrewdly calculated. But the sorcerer was still haughty.

"I also can show you strange things, white men," he said. "Shall I tell you why you have come? To ask me to give you a token that will serve you with the Mafulu, who do not love strangers, save in their bellies. So you may pass through them, so you may find the yellow stones you seek—soft stones that will buy many things among white men, that make ornaments for their women. Now tell me why I should serve you?"

Gold! Somers started. Was that what Chance was after in the cannibal land? Masking his purpose under the talk of collecting beetles. Had he knowledge of rich deposits? No wonder he offered high wages! It was largely guesswork on the wizard's part, Somers surmised, but if there was gold, Morimori would know it. As for needing his passport, that was easily arrived at.

"We seek nothing that will harm your people or the people of the Mafulus," said Chance. "We come to you because we know that you are a great wizard. With whom we would be friends."

"Are you then all sorcerers?"

This was a challenge and Chance took it up.

"Let us have plenty of light," he said. "I will ask one more of us to show you something."

Torches were brought and held high while Wang stepped forward. Slowly and fearfully the natives gathered about in a circle, the chief to the front with Morimori.

Wang thrust his hand into his pocket and brought out a mango seed, which he exhibited, passing it to the chief and the wizard. He called for dirt and made a little pile of it, burying the seed and covering it with a cloth. Somers knew what was coming, but the savage audience had never seen the mango trick and they watched with awe. Morimori frowned deeply, as the cloth moved, was lifted and disclosed, first the twig leafing out, then the little tree with a ripe fruit upon it which Wang showed, bit into, and ate.

Somers was unprepared, but he fancied there had been enough of marvels. But the wizard was stubborn.

"You are three," he said. "One of you lacks magic to protect him on this journey. Is it the third one?"

Chance did not hesitate. He turned to Somers.

"Light some of your matches," he said, "then pass the box to me."

It was a chance. Morimori might or might not know a match when he saw one. Might have heard of the firesticks and thought them magic or known them through some other trader as an article of common commerce. But it was a chance that the skipper was evidently determined to take. They were far from civilization now.

Somers did what he could to make it impressive. He took out a match and whispered to it, blowing on it as if he breathed the power of his spirit—his *mana*. Then he ignited it, with two more, and passed on the box to Chance.

Morimori had intently watched the performance.

"Perhaps I can do this thing," he said.

Somers thought the jig was up, but Chance handed over the box.

There was no breath taken while the wizard took out a safety match and struck its head against the prepared side of the box. There came the merest flicker of light and then failure. He tried again, and a third and fourth time, before his painted face twitched and his eyes glared crimson with anger.

Chance put out his hand for the box.

"It is because these answer only to the white man's *mana* that you have failed, Morimori," he said. "Behold!" And he lit one. "Yet you may acquire this power later, being what you are. Only it is dangerous for the spirit of a white man to enter into the body of one who is of another color and race. Touch my hand with yours."

Slowly Morimori obeyed. The desire to achieve this magic wrestled against his growing fear of the visitors, desire bolstered by pride. Black fingers touched white, and then Chance again handed him the box.

This time the match flared and an *ah!* went up that brought a smile for the first time to the wizard's features.

"Keep, them Morimori," said Chance. "Only I will not promise you how long my *mana* will live within you."

Somers guessed the jugglery that had gone on. A box of trick matches, a little palming in the deceitful light, the final handing over of a box with some good matches on top, fake ones below. A simple thing but startling. Morimori would use them up on proper occasions and, finding them fail him later, would surmise that the *mana* had passed, loaned by Chance, returning to him.

"It is good," he said. "To-morrow we shall talk together. And we will exchange gifts. Now we shall eat."

There was a bustle as young men began to bring in the huge carcass of a pig on a plank, which had been steamed in a dirt oven with enormous yams and plantains. The etiquette was crude and a little disturbing to Somers. For the chief tore off juicy gobbets, bit them in half, and then pressed the remainder into the mouth of his guest. Morimori did the like with Chance and with Wang, who bolted the morsels with much smacking of lips, and Somers copied them though his stomach revolted. He doubted whether the Mekeo ever washed, judging by the odors that came from them as the clubhouse grew closer and warmer. But he managed to retain the food and was relieved when he found that the chief only did this as a preliminary to his own gorging.

They slept in the clubhouse that night, or attempted to. The place reeked from uncleanliness. Lying awake, looking at the ranks of skulls above him,

Jack Somers reverted to Morimori's grim prophecy that three of them went out but only two should return. Which of them was to stay in the jungle?

He lacked superstition, or thought he did, but there was something in the ordeal of the night, the primitive dances, the weird, charnel-like interior, that seemed to carry his spirit back to the times when he, too, had shuffled to barbaric drums, had stuffed himself with food and been little more than an animal in his manners, listening with awe to the voice of a tribal wizard.

It was hard to shake off. He thought of Mitchell, on the sisal plantation, of their own future plans, but all seemed hazy. Out of the jungle that surrounded them, down from the mysterious mountains which they were yet to cross to cannibal villages where apemen lurked in the tree-tops with their bamboo tubes of death, there seemed to steal down something that dwarfed Jack's white heritage, that threatened him, that shrank his soul with a vague prescience of evil.

He touched the butt of his gun in the darkness, and the cold, hard grip of it brought some comfort. If he had to go out, he told himself, he would go fighting.

But his soul, which had retreated into the past, could not see into the future.

The place was full of snoring and fetid with rank smells, when the dawn finally stole in through the mats that closed the entrance. It touched the rows of skulls and flamed upon the fish god, hideous emblem of idolatry and ignorance.

The birds began to chatter and screech. It was day again, and the white men had shown their dominance. White men questing for gold on hidden trails.

III

MITCHELL MOVES

MITCHELL'S MIND WAS UNEASY. Though he was soon busy beyond the ordinary at the sisal plantation at Ikoiko, he was infinitely lonely without his chum. It was practically the first time they had been parted for eight years. Nothing had come between them. They had starved together, feasted together, slept together and worked together in plenitude and poverty until they were far closer than brothers. They had tested each other to the limit and out of this had come the welding of a bond that now, parted, however temporarily, left a gap—a vacuum.

Mitchell had always looked up to Somers. The other's education, his knowledge on many subjects, his faculty for mathematics, his trick at languages—though in this particular, without grammatical consideration—he matched his pal. They were equals, they joshed each other and even baited each other at times, knowing each other's faults and liking none the less because of them, but, secretly, Mitchell considered himself Somers' inferior in all but physical strength. There he had perhaps a little the best of it. A certain doggedness and toughness of fiber offset the flaming spirit that had sustained and prompted the other man in times of stress and peril. There were those who called Mitchell stubborn. It was certain that he was loath to change his mind, or alter any course that he had determined upon, once having done so.

So Mitchell welcomed the work and the problems at Ikoiko. The owner was often away, having a string of plantations and being now busy with the start of a new native rubber industry. Ned was constantly combating the indolence of the natives, to whom work in the sun was almost a sacrilege, an insult to their tutelary deity. The previous superintendent, Whittingham by name, had been the unfortunate combination of a "new chum" and a "younger son," whose ideas of work in the tropics meant wearing faultlessly cut linen riding breeches, polished riding boots, a drill sleeveless polo shirt, a solar topee and an eyeglass, with many servants to wait upon him, cool verandas and iced drinks, a good horse to ride and cheery calls with a Scotch and soda and a game of bridge with the neighbors.

There was nothing of that kind at Ikoiko. The quarters for owner and superintendent were primitive, the porch was unscreened, there was no ice, and the house help, taken in from the most promising of the field hands, was almost, impossible. They were dirty, lazy, always scratching themselves, stealing, lying, shiftless and incompetent. They could not sweep nor make a bed any better than they could boil an egg. With the latter they either left it in the water for half an hour or brought it barely warmed through. The nearest white neighbor was fifteen miles away, with swamp and jungle in between. He was a Scotchman named Menzies, who played the pipes, read Robert Burns, got drunk on Sundays and the rest of the week worked so hard that he turned in with his clothes on.

"You're going to find it a bit hard, old chap," said Whittingham to Mitchell on the latter's arrival and after his introduction. "I wish you luck, I really do. The place is a bally washout, and these blacks are a bit thick, to put it mildly. I'm being fired, I suppose, and I'm glad of it. You know a chap can't even get a cold tub in the morning. The mosquitoes are winged tigers; the whole shop is nothing but mud and malaria in the lower half, and the rest of it must be remarkably like a suburb of Hades. My word, Mitchell, if you stick it out you're a wonder. I might have got along better if I'd learned to talk their lingo. But they've got a dozen dialects between 'em and I never was any good at languages. Never carried off any of the jolly old prizes, you know. And those beggars will always pretend not to understand this pidgin beach talk when they don't want to.

"Drop in and see me when you get down to Port Moresby, if you ever do. Between you and me, Howell is a bit of a slave driver—expects a Johnny to be on the go all day and sit up all night thinking of improvements and odd jobs."

"What are you going to do?" asked Mitchell. He had taken a liking to the Britisher, fancying him more naturally incompetent for this sort of executive work than actually a loafer.

"Me? I hardly know. I've got a bit of change coming in, you see. Uncle left it to me for merit. Fact. He was nutty over cricket and, if I do say so myself, I have a neat break from the off. He was on the eleven when he was a kid at Winchester and New, and so was I. So he watched my bowling average and approved. Stood between me and the wrath at home when the jolly old reports came in on the educational end of it. He had matches at his own place in Surrey, and I used to trot down there and bowl for his home eleven. So, when he passed on, he left me a cool five hundred pounds a year. It don't go far in London, but in the merry old Antipodes it's all to the mustard. I'll knock about a bit, look for gold, nose round for pearls. Get a sloop maybe. I've got a quarter's allowance due and I've got what's coming to me here intact. You simply can't spend money at Ikoiko, and the chaps you run into at Port Moresby are rotters, outside of the government crowd, and they're spineless, positively spineless. So long, Mitchell. Look me up. Might go on a trip together if you ever get a vacation out of Howell."

He slid into his saddle and went cantering off, with the easy seat of a polo player and one born of generations of fox hunters. Youth on a blooded horse; a good-natured, happy-go-lucky, likable kid, Mitchell considered him, and was sorry to see him go, wondering a bit how he would make out. But he had seen just such chaps stiffen with duty, and fight like old veterans with a cool courage that had long ago won his admiration. There was the right stuff in Whittingham, he decided, only it would take time to settle itself.

Ned soon found out that the Britisher's remarks on the amount of work to be done were not exaggerated. The Papuan boys were not to be worked more than fifty hours a week under government provision, but the superintendent's only limit was the end of his responsibilities.

"There are some folk who like the eastern natives," said Howell. "Some the northern Orokaiva. The boys from the Kiwai have a name for being sullen but determined, and those from the Purari Delta are a bad lot. We've got some of all of 'em. The truth is it all depends on the way you handle 'em. You've got to be firm but not so as to get them sulky. You've got to watch 'em close. If they put one over on you they'll make a joke of it and soon they'll all be loafing. You've got to make 'em be clean or we'll have dysentery wipe 'em out in jigtime. One bad attack queers a plantation if there are many casualties. Then there's the store. Don't let 'em spend too much.

"They look forward to a jamboree when their contracts are up and, if they haven't got anything coming then, they'll go back to their villages and tell 'em we're crooks at Ikoiko. That means no more boys coming in to work of their own account, and one volunteer is worth two recruited boys. Pick out your best workers and jolly 'em along. They'll set the example to the rest. Give 'em a bit of tobacco, now and then, but go easy. Ikoiko is paying by the skin of its teeth right now. They raised the pay of the boys to fifteen shillings a month and their living, including smoking, and they cut down the signing on to not more than two years. There's always a government officer nosin' round and, because this is an American plantation, he thinks we're all Simon Legrees. Goes round asking bush boys if they've got any complaints, instead of waitin' to hear 'em. They find plenty to kick about."

Mitchell saw that he was to be field overseer, storekeeper and health inspector, all in one. Howell also suggested the necessity of learning dialects and showed him how he had picked them up himself, getting together a vocabulary of a few words at a time, which he would write down phonetically and pin the list up next to his shaving mirror or in his sun helmet. Most of the dialects interlocked, and Mitchell soon found himself getting some fluency. The boys were like big children, their minds unstable, overexcitable at times, incapable of sustained thought or any train of thought, sometimes singularly dull and apathetic. They had spells of homesickness for their villages out of which they had to be coaxed. They were subject to sudden fits of petulance over some fancied grievance; but the new superintendent was patient with them, and he began to get along.

Now and then a boy came down from a village looking for work, though there were professional, licensed recruiters who were the main source of supply. Labor was scarce and Ned had to take the new hand without delay before a government officer, who explained to him, or at least tried to explain, the terms of the contract of service. There were boys whose terms were up and who had to be sent back at the plantation's expense to their homes. All these were extras. But Ned, who had once been a corporal, developed executive capacities that pleased Howell so much that he left him in complete charge. It was the first time that such responsibility had been thrust upon him and, in a way it was pleasantly flattering. It was the butter on the dry bread of his hard work that gave him appetite.

But he did not cease to think of Jack Somers. That hunch of his was something more than superstition. It was a persistent suggestion that almost amounted to a positive message that something was wrong.

It assailed him at odd moments in the fields when he was riding under the scorching sun between the rows of fleshy, prickless, sprawling agaves, or watching the planting of suckers. It smote him out of the clear sky while he bossed the cutting off of the big leaves, the removal of the spiny ends and their bundling for the machines.

This part was all automatic and the machinery simple, merely holding the leaves while one half was cleaned and delivered at the far end, then repeating. The yellowish-white fiber, straight and clean, was then gathered from the wheels for final treatment. The machines clanked on regularly, until suddenly the feeding would slacken and Ned would come to with a start from a vision that seemed on the point of materializing from the air, which left the baffling impression that Jack was in danger—imminent danger.

At night he would wake to see eyes in the blackness, the unmated orbs of Chance in his satanic face, the marble-like blue ones of Hansen, the squinting eyes of Tufu, the lascar, and the dead white optic of the too unctuous Wang. It was uncanny and it began to get on his nerves so that he strove to reason things out with himself, to make inquiries of the recruiters—men of wide travel—and of the government agents on his trips to Port Moresby with a new hand. On the first of these occasions he found that Whittingham had chartered a sloop and was off to the Louisiade Archipelago, hoping to find gold.

And he heard things about Chance that were not reassuring. The schooner seemingly was still at Yule Island, awaiting the return of the expedition, for bugs or whatever Chance had in mind. For all the display of entomological specimens in the cabin, Mitchell was not at all convinced that Chance was out for more specimens. There was, he believed, something deeper, more sinister to the man than the collecting of insects.

The tales were not pretty. Collectively, they left a grim smear upon Mitchell's mind. Once, it seemed, the *Molly* had run down a canoe load of natives in a channel between mushroom coral reefs. The place was shark infested. The schooner had sailed on, with Chance at the helm. The exact place of the casualty was hard to place, even by the survivors of the canoe who escaped the sharks, but other skippers had suggested there was no necessity for the collision, that a little combined seamanship and humanity could have averted tragedy.

Once, admittedly in a gale, a man had gone overboard. Chance had kept on his course without so much as a flung life buoy. There were no buoys handy; it was not within British administration to censure the skipper of an American registry schooner. No complaint had been made, but these tales had leaked out, as they will, and the recruiting men had picked them up as they toured the friendly villages.

Chance had undoubtedly killed a man in Brisbane some time before. Some cited it as cold-blooded murder. The man was drunk and without doubt insulting. He had damned Chance's eyes, for one thing, and declared them a hoodoo. According to the witnesses Chance had said nothing, only looked at him, and the liquor-crazed man had suddenly gone amuck and reached for his gun. It was in his hip pocket and it caught in the lining, held there while he tugged and swore.

It had been a matter of a second or two—some said more. Chance had slid out a weapon from a shoulder holster, and there were those who said that he deliberately watched the efforts of the drunkard to get his gun loose, with a smile on his face, before he pulled trigger and turned away, leaving the man on the floor. The inference was that Chance had ample time to cover his man and disarm him but that he had killed him with less sentiment than he would have felt in putting a beetle into a cyanide bottle. He had been discharged. The dead man was a notorious nuisance and had a rotten record. Chance's, before the court, was clean.

An extra touch was given Mitchell by a bartender in Port Moresby, referring not so much to Chance, as to the first mate, Hansen of the pale-blue eyes that were like marbles.

" 'Im," said the dispenser of whisky, " 'e's plain swine, 'e is, that 'Ansen. Beat 'is wife up till she's a crawlin' cripple. Lost 'is ticket for 'itting a man over the 'ead with a belayin' pin because 'e didn't move fast enough ter suit 'im. Kicked in the ribs of a pore blighter who tapped 'im for a drink one night, after 'e'd bashed 'im in the face an' blinded 'im. You mightn't think it to look at 'im but 'e's got the eyes of a killer. 'E ain't got no feelin's, no more'n a blood-sucking spider, 'e ain't. An' 'e's syling with a proper skipper. No one else wants 'im. They say Chance 'as got somethin' on 'im, at that. But they're a pair."

Chance had said that Hansen was slow, no good with the natives in an emergency. He seemed to be over handy, to Mitchell. And Chance had left him behind with the schooner.

The question that really bothered him most was why Chance had gone to the trouble of getting him the job with Howell. Howell, it turned out, was by no means a special friend of Chance. The planter did not like Chance particularly. But they were both Americans and in an accidental meeting, Howell had happened to say that he wished he had a live American as superintendent. Whereupon Chance had said he knew of just the man.

This was before Chance had talked with either of them. The skipper knew nothing about them, beyond the gossip that the two were stranded.

Perhaps he *had* only wanted one of them, offering the good wages he did, but why had he gone to such pains to bother about the partner? Not from kindliness or good will. Mitchell did not believe he possessed such virtues in even a minor degree. It might be that he was eager to get one of them and took the means to offset refusal. But to Ned, pondering the thing over and over, it seemed suspicious. A film seemed to come over the sun at such times, a vapor to rise up from the baking dirt like a screen on which a grim picture would presently project itself but which never materialized, except in its suggestion.

The thing grew to be an obsession. Mitchell was overworking, strained by new responsibilities, and his strong nerves began to suffer. Sleep was insufficient and he grew gaunt. But he was of tough caliber, the sort that rose to emergencies, and, when the dysentery struck Ikoiko, he braced himself to meet the epidemic and his premonitions concerning Somers vanished, for the time.

Howell was away and stayed away. Later, Mitchell learned that he too had encountered the disease where he was, the scourge that has been most fatal to Papuan field development. Aside from the actual mortality, once a plantation got a bad name on account of it, it might be accounted as a failure. Nothing could convince the native boys that here was not sorcery of the worst kind, and henceforth the spot would be tabooed by labor. The news spread swiftly to all recruiting village stations. In this case the disease was endemic, appearing in a dozen places at once, widely separated. Its source was undoubtedly dietary. The water at Ikoiko was carefully filtered but it was impossible to prevent the hands from eating fruit that was too ripe, or unripe, and probably the cause lay there.

Howell had left Mitchell directions for combating it, and there were supplies of sulphate of sodium, of ipecac and laudanum, but he had no idea of the tremendous and unpleasant task that lay before him. Those who were not attacked were panic-stricken; they could not be convinced of the necessity for constant cleanliness. Mitchell had to drive them to the task of removing all foulness, and sickening odors vitiated the air despite all disinfectants and enforced discipline.

Native boys were stricken in the fields with the terrific griping and lay down there and then to die, their chocolate skins turning blue-gray with fright, their teeth chattering, their bodies twitching and their eyes rolling in appeal like so many sick apes. A week of it found Mitchell red-eyed from loss of sleep and worry as he went his rounds of the sheds, fearing to find a patient dead, making that discovery, ordering the corpse carried out for burial by men who were either cowed or surly to the point of revolt. There were boys there, marked with tribal weals, little short of savages, accredited cannibals, and these he had to drive with blows or at the point of his gun.

The sheds were shambles. The flies buzzed and settled down or rose in clouds, the air was a pestilence. Many of the sick men were covered with sores. Some could not take the ipecac and had to be given laudanum or a saline solution four, six, even eight times a day.

It was a heroic task and it left its mark upon Mitchell. His face acquired a gravity that it never lost. He matured and deepened and his spirit toughened. He had to crack jokes, to force himself to go down the line singing, with his voice hoarse from exhaustion, to urge sick men to build additions to the sheds, to burn one building that was utterly untenable. Now and then he rose to wrath that made them flinch, but he never dared to lose his own temper. His self-control was their salvation as well as his own. It was his will that kept them alive as much as the medicine.

The heat was tremendous, exhausting his ebbing vitality. The air was rank and stifling. He had to look after his own health, to cook his own food and bathe himself in disinfectants when he was dog tired. Often he was close to collapse, making his four-hour visits on feet that were like boils, with limbs that were limp as rags yet heavy as lead. Always his head ached and the swallowing of any nourishment was an achievement.

He took dozing cat naps, setting his alarm clock, fearful that it would not waken him, afraid to find fresh cases. Field work was abandoned. The sisal plants raised their long stems and flowered, dropping off the ripened pole plants that rooted where they wished, undoing the work of weeks, destroying the symmetry and efficiency of the plantation. For that Mitchell did not care. He was past caring much about anything, keeping on with a doggedness that he was later often to marvel at. His endurance was truly phenomenal.

Other plantations were in trouble. Ikoiko was shunned, quarantined by selfishness as much as by any regulation of the government. Ned's medicines ran low and he had a nightmare ride to Port Moresby and back for more. People questioned him, shrugged their shoulders, and watched him reel from the store. At the government hospital they could give him no aid and little advice. He was doing all that could be done.

He crawled back into his saddle, a haggard, unshaven tramp who could barely keep awake, and rode out of town, making for Ikoiko, when he was hailed by a man spruce and clean and cheery. Whittingham!

"My word, Mitchell, what's wrong with you?"

Mitchell essayed a ghastly grin.

"Dysentery," he croaked. "Howell's away. I've just heard he's bucking the same thing up north. Eleven dead and the rest of 'em ready to pass out the first time they think I'm not on top of 'em. Been away seven hours now, missed two rounds. Devil knows how I'll find 'em when I get back. They're helpless. Can't make 'em keep the place clean."

"Doing it all alone, what?"

"On my own. The others have troubles of their own."

"Look here, old top, I'm going back with you. No spoofing. I know those swine. You can't do it all. I'll get my horse in a minute."

Whittingham appeared as an angel of light, almost as a miracle. Mitchell was too tired, too dazed to express his actual gratitude. He dimly knew that if Whittingham had not showed up and made his offer he could not have gone through with it. For two weeks he had eaten little and slept hardly at all while his labor had been practically incessant. The crisis for most of his patients would come within the next few days. Ten per cent—a little better than ten per cent of them were gone already. If the mortality grew much greater the prosperity of Ikoiko would be doomed, and Mitchell felt that responsibility as well as the lives of his charges.

They were wild creatures, alternately turning to him for succor and ready to rebel against him. Why they should be forced to clean up for their fellows was incomprehensible to them. In their villages a sick man was set apart with only the sorcerer and his womenfolk to see him through. Here they were herded together, sick and well—though Mitchell kept the worse cases apart— in an atmosphere fetid with decaying humanity and charged with fear.

Fear brooded over Ikoiko accompanied by its twin brother Horror. They hovered over it day and night, through the broiling, stifling hours and through the hot, breathless nights when the sick moaned and shrieked and gibbered. When those who were not stricken hunkered down with eyes that were sullen against this white man who drove them, brooding savage instincts that roused them to leap at him, butcher him.

If they ever found him asleep, if he ever collapsed, Mitchell knew that moment would be his last. It was not so much the menace of his gun as the unseen barrier of the white man's *mana*, his ghostly power, that saved him from their rush.

Now Whittingham had come to help him.

"You're a damn good sport," blurted Ned.

"Rot! Might have happened when I was there. Couldn't have handled it the way you have. Can't see you carry on alone, old top."

Mitchell was vaguely aware of Whittingham's overtaking him, of their riding on through the scorching bush, through high, rustling reeds, over the swamp and through the stretch of forest up to the slopes of Ikoiko. Whittingham insisted upon being shown immediately through the sheds. Mitchell half feared to find that his mutineers had bolted into the bush. He had locked up all weapons and stores before he left but, if their monkey brains held purpose long enough and sufficiently in accord, they would make short work of locks. He half dreaded to see smoke rising.

He had installed a foreman, of sorts, a boy who had come in voluntarily to work and had shown signs of executive efficiency, of control over the others that Mitchell could not fathom but accepted gratefully, hoping that the man would prove faithful to him in the emergency. His name was Lipako. He stood some five feet six and he was beautifully muscled. His costume had been only a gee string, but he had adopted the short kilt that the others wore in the fields. His features were not unpleasing though his nose was depressed at the bridge and the nostrils over wide. His breast was tattooed with a decoration that told—though Mitchell did not know that at the time— that he had taken human life and was a proven warrior. He carried himself with a pride that was curious in a voluntary hand.

And he had been faithful. The boys were still there, sick and well, save for one who had died while Ned was away. Lipako greeted the two whites without emotion. Mitchell saw that his usually glossy skin was dry; it felt hot and his eyes glittered. If he felt pain he showed none, but he was sick. Mitchell gave him a dose of ipecac.

"Can't have *you* sick, Lipako," he said in the man's own dialect of Mekeo. But Lipako chose to answer in the beach lingo, as proud of his swift acquirement of that as Mitchell was of his own progress in Papuan.

"Me savvy me sick. Bimeby big fella sick. Him fella die too much. Lipako no like finish up. Lipako live. One fella finish, three fella sick too much. Lipako make fella chase um fly, wash um sick fella, clean um shed."

Whittingham went with Mitchell as he made his rounds, noting the dosage and the routine on a pad. When they went back to the shack that was facetiously called a bungalow the Britisher produced from a saddlebag a bottle of Scotch.

"Brought along four jolly old Johnny Walker's," he said. "We'll have a stiff peg, old top. I'm going to fix you up a regular snorter."

He fished around in the little kitchen and brought Mitchell the drink, steaming, in a long glass that smelled of fresh cloves. It was over sweet, Ned fancied, but he was not in a capricious humor and it was soothing. The liquor brought an instant glow to his stomach and relaxed him.

He came to on his cot. The sun was low. He must have slept for hours. He was still drowsy but he felt stronger. He did not remember turning in, in his pajamas. Shouldn't have done that, he told himself. Rounds to be made. More dead, maybe; graves to be dug, flies driven out, disinfectants sprinkled, mopping, medicine mixed—

A man stepped in through the door with a "Cheerio!" Ned had forgotten that Whittingham was with him.

"Have a good snooze, old top? Fine. No more casualties. That chap Lipako is down, but he's game as a fighting rooster. He don't want to die and he won't. First native I ever saw that way. I've dosed him, dosed all of 'em. Want to look around while I rustle up some chow?"

Mitchell found the sheds fumigated and clean, and the sick men were in good shape, save for their spasms of pain. As for himself, mentally and physically he felt in better shape than he had done for days. The drink and the nap had done him good. The calendar did not bother him those days. He did not know until a long time afterward that Whittingham had put laudanum in his toddy and that he had slept for almost thirty hours while the other carried on.

That was the turn of the tide. They lost no more men. Lipako put up a gallant fight. Of all the boys, he alone seemed really grateful and understanding of the white men's efforts. After a while he talked with Mitchell in Mekeo, letting down a screen between them by so doing, in some subtle way.

It appeared that he was the son of a chief, a warrior, the nephew of a great wizard, whose fame, it appeared, was known beyond the "Big Rivers," who sent out drum messages that were taken as oracles. He loved a girl, dark as ebony, with skin as smooth as polished shell. The village beauty, haughty and disdainful, was mindful of her too-short time of queening it over the bucks and she was making the most of it. There was an old chief, whose skin was like an alligator's—skin conditions seemed a standard of beauty—who desired her and had offered many pigs. But she had put all her suitors off, and Lipako had come down to earn money, so that he could take back gifts which would make the maiden's eyes soften, satisfy her parents and show up the old suitor with the pigs as a four-flusher.

Love had tamed the man-killer. The gentle passion had made him relinquish his dignity and serve for her favor. Her name was Vuuni, which meant the wood dove, but Mitchell gleaned that she could be fierce enough in repulsing gallantry.

No man could take the place of Somers, but Ned speedily grew fond of Whittingham. The Britisher had a certain shyness about him that would ordinarily bar intimacy, but circumstances had dissolved that insular aloofness and he revealed a personality that Mitchell came more and more to appreciate if not to entirely understand.

For one thing, Whittingham evidently regarded his voluntary aid to the pestilential camp, with its nauseating work, as a sort of duty, and duty was a matter that he entered into with a thoroughness and an almost fanatic zeal. Mitchell gathered that here was the inherent idea of the empire builder, considering the natives of the lands where the Union Jack flew as charges of all Britain's sons. They treated them as they would hound or horse, knowing that they were merely children. They gave them justice, tolerated religions and tried to understand them and ameliorate conditions. Where other nations used and neglected, exploited and abused, the British strove to build up. This was perhaps the secret of successful colonization.

"Can't let the poor beggars snuff out," Whittingham said. "They haven't savvy enough to help themselves."

It had not been a spontaneous impulse of one white man to help another in extremity, after all, though Mitchell knew the other would have come to his personal rescue if there had been no natives involved at all. Therefore, the two grew almost chummy, and, while Whittingham was still reticent, Mitchell found him sympathetic when he spoke of Somers and his fears for his safety.

"I wouldn't worry over that, old top," said the other. "You've been working overtime. Chap gets the bally hump and you can't see over it. What? I've heard a bit about this Chance. To my mind he's a cold-blooded polecat, but, why should he want to take your pal out into the bush and scrag him? What would that get him?"

"I don't know. It's just a hunch."

"You've let your jib down, that's what's the matter. Somers sounds to me as if he could look after himself all right."

"It isn't that," Mitchell replied. "Just a hunch. I know one thing: if he don't come out of the bush before long I'm going in after him."

"Good egg. We'll both go. With gold as a side issue. There's oodles of the jolly stuff back in the mountains. Dust in all the rivers, but a lot of it's flour gold, and these rivers are not easy to work as a placer. All mud and no gravel at the mouths for miles up. Too many mangroves, too many merry mosquitoes, and too many crocodiles. Some fun potting those last. And it would be a sportin' trip. No end of a lark. But we'd have to go in right. You can't trek without natives. You've got to know how to get along with 'em and you've got to trickle out gum drops and tobacco all the route. But your man'll be out all right. I saw the schooner at Yule Island, careened. They're overhauling her. How long is your contract for, with Howell? Decent chap, Howell, though he thinks I'm a loose end."

Ned smiled.

"He won't think so now. The two of us have saved Ikoiko for him. He ought to come through for your share in it. I'll speak to him about it."

Then occurred one of those changes in Whittingham that puzzled the American. He seemed to stiffen, to set back military shoulders that he had gained in the war; his eyes altered, he stuck his monocle in one of them, and his voice drawled. He had put on his British mask.

"Thanks, old chap. Rather you wouldn't. Couldn't think of drawing pay for a thing like that. I was inefficient enough when I was super here. Mebbe I've evened things up a bit."

Mitchell nodded. They were both smoking on their shaky porch after a supper that Whittingham had cooked, in his turn. He had a good knack at that, as had Mitchell, and they fared well. A message had come through from Howell that he was on his way back, and the two of them were now taking the first chance of leisure for a chat rather than sleep.

"I said I'd stay with him till Chance got back," said Ned in answer to the other's query. "I understand he wrote home—to the States—some time back, and that a man he knows is coming out in the fall." Mitchell suddenly reddened. This letter had been sent because of Howell's dissatisfaction with Whittingham, and here he was rubbing it in after all his friend had done for him.

"Quite all right, old top. I was a bit of a waster, you know. Did me good to get the sack. Stiffens a chap up, I fancy."

They were both lean as greyhounds after their travail. Whittingham possessed a really splendid physique, though his flesh, fair almost as a woman's where it had not been burned by the sun, was marred with shrapnel scars. Of his war record he said nothing.

Mitchell admired him, and he, in turn, criticized approvingly Mitchell's rangy figure. It ran a bit to over-broad shoulders and spidery legs but it was powerful and well knit.

"I fancy you'd put it all over me with the gloves," said the Britisher. "You've got a whale of a reach. I can fancy you poking that left of yours into my face and jabbing the daylights out of me. You Americans have got the Old Country lashed to the mast when it comes to the ring. Not to mention a few other things of late. Tennis and polo and golf. Shall we have a snifter? There's a little Scotch left. Shame to waste it on Howell. The main thing he had against me was rooting me out mornings. There's a rooster strain in him somewhere. I was born with an affection for my bed."

Mitchell grinned. There had been no indications of laziness in Whittingham through the stress of fighting the pestilence but now he affected it. He would lie under the mosquito nettings of his cot and yawn as he sang in a pleasant baritone:

> "Some day I'm going to murder the bugler,
>   Some day they're going to find him dead;
> And then I'll get the other pup,
> The guy that wakes the bugler up,
>   And spend the rest of my life in bed."

Good company. Clean of mind and body, full of pluck, generous and unselfish. When Somers came back Mitchell was minded to make a proposition to take Whittingham in with them. He had never expected to get along so well with an Englishman. He hoped Somers would like him when he returned. *When* he returned. And once more the blighting premonition came over him. But it was better with Whittingham there. He would miss him when Howell came back and Whittingham left Ikoiko. They were calling each other Ned and Buck now, Whittingham's first name being Buxton.

Howell came, gaunt and worried from his own battle, approving and praising when he saw what had been done. Lipako came in for honorable mention and suitable reward. Howell offered him a permanent foremanship under the superintendent, a chance for authority that the ordinary native would have jumped at. But Lipako refused. Mitchell had not had time to take him before the government officials for signing and a hand was allowed three months of service without contract. So that he was free to leave. Whittingham had made the young chieftain a present of five golden sovereigns with which he could discount many pigs. He promised to stay his voluntary term and to send in boys from his village later on.

Whittingham waved off any idea of pay.

"Check it against lost time and mistakes," he said to the plantation owner. "Plenty on that score. If you like I'll stick around a bit and do what I can, for the fun of it. You're behindhand. I can run the machines while you go the round of your other places. Must be a bit keen on inspecting them, what? And Ned and I get along like a couple of pups in a blanket."

It suited Howell and he said so. He had mail from home and his man would be coming out before long, as soon as he had arranged affairs.

"But I can use you any time," he said to Mitchell. "I'll find a place for you and raise your pay if you'll stay. I reckon I was mistaken in you, Whittingham. I'm in your debt. I can use you, too."

"No. Thanks just the same. I'm too constitutionally lazy. My word, Howell, you've no idea how Mitchell has been abusing me, kicking me out of bed at one bell in the morning watch. I'm fed up on it. But if he'll give me decent hours, I'll stick around here till his pal comes out of the jolly jungle. I want to meet him."

"You're welcome," said Howell a bit crisply, though it was plain enough that he was glad to have Whittingham stay. "By the way, I ran across word of Chance. He's gone up beyond what the natives call Big Rivers, into the mountains. He got in right with a wizard named Morimori, up Mekeo way, a high muckamuck in the sorcery line. Your friend was with him and another white man. They call the Chinese white men so I imagine that was Wang, and they're all right so far."

"Morimori!" exclaimed Mitchell. "That is Lipako's uncle. And he spoke of Big Rivers."

"Good egg!" said Whittingham. "We may be able to use Lipako, though I hope we won't, hunting for your pal. But, if we take a little trip that way on our own hook, he should come in useful. I wonder what Chance is snoozing up in the mountains for? I think that butterfly hunting stuff of his is the bunk. There can't be much money in it and Chance is a spender. They say he chucks the coin around like a dog shaking water. Goes into some dive and buys it out. Prowls round with that Wang cook of his. I don't savvy that. Chinks are all right. I've known lots of them who were prime chaps. But when a white man chums round with them, it's a bit messy, to my mind."

IV

CHANCE RETURNS

THE WEEKS WORE ON THROUGH THE TRANSPLANTING SEASON. The crop was harvested and turned into sisal fiber of prime quality. Howell insisted upon giving Mitchell a bonus of a hundred pounds, saying that he had virtually saved the crop. And he came back from one of his inspection trips with a gift for Whittingham. It was a high-powered rifle of German manufacture, a masterpiece of gunsmithing, the parts interlocking, hand-forged and fitted.

"It belonged to a man up in what was German New Guinea," he explained. "He left it behind when they cleared out. You know the natives turned against a lot of them when they savvied how things were going. I'll wager there are plenty of skulls in the racks of what used to be Kaiser Wilhelm's Land. The blacks are a wild lot."

"It's a ripping gun," said the delighted Whittingham. "Shoot a mile and then not get started. Takes the Germans to make 'em. It's a beauty. Slathers of ammunition, too. Mighty decent of you, Howell. Too bad there's no big game in Papua."

He was like a boy with his first weapon as he took it apart and examined it with the manner of an expert.

"We'll take her out and try it," he said when it was assembled. "Got no end of a kick in the butt, I'll bet tuppence ha'penny."

"I don't know how the trader got hold of it," said Howell. "He couldn't make butt or muzzle of it. Sold it cheap, shells and all. Glad you like it."

"Like it? Wait till I get the hang of it. I wish I'd had this on the front. There was a sniper there who outranged our rifles. But that's over."

It was the only direct reference Mitchell had heard him make to the war. He set up a target and showed himself by far the best marksman of the three, though both the Americans could handle a rifle. But Whittingham was a born shot. He plugged bull after bull at lengthening ranges until they gave up vying with him.

The Britisher was modest.

"It's a snap in this climate," he said. "No wind to speak of. Good visibility. I could make a crocodile jump like a trout with this at half a mile."

It was Whittingham who brought news of the return of Chance to Port Moresby, riding back in a hurry from a trip that he cut short.

"The *Molly* is in," he said, "and Chance is aboard. She's anchored well out and the skipper hasn't been ashore yet. Schooner got in this morning, from Yule Island. They're back."

Mitchell turned white with what seemed a sudden clutch on his heart.

They were back. Then where was Jack Somers? Jack knew where to find him. He would waste no time showing up unless he was sick, or something else had happened.

"Buck up, old top," said Whittingham. "Get your crock saddled and we'll make a social call on the schooner. They sent a boat ashore for stores. Looks as if he might figure on slipping out in a hurry. He's as easy to hold as an eel, that Chance, I imagine. But we'll nail him. If anything looks fishy I've got a bit of a drag up at Government House. Never used it yet, but I can make those official Johnnies sit up a bit. Chance'll talk turkey, as you say, before he leaves."

He did not attempt to make light of the situation, and Mitchell fancied that he had heard, or surmised, more than he said. Howell was at Ikoiko and, in five minutes, Ned and Buck were galloping through scrub, forest and swamp, at top speed. Mitchell had a Colt automatic in a belt holster and Whittingham carried an English .45 with which he could spot designs on a playing card at thirty feet. They were in a grim mood. Chance had had plenty of time to send word of accident, sickness or disaster.

"He's probably heard that I was in town," said Whittingham. "Know I've been up here with you. He'd inquire about you anyway. He'll either duck or be Johnny on the spot to meet us."

Mitchell nodded, his jaw set. His hunch was working out. Jack had not come back—was not coming back.

They came out upon a brown, sun-scorched hill and looked down on the roadstead. The horses were blowing and Mitchell's was a sorry case. He was not the horseman Whittingham was. They could see the ships in the harbor, the water of which was wrinkled like blue crape paper from the smoky northeaster that blew gustily, now they were out of the bush. Whittingham pointed out the schooner *Molly*, but Mitchell had already identified it. Then Buck gave a cry.

Coming in from Torres Straits moved a gunboat, the British patrol in those waters.

"Look here, Ned," said Whittingham, "you've got to breathe that nag of yours or you'll walk in. He's not far from foundering—we've come at a desperate pace. Mind if I go ahead? I've got an errand. Important. Meet you at the wharf. If I get there first I'll have a shore boat commandeered."

"Go ahead," said Mitchell a little stiffly. It was natural enough for Whittingham to have affairs of his own, yet somehow this attention to them jarred. He dismounted and loosened the girths of his saddle, as the other cantered off.

Ned stayed beside the winded horse for several minutes that seemed like hours. His lean face was hard, and his eyes were steely. He took out his automatic and inspected it, although he knew it was in perfect shape. Then he told himself he must get in hand. Chance was the key to whatever situation might develop.

He could see black specks moving on board the schooner. Her canvas was down, but presently he saw men busy about the booms, ungasketing, and he mounted his tired and galled steed. What was a horse compared to news of Jack? Let it die on his feet.

But the beast lasted, though Ned thought it would drop when he reached the wharf. Whittingham was there with a shore boat ready, the native crew at the oars. Mitchell started to jump into it, but Buck checked him.

"Boat coming off from the *Molly*," he said. "Chance is in it. Bet you a shilling he's figuring on meeting us, or you, not quite so soon perhaps, as he will."

They sat on the stringpiece, the boat crew idling, chewing betel, spitting the crimson saliva into the rippling tide, while the boat from the schooner came on smartly. Chance recognized them and stood up in the stern where he was handling the steering sweep. Holding it with one hand, he waved his hat to them. Ned and Buck did not respond. The whale-boat came alongside the wharf, and a native sailor jumped up with a rope like a trained ape, making fast.

Chance mounted nimbly by slippery cleats. He looked more like Mephisto than ever, Mitchell thought, smug with some secret satisfaction, and an almost irresistible desire raged through him to smash a fist into the satiric face. But Whittingham's hand was on his arm.

"Steady, old top! Go easy. I've got an ace up my sleeve."

Chance held out his hand.

"I was coming out to the plantation to see you, Mitchell. Hard to get away before. I'm sailing on the tide. And I wanted to go over what I have to say to you. First of all, let's get rid of this."

He took out a package from his pocket and gave it to Mitchell, who thrust it away mechanically in his coat.

"Where's Jack Somers?" he demanded.

"It's a hard thing to tell you, Mitchell. He didn't come back. He had an accident. Slipped on the grass, I'm afraid. It's like walking on ice. We found him at the foot of a cliff. Couldn't bring the body back. Impossible, naturally."

Whittingham's grip bit into Mitchell's forearm, as the latter took a step forward with blazing eyes and words crowding, clogging speech. Chance did not flinch. His mismated eyes gleamed, and his hand slid toward his open tunic front.

"We'll go aboard and talk it over, if you don't mind, Captain Chance," said Whittingham. "Too many ears round here."

The gleam was a flash of satisfaction now, diabolic.

"You're interested?" he asked of the Britisher.

"Quite. So much so, Captain Chance, that I sent a message up to Government House some time ago. It's there by this. I wouldn't wonder but what they had radioed something about it to the gunboat that just came in. We'll have our talk aboard the *Molly*. I hope you will not be delayed and lose this tide, or any others. You see," Whittingham added blandly, as Chance's bristling eyebrows drew together, "the lieutenant governor and chief judicial officer of Papua happens to be a relative of mine. I don't like him very much. He's a bit stiff in the neck at times. I haven't called on him up to date, but I sent my card up with a note and certain other credentials. So, I think we can all go aboard the *Molly*, captain, and have a quiet talk."

He emphasized the "quiet" ever so slightly.

The strange eyes flamed. Chance's teeth were bared above his goatee in a snarl. But Whittingham stood coolly filling his pipe, so quietly assured that Mitchell took cue from him, getting a grip on himself. This was the reason that Whittingham had ridden ahead—to get in touch with Government House, with a relative he had never mentioned, had never cared so far to link up with. Mitchell knew the reputation of the governor, stiff and official, prompt to resent any breach of his authority, none too cordial to Americans, though formally polite enough. The *Molly* would not sail until he was satisfied that the hint from his young connection was unsustained by circumstance.

Looking over the water to the gunboat, Ned saw a sailor go up to its deck officer, both like marionettes in miniature but plain enough. The man handed a message, saluted. There was some order given. A run of men toward a canvas-covered, rapid-fire gun. It swung casually but inevitably on its base, covering the *Molly*.

Chance saw it and caught up his goatee between his strong teeth, chewing at it. Mitchell felt a sudden sense of relief. He was going to get a fair show at Chance, backed by the power that Whittingham had evoked. It was good to have a pal like that. He got back his poise and nodded calmly enough when Chance, with a half bow, said that he would be delighted to play the host and invited them into his own boat.

Mitchell declined, and Chance cast off and led the way for their shore crew.

"That's your ace?" Mitchell asked Whittingham.

"Haven't played it yet, but he got a glimpse of it. There won't be any monkey business now. He'll talk straight."

On board the schooner, they listened with set faces, declining refreshments. Chance called in Tufu and Wang to corroborate his yarn.

"Of course, there will be affidavits from my own men," he said. "And corroboration can be had from my carriers. A tedious job to collect them. But they'll all tell you just what happened. Poor Somers was on the cliff above the big pool, as I told you. I was busy with the men. We thought there might be gold in the pool—"

"Was there?" flashed Mitchell.

"Not as much as we hoped. This was way back of Mount Pitzoko, far in the interior valleys of the Anabunga tributaries. The river flows in the Aduala Valley between Pitzoko and the mission station. There's quite a decent road that far, considering, but it's all wilderness beyond. We wanted to take the body back to the station for Christian burial but it was quite impossible. The climate, you see. At least a week's travel—"

Again to Mitchell came the desire to smash the man between the eyes. He knew that Chance was lying. Every instinct told him so. His spinal marrow crawled and invisible hairs seemed lifting there. Some forgotten sense came alive and told him that here was a hypocrite and an enemy, a man who was wholly evil and clever enough to cover his story with a tissue of falsehood that could not be lifted to reveal the truth.

"Tufu found him," said Chance. "Tufu and Wang. He was badly mangled by the fall. Lit on rocks. That was against bringing in the body, of course."

Mitchell's veins swelled. The man was mocking him. There were devils in his eyes with their uncanny look.

"I wouldn't call Somers careless," he went on. "He was intrepid—took too many risks, perhaps. But he was a valuable man. His loss is a sad one. You will find his effects in the package I gave you, with other matters. There was no message. Would you like to talk with Wang—or Tufu?"

Mitchell controlled himself with a prodigious effort. Chance had full assurance now, but just the same Whittingham had upset him. For a moment he had been rattled.

"Just where was this place?" Mitchell asked. "I'd like a map of your route, the villages you went through, their headmen, the names of your carriers." He snapped the phrases out while Chance palpably sneered.

"As far as I can do so, my friend," he said. "You are upset, of course. Are you proposing to go over that trail?"

"You bet I am. And, if things don't match up with what you are going to tell us, I'll have a reckoning with you, if I have to go round the world twenty times to find you."

Chance's sneer grew more open.

"I'm afraid you won't find much," he said. "The natives have a way of collecting trophies. And they don't like to give them up. Of course, we buried your friend, but I wouldn't be surprised if you ran across his skull grinning at you from a rack in a clubhouse, if you ever get that far."

Now there was open enmity in the cabin. Whittingham alone, with the Britisher's birthright, sat calmly puffing his pipe.

"I am going to suggest," he said, "that Captain Chance bring his witnesses and his maps up to Government House and we'll go over the thing there this evening. Sorry not to invite you to dinner, captain, but matters seem a bit strained. We'll meet you at Government House at, say, eight o'clock. Meantime, you and I, Ned, will paddle over to the gunboat. I know the skipper. Let's toddle."

Mitchell got up, leaning over the table.

"You may have cooked things up," he said to Chance, between teeth that were close set, "but I'm going to check you up. My pal's dead and I've got a hunch, the same I had before he went with you, that you've done some rotten work. I'll take a shot that you expected to find gold and didn't want any one to bring back word of where it was."

He saw a flicker in the strange eyes, the momentary dilation of pupils.

"But, by Heaven, you'll come through with where you went!" Ned went on. "I'm going to check it up, I tell you. And if you did Jack Somers in, I'll get you if I have to wade hip-deep through blazing hell to find you."

The flicker and the dilation came again, passed.

"You are hasty, Mitchell. Upset. I am quite sure that I can satisfy Government House and our suspicious friend." He bowed to Whittingham. "I wish you luck—back of Pitzoko."

There was a fiend's malice in that wish, but Mitchell turned and went on deck, his fists tightly clenched.

If he had not known that the visit to the gunboat was a move in their game he would not have gone. He was in no mood to eat, to talk with strangers. But he was glad he went.

"We've got a message from Government House to keep our eyes peeled on that beggar Chance," said the commander of the *Thetis*. "I'd give something to plunk a shot at him. He's a rotter but a slick one. His Nibs will put him through a course of sprouts, but I doubt if they'll be able to hold him."

"If there's occasion, I'll find him," said Mitchell, tight-lipped. He remembered the package in his pocket, but this was no place to look at it. It could wait until the conference at the governor's. Whittingham sent a wireless and received one.

"He'll have to come clean with his trail," he said. "And I've a notion that's about the last thing he wants to do. I've an idea he struck gold all right. Couldn't take out all he wanted to, of course. Figures on going back. Greedy beggar, I'll bet. Well, I'm with you, Ned, to check him up. And we'll tap his little treasure-house, just for fun. If you're going to have to chase after him, hard, cold gold dust and nuggets will come in mighty handy."

Ned nodded. He did not wish to seem churlish in that kindly, tactful mess room, but gold seemed less than dirt to him at the time. He was to consider differently.

If he ate he was not conscious of it. Jack was gone, done to death, killed to hide the secret of a discovery. And he knew that Chance was going to slip through their fingers. If he attacked him, and he itched to do so, he would lose all his chances of finding out the truth. These might be slim, but now another hunch was moving in him. He felt that he was going to discover the truth. There were, too, Lipako, Morimori, and Whittingham stanch comrade, unexpectedly equipped with access to authority. Their pat assembly could not be just accident. He would run down this covered trail, unearth its grim secret and then—Chance would pay the reckoning. Jack was to be avenged. Gallant Jack Somers, the pal whom he had almost worshiped, comrade of several thousand days and nights! Gone!

The inquiry was official enough, though the governor wore only his tropical evening clothes—mess jacket and trousers of fine white linen, with starched vest and shirt. He was an imposing figure with his red horse face, looking a great deal like a chessman knight's head, wooden but impressive. His secretary was present and a stenographer. Chance had brought Wang, Tufu and two of his crew, but the governor did not examine the natives. He kept them outside. Wang he put through a separate cross-questioning. But in the end Chance went out, free to leave in his schooner.

His face was not pleasant to behold. Sardonic at first, it held something of bafflement when he left. It was an evil countenance he turned at the door with a half bow and a "Good evening, gentlemen." His eyes were cruel as a cat's that see a mouse going into its hole. Mitchell felt its malignancy and knew that he was the mouse.

But the skipper's hand had been forced. He had been obliged to show the object of his mission—to open for inspection a mining license he had taken out before he left Port Moresby. The trail he had thought covered was traced on official maps. He might have juggled a little at the last about the exact location of his golden pool but he had had to give names, to display logs and diaries, to furnish dates, to answer shrewd questions by a man who knew his Papua better than any other white man. He had not dared to lie too much. Before he could get out of the zone of British administration, swift runners might check his story, far-flung radio messages halt his progress. He was not going to be welcome if he came back for more gold—if he dared to come back.

Much depended upon the impression he had made upon the governor, as to whether the latter would start the official machinery to corroborate his tale, or find it false. That the man who had not come out was not a British subject helped, but Whittingham had put a spoke in that wheel.

The executive countenance betrayed nothing. It was judicial, symbolic of the really vast authority that was vested in the man.

But he spoke some of his mind after Chance and his men had gone.

"That fellow is an unprincipled scoundrel," he said. "Without a doubt. I question whether he possesses more than the rudiments of a soul. I imagine him to be an unqualified and accomplished liar, but I think he has spoken the truth in large measure. Or if he has not, his lies are too well based. I should dearly like to catch him in some act that would bring him under my jurisdiction, but I am afraid there is nothing—"

He broke off, muttering something about international courtesy, before he turned to Mitchell.

"He said something about the—er—missing man's effects. Did he give them to you, Mr. Mitchell?"

Mitchell took the package from his pocket and opened it with a gush of emotion he was hard put to it to master. There was Jack's wallet, with a few letters and papers, his watch, some cuff links and studs, and a stickpin that Mitchell had given him, made from a curiously shaped pearl. And there was a little crisp bundle of notes to the value of five hundred pounds. It was his first instinct to tear these across, and only the tough paper kept him from doing so until Whittingham interposed.

"Somers earned those, old chap," he said. "I've a notion that if he's been done in he'd like you to use them in finding out about it."

"You're right. I've got the first payment intact and what I have myself. I'm going into the interior to see what I can find out, governor," said Mitchell. "If he's been murdered"—his voice shook a little—"as I believe, I'll track down Chance and punish him as sure as there is a God in heaven."

"A God who reserves vengeance for Himself, Mitchell," said the governor. "Bear that in mind. If you bring proof I will aid you to fetch the man to justice."

"Justice! To hang a cold-blooded murderer like that? By process of law. With a dozen loopholes for him to wriggle out of. If he's done in my pal, he'll suffer for it, not by swinging, but by the fear of death. He'll not know when it'll strike, or how. I'll make him afraid. He likes to live, in his own devilish fashion. I'll make him afraid of his own shadow. There's a soul somewhere in him and I'll reach it until it crawls. I'll—"

The governor held up his hand.

"I cannot listen to talk like this, Mitchell," he said. "You've said too much, as it is. I am disposed to help you but I cannot give audience to wild talk. I know that you are upset, convinced that harm has willfully been done your friend. I consider Chance quite capable of it, but I must weigh facts. The evidence is in his favor." He turned to Whittingham.

"Buxton, your aunt would like to talk with you. I trust we are going to see something of you. I had no idea you were in Papua. Why did you not use your right name?"

"I used one that belongs to me, sir."

The governor grunted. Mitchell, mixed up in the maze of British high rank nomenclature, remembered dimly that the royal family's actual name was Guelph, or something of the sort, that the nobility had surnames seldom used. Whittingham was no commoner.

"That hardly excused you from not paying respects to your aunt—and to me."

"I had a better reason, sir. I have no evening things with me."

Astounding as it seemed, the governor accepted the evasion.

"Your aunt will excuse that to-night," he answered. "I will join you later. Mr. Mitchell, if you are resolved upon this trip, which I fear will bring you nothing—unless, indeed, you find gold"—Ned made a gesture waving that aside—"we will do what we can for you in the matter of carriers, and advice. Consult with my secretary. I am sorry for the misfortunes of your friend, and your own natural grief. Good night, sir."

He rose, his shirt front creaking. The audience was over.

"Good night, Buck," said Mitchell.

"See you in the morning. I'm going with you."

The governor gasped at his nephew.

"What?"

Whittingham nodded.

"Surest thing you know, sir. Just suits my book. Good night, Ned. I'll be out at Ikoiko for breakfast."

V

BIG RIVERS

HOWELL WAS ALL SYMPATHY when Mitchell returned to the plantation. Ned had recovered from his first emotion. That had its outlet during his ride back to Ikoiko, and he had not been ashamed of the tears that flowed on his cheeks as he cantered through bush and swamp and forest. By the time he arrived he was hard, set to uncover the crime he was certain that Chance had committed, to follow the latter and punish him, by the law of man to man, of friend for friend. The thought of the red tape of regular justice he set aside. There were too many ways out. The British government would conduct the inquiry and, scrupulously fair as they were, they moved slowly. Unless his evidence were utterly convincing they would hesitate to move, or, moving, to administer a supreme penalty. Chance had got away—he might get into American or French territory before Mitchell returned. And then there would be international complications, extradition, the mesh of justice stretched too far, too great a likelihood of the fish getting through.

Also, Mitchell realized that what evidence he might find would be stale, that he would probably have to base it largely upon the accounts of natives who might object strongly to accompanying him back to Port Moresby to give their testimony, never held very highly by the courts.

He knew how difficult it was for the government to enforce obedience from the natives, even in territory patrolled by the native police themselves. There was the story of the time the governor could not get carriers for an up-river expedition of his own, despite official authority, until the unwilling men were threatened with jail. Even this would not have sufficed, except on threat of the cutting off of favors from their village. Jail meant free board and had no terrors. To bring in a wild savage from a cannibal and practically unknown district would be a stupendous affair. The man, or men, might have to be kidnapped—no easy matter, likely to cause a general uprising against the abductors, and then the enforced witness would probably turn sullen.

The only thing was to convince himself and then to act. Whittingham was a trump. His help just halved the difficulty of getting away and he insisted upon sharing the expenses.

"This is just the sort of trip I've always wanted," Buck declared. "There's more than the chance of getting gold."

They held a consultation that morning.

"I can manage nicely until my man arrives," said Howell. "The sooner you land up in the Mafulu country the better. Lipako is free to go. He's grateful to you for bringing him through the dysentery, the first of his kind I have ever known to show that virtue, and he'll be more than useful. This wizard, Morimori, has pulled off some great stunts. Chance had to deal through him and if you can get his good will you'll have the odds in your favor, at least until you get back of Mount Pitzoko.

"There's an old chap, a sort of beach comber, though he's not a bum, but just satisfied with living in an old shack with his native wife on the beach near Moresby. He's been out here for years. No one knows just where he has been in the interior, but all the traders know him and his name is recognized in remote villages. He's close to eighty now and he's got enough to live on. Some say he's worth quite a pile but that is probably just gossip. He can give you more real advice in half an hour than the governor's secretary can in a day. I'm friendly with him. I managed to fix things once when they wanted to take his woman into the hospital. If she had been a white woman it would have been the best thing for her but, being a native, she'd have died of fright. I diagnosed it as appendicitis and we got some ice and reduced the inflammation and the fever so that they didn't take her. Old Joe Davis didn't say much, but I think he'd go a long way to help me.

"Your main trouble is going to be carriers. You've got to take grub that you two can eat and you've got to pack trade goods and gifts. The government officials generally manage to get a train of police boys and carriers to stay with them through their whole trip, but those are short compared with yours. You'll want to avoid all suggestion of having a thing to do with the government. The natives are always afraid they are going to be punished for something. The best you can do is to get relays of carriers from village to village, unless Morimori interests himself, and you'll have a hard job at that to get any one to go with you behind Pitzoko. The Mafulu have threatened to wipe out the mission up there more than once—probably would if the fathers hadn't managed to put through a road of communication which ends at the mission itself.

"Davis'll tell you of some things he's seen. He's been up the Fly farther than any other white man and he's got a yarn about pigmies that is probably true enough, though they laugh at him for an old long-bowman so that it's hard to draw him out. But I've proved, and traders have proved, a whole lot of the tales he spins.

"I've done pretty well this season. If you're short of money, Mitchell, I'll loan you some. I believe you're dead right about Chance; he'd kill and walk away any time to serve his own interests. If he found gold—and I don't doubt that he did—he undoubtedly was pretty sure of it before he started. For some reason he didn't want to take Hansen. Probably wanted to leave some one responsible in charge of his schooner and have it careened. He had to have another white man. Wang is white to the natives but not to Chance. Wang is probably onto a lot of his tricks and very likely none too amenable to discipline. Somers or you suited him. Some one who could shoot well and stand guard—until he got what he wanted. When he was through with Somers at the end of his trip he had no more use for him. He'd think no more of putting him out of the way, or of having him put out of the way, than he would of shooting a dog. I wouldn't talk this way but I'm afraid there is no hope of your finding your pal alive. The return trip would be comparatively easy without him over known trails, with definite distances for each day's travel, knowledge of where to get food and find water.

"You can get food for your carriers at the native villages. Don't pack in any grub for them. And watch 'em. They've got a knack of loading up with the lightest pack and bolting off along the trail, leaving the heavy stuff without enough men to tote it. They've got another habit of being dumb when you call them for it and, if you overdo that, they'll quit on you. I don't want to magnify your troubles but to warn you of them. You'll be better equipped than most outfits with a chief like Lipako along. I'd advise you to do all you can to get him to go into the Mafulu country with you, if you can get him to leave his girl."

Mitchell listened attentively. Howell was a bit garrulous; Ned had already determined on several of his suggestions, but the planter meant more than merely well. Joe Davis sounded like a find. Ned chafed at any delay but he knew that it would take time to get their first carriers and obtain and prepare their loads. Howell was eminently right in one thing. The more they learned, the more trouble they might avoid. But, if Chance had got there and back, unless he had misused some of the tribes on his way out, he and Whittingham ought to get through. Therefore he thanked Howell heartily and took down the names of villages and chiefs, of traders he might run across or whose names he might invoke. Howell had been in the interior himself fairly extensively. But it seemed plain that their mainstay would be Morimori. His influence for or against them was likely to prove a determining factor in success or failure.

Back of Pitzoko they entered the unknown. There all trails ended. There the Big Rivers rolled black and swift in the valleys of the lower ranges. Beyond, lifted ridge upon ridge of mountains set like the teeth of a comb, so steep that the gable of a house seemed comparatively level. They were set with matted jungle, woven together with thorny, poisonous growths far worse than any tangle of barbed wire. On top of the ridges, on the narrow tracts of level ground, were the villages, the backs of the houses high stilted to the slope. Here were men so primitive as to have only recently advanced to the use of bows and arrows, abysmal brutes of the stone age, but for the puff darts that they had adopted from the negrito pigmies whom no man claimed to have seen, save Davis. They wore armor, crude cuirasses of wickerwork to catch venomous darts; and they had achieved shields, dating back to the time when they hurled stones at each other, and these bucklers were their main protection. But they were apemen, who, worse than the primates, devoured each other and united against strangers, drumming their messages ahead of the coming in of visitors.

Morimori's protection would help, but most of all their own unceasing watchfulness, the ghostly influence of the white man's superior *mana*— literally to native understanding, his magic. Their carriers would be afraid, with the saving condition that their fear would keep them with the caravan, unless panic made them bolt, to certain butchery.

It was a large contract but, aside from Mitchell's determination to assure himself of and have vengeance for his pal's death, it appealed to them—to the adventurous spirit of the white man, the Nordic, explorer by heritage, to whom danger is merely one spur and the lure of the unknown another upon the heels of their errantry.

Joe Davis lived at Elavera, an island at high tide, joined to the shore between Government House and the mission at other times. This was essentially a native village, and Davis was the only white man living there. He had himself "gone native" but he had not lost his pride of race. The natives lived in thatched shacks that were set on poles, twelve feet above the tide that flowed in and out under these foundations, serving the double purpose of fishing grounds and sewage conveyors. The shacks were reached by primitive ladders and their floors were of uneven, unsquared logs. But though Joe's wife was an Elavera woman, his hut, made out of the upturned hull of an abandoned cutter, was as clean as the cockpit of a man-of-war cleared for action.

Joe was a venerable-looking man, deep-tanned and bald, with a gray beard, carefully combed, that covered the front of the upper part of his body, which was unclothed but tattooed in designs that gave him the appearance of wearing a lace undershirt of exquisite design. His nether garment was a pair of faded blue-denim pants, sagged at the knees. His sight was filmed and his voice quavering, but there was strength in him and he stood up easily enough as his wife told him of the approach of visitors.

She, half his age, might have been twice it. Her skin was covered with deep wrinkles, her hair grizzled, and her mouth held only a few blackened teeth between which was set the stub of a clay pipe. But she was clad in a sleeveless cotton gown that was clean and stiff with starch. As the three white men came up, she retreated, leaving Joe peering at them.

He seemed relieved at the sound of Howell's voice and bade them sit down on a rude bench.

"You're welcome, gents," he said. "There's them as makes a show out of me, bringin' folks to look at the 'bloody 'ermit.' Me, I'm no hermit. I've had three wives in my time, and twenty children—don't know how many grandkids. I'm human, though some don't think so. Call me an old liar and wink at what I say. I know, if I am half blind. I live here because it suits me. They're pigs in Moresby, most of 'em. My shack ain't a sty, is it?"

Whittingham produced a bottle and swore afterward that he saw Joe's hairy ears prick at the sound of the withdrawn cork. The old beach comber grinned as he took the liberal swig poured out for him.

"Gin's my fav'rite medicine as a rule," he said. "But this now is the real stuff. My belly don't warm up like it used ter. It's good of you ter come an' see old Joe, Mister Howell. Time was—but that don't matter now. But I've held palaver with a hundred chiefs who came to ask me what they sh'u'd do. There ain't much of the South Seas I ain't bin in an' lived in, east an' west, since I come to Lahaina in Hawaii, aboard a whaler—sixty-four year ago, gents. Seems like I've lived two or three lives; now I've got nothin' ter do but sit in the sun an' smoke my pipe an' think. I've lived, I have. Out of New Bedford, I am, an' I'm windin' up in New Guinea. They'll tuck me in the sand by an' by, an' the land crabs'll pick my old bones. Not much pickin' on 'em now. But—look me over, thar's my record underneath the tattoo. Bullet marks an' spear marks, sharks' teeth jags an' arrer wounds. Swipes from wooden swords an' bumps where clubs have cracked my bones. But they c'u'dn't kill old Joe."

He cackled and Mitchell feared they had given him too much Scotch, but it was soon evident that the old chap was merely garrulous, glad to talk with his own kind.

"We won't let you be buried in the sand, Joe, when the time comes," said Howell.

"What odds? If you put a headboard over me, they'll p'int it out an' say: 'Here lies Joe Davis. Like he allus did.' Man, if they'd seen what I've seen, they'd believe ennything.

"If I was ter tell you I've seen natives with tails like cats, so they hang down through round holes in the flooring when they squat in their huts of nights; tell you how a smart man come erlong an' tied the tails in knots an' then went up an' killed them all one-handed, becos they had et his father, w'u'd you believe me?" He squinted at them.

"If you told me you believed it, I would, Joe," returned Howell and the old whaler grunted.

"I've told many things thet was true an' got laffed at. I've seen the dwarfs, black as coal, no higher than my elbow, livin' in tree houses. They held me there prisoner while they tried to fatten me up. Never mind how I got erway. I did. After dark, you can bet. I didn't want none of their pizen darts puffed inter me.

"I've seen a canoe load of human flesh. Erlong the coast they bile man meat in pots. Up in the mountains they roast it. Just chuck it in the fire, some of 'em. I read a piece a while back before my eyes got so bad that some fool wrote thet claimed he was an explorer. Said there was no more cannibalism in New Guinea.

"Wot the hell does he know of it? The place ain't bin scratched. Down in the Solomons, where they bake long pig, in the ovens same as the reg'lar kind, they eat a man ter git his *mana*, serve his heart up ter the chief so he kin absorb his bravery. In Papua it's jest meat, better than fish or birds."

There was no stopping him, and his gruesome tales were not without their elements of education. Moreover he gave the impression of telling the truth. His scars bore witness to much of it. At last he stopped, asking Howell if there was anything he could do for him.

"I owe you a heap," he said. "I like ter pay my way. Allus hev. Even got my coffin bought an' waitin' fer me. So mebbe I'll fool the crabs, after all."

"There is something you can do, Joe. I came here on purpose. These two men with me are my friends. I'm in their debt. They're going in back of Pitzoko and they want your advice."

"Back of Pitzoko! Aye, thar's gold in thar. But you're like ter pay dear enough fer it. Pearls now, you kin carry a fortune in pearls, but gold you've got ter tote out. Dead weight. You try an' pack thirty pound of it through the bush. Five mile a day if you're goin' good, up an' down mountains steep as haystacks an' burred with jungle. Yore carriers don't savvy the value of it. I know one man went way up inter the Boboi district an' found a lot of it. He had fifteen carriers with him. He told me he was bringin' out an average of twenty-five pounds of dust a man, goin' light on grub, though he had to tote his trade stuff ter feed 'em. He had a fortune. Five thousand dollars to each boy. Figger it yoreself. What happened? They chucked it erway on him. Said it was no use ter tote ennything but trade. Chucked it erway on some

mountainside whar you don't know if yore next step is goin' ter light on
dirt or not as you shove it through the tangle. It's thar now, somewhar in the
bush. A quarter of a million dollars lost in the jungle. Try an' find it. He did.
Needles in haystacks aire a joke ter it."

"They're not going just after gold, Joe. There's something bigger. I guess
you'll agree with them. Mitchell, you spill the story."

Whittingham gave Davis another drink and a cheroot before Mitchell
began to talk. The old man did not light the smoke but chewed it listening
quietly. When Ned had finished he said:

"If I was twenty years younger—if I was ten, an' had my sight—I'd go
erlong. Hell blast a white man who does in another in sech parts as this! Enny
place, fer thet matter. A native kills because he don't know enny better. But
a murderer ought ter hev his bones broke an' be staked out fer the sharks ter
git at high tide. Chance! I've heard of him. Come out here huntin' bugs an'
beetles an' pretendin' he was a scientist. Lookin' fer a fortune, he was. He's
spent a few stakes. In Levuka and Suva, in Papeete an' ashore in Australia.
He's a rampin' devil in his heart an' smooth as Lucifer. A woman ter him is
less than a plaything an' a man less than a dog ter be kicked out of his road.
I'd believe ennything of him.

"I wish I c'u'd go with yer. He'll have covered his tracks or thought he
has, but the best of 'em ain't so smart. The Lord fixes murderers so's they
trip up sooner or later. Allus. I've seen 'em found out twenty—thirty—aye,
fifty years later. Hangin's too good fer him. An ant heap, with him tied ter
a tree close by an' the trail set with molasses, an' his body smeared with
it—thet's what I'd do with him if he'd done in a pal of mine. You remember
thet, mister. You're right ter go after him. A woman's a good thing ter have
when you're old but thar's nothin' like a friend. I've had 'em an' lost 'em.
Pals thet 'u'd go through hell fer me or me fer them."

"I'm going to get even with him," said Mitchell, his voice holding its new
quality of hardness. "And not with his body, to begin with. He's proud to
think of the deeds he's done. I'll make him squirm. I'll take his pride away
from him, with his sleep and his courage. I'll haunt him with the fear of death
and the knowledge of where it comes from, without the knowledge when."

The three listeners sat in a sudden silence that seemed to have surrounded
the little cabin. The tide hissed softly on the beach and grated among the
pebbles, but there was no other sound. Foreboding fell upon them, a grim
feeling of vengeance to be awfully fulfilled. Mitchell's face was a stern mask
of hate, his eyes hard as agate.

"Thet's yore affair," said Davis at last. "I don't hold much with courts of
justice out here in the wilds. An eye for an eye, I say. I hope you git him."

"I will."

"An' I'll do what I kin. I've bin called a cracked pot but I ain't leakin' none yet. An' what I tell you is truth, the same as gospel, told in the name of friendship."

Davis had put on a dignity that he carried well. He spoke out of the wisdom of his years, of the beliefs that he had tested, the fealty of true man to true man, the deceit of villains. He talked simply and with conviction.

"I ain't goin' ter talk ter you about the A.B.C. of jungle trails. You'll have this Mekeo boy with you, Lipako, and he'll help eddicate you but, if you're greenhorns at it, Heaven help you, fer you don't know what you're up ag'inst. Leeches an' crocodiles in the swamps, mosquitoes everywhere except in the high mountains. Mosquitoes so thick you eat 'em with every mouthful of grub and you breathe 'em. An' thet means malaria. Pizen thorns an' pizen snakes an' spiders, places after you've left the trade trails what if you make four miles a day you're lucky. It takes guts an' it takes good health ter start with; ter git in. Every scratch you git'll turn inter an ulcer, an' them sores'll spread till they're big as the palm of yore hand. Scrub itch, ants that'll nip through leather. I'd like ter know right now if you've had enny experience of thet sort."

"I've been in the South Pacific, knocking round, including the New Hebrides and the Solomons for four years," said Mitchell. Whittingham said that he had roughed it a bit, and Davis seemed inclined to appraise his quiet statement at top value.

"Then I won't talk erbout thet end of it. I kin probably start you right with carriers, mebbe ter go up ter Mekeo district. Thar's some Mekeo men here on Elavera and more close by at Hanuabada and Tanabada. I'll git my woman ter scoutin' round. After thet you'll hev ter do the best you kin.

"The main thing ter remember is thet New Guinea is run by the wizards. Thar's a slue of 'em—rain wizards, sick wizards, thief takers—all small magic men, besides the main sorcerer of a district. Once in a while thar's one like Morimori. Mebbe they kin do things with ghosts, mebbe they can't. More I've seen of 'em the less I figger ter explain it. I've seen 'em do mighty funny things an' I know they believe in their charms themselves. They're the wise men of the tribe all right. They fake a lot of stuff an' they take chances now an' then, allus fixed ter kivver up if they lose out an' take a heap of credit if the breaks come right. Look at Morimori. His people had trouble with the Mafulu an' he throws a bluff an' threatens 'em the worst way. A comet comes erlong an' they think he did it. If a volcano bust out they'd figger it happened jest on their account. Now, mebbe Morimori had heard of comets before, might hev seen one, an' these top wizards hev all got a lot of knowledge handed down. He ses he'll stop the comet burnin' 'em up if they'll be good, but keep it in the sky till they behave. Now he's the kingpin. They figger he kin trot out a comet enny old day he wants ter.

"But even the biggest of 'em figger we kin go 'em one better. They know

how fur they kin go but they don't know how fur *we* kin. D'Albertis used ter
eat fire, stuff his mouth with tow soaked in alum. He used alcohol, lit it an'
pretended he c'u'd set water on fire. The wizards aire on to thet trick now.
They've heard of gasoline if they ain't seen it. But thar's a lot of things kin
fool 'em. I mean tricks like they sell kids in a box of parlor magic. I'll tell
you one I never used here. Mix up white sugar and potash that'll git afire
from a drop of acid. Make 'em think you're a fire master. Work it up like they
do, with a lot of hanky-panky an' taboo sticks. But don't hand 'em ennything
too deep. What they can't savvy they ain't impressed with. A phonygraff ter
them is jest the white man's god talkin' in a box. Moving picters don't feaze
'em at aill. I've made a hit with a cupple of screws ter hold blocks of wood
tergether an' got nigh mobbed in a scramble fer a package of safety pins.
Stand in with the wizards an' you'll not go fur wrong. Jolly 'em erlong an'
don't make 'em lose face. Tell 'em you've heard of 'em. If you kin do it in
their own lingo, so much the better.

"Don't hurry erway from a village if they're fixin' ter give you a dance or
a feast. They'll do thet on enny excuse, but you swaller yore hurry an' stay.
If you don't they'll drum word on ahead you're no good, an' the next village
won't have enny grub for yore men. Lipako'll steer you. When you cured
him of dysentery you made a ten-strike.

"Don't git bluffed an' don't shoot until you're dead sure you'll hev to.
Then shoot straight. Killin' a man means all manner of trouble, but it has ter
be done sometimes. When you git in the high hills, one of you keep erwake
all the time. They're plumb scared of ghosts in the nighttime as a rule, but
I've known thet rule broken.

"Thumbtacks, long uns, strewed on the ground with their p'ints up, is a
good idee if you've got ter sleep. An' I know one trader who saved his life
by spreadin' sticky fly papers all over his porch.

"You want ter take erlong axes, knives, terbacco, an' some sun cholery
cure ter treat the chiefs an' wizards with. Warmin' their bellies is a sure way
ter their hearts. Screws an' safety pins, brass curtain rings an' a cheap watch
or two for speshul gifts. If you git real sick, make fer the nearest mission, an'
keep posted on whar they aire. The fathers'll look out fer you an' they ain't
molested enny more.

"I wish I c'u'd go erlong but I'm run down like an old clock. I'm tough
though an' I'll be waitin' fer you. I'll git after yore carriers an' I wish I c'u'd
do more fer you."

"You've done a lot," said Mitchell as he shook the ancient by the hand,
the others following. Whittingham left the bottle of Scotch and suggested
sending out more. However, Howell vetoed this.

"The old chap is proud," he said. "He wants to feel he's helped you freely.
And his advice is good."

VI
MITCHELL'S PROOF

SEVEN WEEKS LATER TWO WORN WHITE MEN camped on the banks of a river that rolled sullen and dark between the matted ranks of great trees. With them was Lipako. His gratitude had proved greater than his love, which had promptly and properly died when he found his chosen one had been encouraging the advances of the old chief. They had with them four Mekeo men and ten carriers from the last village, who now gazed at the swirling, bridgeless current with something closely akin to panic.

Beyond, hidden by the jungle save at rare intervals, towered ridge upon ridge, thick with forest bush, interlaced with creepers that were barbed with cruel thorns. So far they had found trails. Across the river they had no knowledge of any, save as the craft of Lipako or his fellows might discover some narrow track. They were worn to the bone, their clothes in tatters, their boots well nigh gone, but what they passed through was only a suggestion of what lay ahead. Morimori's favor had protected them, furnished them with the friendly greetings of village chiefs, procured them food. It might prevail on the other side of the Big Rivers. Always they heard drums throbbing out the news of their marching, found their numbers known on arrival. The drums were beating now and they seemed to hold a more sinister note.

"White men crossing the river. White men with gifts. White men who are wizards and warriors. Two white men. Lipako, the nephew of Morimori, is with them. They have many valuable things."

Was this what the drums said? It was a new code to Lipako, who seemed disturbed by his inability to translate it.

"How the devil do we get over the river?" asked Whittingham. "Lipako said there was a bridge. It ought to be here on the trail."

"Storm may have swept it away at high water," suggested Ned.

"No rain. We're stuck."

"For a while. We can fix it, Lipako?"

It was Lipako's opinion that the bridge had been deliberately destroyed, probably moved upstream, whether to arrest their progress or for some local reason he could not tell. Suddenly, as he talked, he made a swift gesture of silence and concealment. The carriers froze into the dark shadows of the trees where no sun touched anything but the high summits. The white men sought cover.

Up the river came the leading war canoes of a strong armada, driven by swift and steady strokes of paddles that moved in silence. In the biggest canoe, the flagship, two big men stood erect, one at each end of the platform deck amidships, each with a spear in his hand. The faces of all were set upstream, wooden as masks.

It was plainly a raid in the making—a raid for human flesh. The two white men thought of Davis' talk of a canoe load of man meat. For all their hardihood and purpose, they felt the gooseflesh rising on their skins, which were suddenly cold under the sweat that the march had brought out on them.

"Mafulu," said Lipako. "Now we have big trub'ble along these fella." He meant the last batch of carriers. Their faces and bodies had changed color; they shivered with terror. Gifts and promises of gifts could not move them. They had seen their own fates if they went ahead into this land of man-eaters. One told how the Mafulus used rattan loops on long bamboo handles, with spikes set at the junction, on which to jerk back the victim's head and pierce his spine.

Besides, the white men could not cross the river. They had no canoes, there was no bridge.

Ned and Buck cajoled and threatened, but the men were sullen. They began to sneak off, leaving their loads, until only the Mekeo men remained. Seven of them now all told. And only the presence of their chief and the magic of Morimori, with the promise he had made them of most unpleasant deaths if they should desert, sustained them. They too felt the journey was ended. It would take a good craft with good paddles to fight across that rolling tide. Lipako said that he could make out a trail on the other side, but neither Mitchell nor Whittingham could discern anything.

There had been a bridge that was perilous enough, a swinging structure of joined bamboos for footing, with a hand line of liana lashed to the bamboos with crisscrossed vines. Its presence showed friendship between the tribes. Its absence was at once a challenge and a menace.

Mitchell surveyed the current, studying it before he began to strip.

"What's the idea?" asked Whittingham. "You'll never make it. Too many crocs, and the current's fierce."

"*Got* to make it. The crocs are your business, Buck. You with your Heinie rifle. Pot 'em if you see one. I don't believe they're so high up. Got to risk it. I've swum worse water."

He began to uncoil a light line, to make a loop in it.

"But what's the idea? What if you do cross?"

"I'll get the line over. You can haul me in with it if you have to. But you won't. Get the boys twisting up cordage from those vines and swinging their axes. Lipako knows which trees will float best. Make some pontoon rafts—enough for the men and the truck. I'll hitch the big rope with the pontoons on the near end. The current'll swing 'em across to the other bank."

"Oh! Good egg," cried Whittingham. Mitchell helped him get the idea into Lipako's brain and the men set to work, impressed by the magic of this naked white man whom nothing could stop.

Ned said he had swam worse water but he doubted it before he was far out from the bank. Undercurrents sucked and dragged at him; great eddies tugged him out of his course, and every swirling wave suggested the rush of a cayman—and the end. Once a slimy, ropy thing, surely alive, wrapped itself about his legs and held him while he treaded water and at last went under and found it was some remnant of the destroyed bridge. He battled with the entanglement, twice coming up for air, while Whittingham called to him from the bank in fear that he was attacked. He got free at last, almost spent, and the swift, inexorable current, in persistent hostility, swept him almost to the limit of the loose line that Whittingham once more paid out freely. He could trust the Britisher not to lose his head in emergencies.

With the end of his strength he made a landing and waded along the shore edge, from slippery rock to rock, seeking a good place for landing the pontoon rafts that the men were making.

The plan was not Ned's own device—he had seen it in operation on tidal rivers—but it was his knowledge of it that was power. He found a fair place and, half an hour later, had a tremendous tussle hauling across the cordage which the natives had woven out of vines. The river snatched at it, and when at last Mitchell got the end snubbed about a tree, he was done up. But he had found during this trip that when his body was exhausted his mind burned on. His will was unflagging, and presently he got to his feet and signaled.

Whittingham superintended the loading, careful of hitches. As the men shoved off with poles, the floating bridge caught the current and was swept swiftly downstream, snubbed by the vine rope, which creaked and stretched—and held—bringing the outfit down to where Mitchell tossed them his light line again and helped them to a landing.

Axes hewed a way through the mat of brush and vines, dodging the trees, until they reached the trail that Lipako had spotted. It was far from an open way—a mere bush track, dim to follow, steeply ascending. When the panting bearers reached the ridge with their second loads they flung themselves down exhausted. Now they were in Mafulu country, their presence known beyond doubt, probably their exact location.

"We'll have to cache some of the stuff that the ants can't hurt," said Whittingham. "We'll get nowhere with double trickling. And we'll have the dickens of a time getting out much gold," he added a bit ruefully.

Mitchell agreed. New Guinea gold! He was as anxious to get the stuff as Whittingham now. They would share it equally and his own half would be devoted to his hunting down of Chance. Nightly he devised plans for a fitting reprisal. He wanted to break the man down, to force him to some realization of his crimes by a punishment that would be a torment. His will was set to the purpose, inexorably, and the toll he set upon it showed in his gaunt features and his eyes, burning like flames of alcohol, as the party pushed deeper and deeper into the wilderness.

They made their camp on the ridge, near the ruins of a long-deserted village. They brought their water from the river and ate sparingly, since rations must now be hoarded. From here on, the trail of Chance was not going to be easy to find unless they ran across friendly natives who could guide them. Chance's expedition was, of course, known to the whole country. They had heard of him at the mission, where the kind fathers forbore to say much of the man, and Mitchell held back his own full purpose from them. It was evident that they had not liked Chance overmuch, though they had sheltered him and done what they could for him, coming and going. But they gave definite hints that he had not been over-politic with the savage Mafulus.

Before he or Whittingham turned in, Mitchell set up his "bogy," a skull that he had secured and painted with radium. It swung at the end of a supple pole, nodding in the breezes, and in its eyes were green lamps connected with a battery in the white man's tent where the thing could be lighted by the pressure of a handy switch. The two would take four-hour shifts, starting from this night, arms ready. The memory of the grim flotilla did not render them less cautious. Nor did Mitchell forget to strew the nightly guard of thumbtacks on the hard-trodden ground of the abandoned village.

There came a week of following trails that dwindled out or led to villages that had been moved entire, owing to some whim, supposed enchantment or epidemic. All villages were built upon the knifelike ridges, but not all ridges, as they found to their cost, held villages. It seemed as if the country were suddenly deserted, but both the white men fancied that they sensed, rather than saw or heard movements and rustlings in the bush and in the boughs above them. Lipako and the Mekeo men declared that they could smell human odors close by a score of times. But the party was unmolested. It seemed the policy of the Mafulus neither to aid them nor injure them but to let them wander in the jungle and prove their *mana* by finding their own way. They might, in this test, hope to wear the little caravan down. Food was low and there was little game. The forest was so thick that it was hard to get a shot at a bird and there was nothing else for the larder, unless they returned to the river and tried for fish.

On the seventh morning after they had crossed the stream Lipako, at the head of the little column with Mitchell, halted and stood like a great dog, nostrils distended, sniffing the air. They were on what seemed to be a beaten path but it had not been lately used and the bush had encroached upon it so that it was almost obliterated. Whittingham came up from the rear to see the cause of the delay, and Lipako motioned ahead, then began to creep through the forest, crawling over vines, carefully holding aside boughs. Mitchell stayed with the tired carriers, who set down their loads, their eyes rolling fearfully, their nostrils also working.

Whittingham, with his gun at hand, followed Lipako as best he could. There were no dry twigs to crack; the danger lay, if there was any, in the waving of branches that might be seen. The wind was against them. Had it not been, according to Lipako, the Mafulus would smell out the white men a quarter of a mile away.

Lipako halted again, peering through a dense shrub that was almost smothered in brilliant crimson orchids. He beckoned to Whittingham. There was a little clearing ahead, and in it were two men walking softly and slowly beneath the trees, their bamboo tubes lifted. One of them halted and set his tube to his mouth. Buck saw his cheeks distend but could not mark the flight of the dart. A mass of brilliant, iridescent plumage flashed gold and copper and metallic green, as it caught a shaft of sunlight, and a splendid cock paradise bird plumped to the ground.

Whittingham stepped forward, gun in holster but with his hand on the butt. In his other hand he held out sticks of tobacco while Lipako, beside him, spoke a greeting in the scant Mafulu that he knew. These men must be pacified, must be made to lead the white men to a village or they would soon have to turn back and abandon the trip. Buck doubted whether he could ever get Ned to return. He could fancy him reduced to a fever-stricken skeleton, stalking on with adamant resolution—alone, if none would stay with him. Whittingham had not the slightest intention of leaving him, but the affair began to look like a very forlorn hope.

And these men—

They stood their ground, as the white man and the chief advanced, seemingly without fear, without a gesture of hostility or friendship, until Whittingham, with his peace offering, was within twenty feet of them. Then the nearer set his puff tube to his lips ready to send out a dart bearing almost instant death, his fellow standing by to back his shot.

Lipako cried a warning. There was no cover. The Britisher's automatic came out in a streak to the level, and he pulled the trigger. The bullet went smashing through the tube of death, splintering it, tearing it from the grasp of the astounded native. Here was a wizard who flung fire from his fingers—fire and some missile that had wrecked his own weapon and plucked it away! He stood goggle-eyed with terror. The other savage seemed turned to stone.

Lipako spoke again—the word for "friend." Then "friend of Morimori." Whittingham put out the tobacco until it touched the man's hand. Slowly they gazed at each other, the dwarfish savage wearing only a skirt of green leaves, held up with a twist of pandanus, and the tall white man, smiling at him, while Lipako repeated words of friendship. The scent of the tobacco tickled the Mafulu's sense of smell. Slowly he reached for the sticks, took them, tasted them, for all the world like a doubtful chimpanzee, then bit off a piece and chewed it with a nod of pleasure. South of the river, in the Mekeo country, the natives smoked great tubes of bamboo, passing the communal pipe around, but here they evidently chewed the weed by preference.

Whittingham dispensed more sticks to the second man, and soon both were grinning. Once the savage whose blowgun and aim had been spoiled, looked at his broken weapon and timidly touched the butt of the Englishman's pistol. Whittingham nodded and walked to the nearest tree with loose bark upon it, a species of gum. He broke the bark to the size he wanted, sent it spinning into the air by one corner and fired twice. Twice the target jumped and then fell. Whereupon Buck picked it up, showing the holes in it through which the savages thrust wondering finger tips. It was an apt object lesson and a timely one. Puff tubes had been shown powerless against this sorcery.

Following the sound of the shots the party reassembled, and Lipako persuaded the bird hunters to take them to their village, which it seemed was the main one, named Livoro. Several times they spoke the word Taangi, which Lipako vowed was a man's name.

The finny summit on which Livoro was built sat high above the other ridges. To the south Ned discerned the river they had crossed and to the north another winding through a gorge. High peaks closed in the sky line. They were between the Big Rivers. And Livoro had been mentioned by the fathers at the mission—not by Chance. Buck doubted if the skipper had told much actual truth concerning the uncharted Mafulu territory.

The houses straggled to right and left, and the place seemed deserted. The women and children were within doors watching through screens, while the warriors were in the clubhouse, a great building well over a hundred and fifty feet in length, sixty feet in actual height at the entrance and tapering down to fifteen at the far end. The baked roof projected like an opened jaw and from it swung long banners of bark cloth on which were inscribed totem signs.

The two whites and Lipako mounted to the high platform where some twenty warriors stood to receive them, all dressed like the two hunters and tattooed with some device on the chest. They kept silence and opened up to let the visitors pass into the dark interior. It looked like a trap, as if they were in fact entering through the jaws of some enormous beast that would close upon them. But the whites marched in without sign of fear to find, as usual, a central passage with the sides divided into square stalls that held oblong painted shields, unstrung bows, bone daggers, mats and dancing gear, with here and there a primitive firestone. At the end was a sort of hall, with human skulls piled on the floor and in racks on one side and the skulls of wild boars on the other, all painted red and yellow.

There were also the skulls of crocodiles and masks of fantastic shape daubed into likenesses of hideous faces. In a recess a half-drawn curtain revealed wickerwork figures, vaguely seen, and a big cage that was also screened, standing on a platform. In it something moved and made strange noises.

The twenty warriors had followed the white men inside, and soon there were two hundred gathered there, all waiting in silence. Ned, Buck and Lipako stood in the hall wondering a little what strange kind of a beast was in the cage, and wondering who was finally to greet them.

Then the curtain was pulled entirely to one side, and they saw a swollen figure advancing toward them seated on a sort of throne mounted on wooden rollers, propelled by unseen attendants.

Here was Taangi, at once chief and high wizard of Livoro. He was a horrible sight, puffed out of human shape by elephantiasis, that had changed his legs to vast columns and enlarged the nails of his feet till an elephant might well have claimed the limbs. He was little more than a mountain of flesh. Either the disease or grossness had made his face a thing of blubbery mounds and creases, in which his nose was hardly noticeable and his eyes deep sunken.

There was the universal fire upon a big stone in the hall, burning coconut husks and candlenuts. The eyes of the wizard were mere points of light reflecting the flames but holding a fixed stare that betokened no friendship.

Lipako spoke his best Mafulu, interpreting Mitchell, offering gifts that Taangi ignored though they made the rest of the Mafulus nudge each other and edge forward. The wizard ignored the statement that the white men had heard of him and his mighty deeds—an ingenuous and needful bit of diplomatic prevarication. When he spoke, the words seemed pumped up from deep within his chest, hollow, unnatural and flat.

"Why do you come here?"

Ned, fearing that to hesitate in replying would be construed as fright, quickly stated his purpose.

"As friends of Morimori, seeking news of a white man."

"There is no white man here. Three came and one indeed stayed, but you will not find him."

There was an ominous suggestion in his tone. Mitchell wondered if the skull of Somers was among that grisly collection, or set apart as a special prize.

"These men also were friends of Morimori," Taangi went on, and Mitchell got the definite impression that the affiliation between Taangi and the sorcerer of Mekeo was one of fear rather than affection, that Taangi grudged the other's reputation. "The biggest tree grows only so big. So it is with friendship. We do not wish white men in Mafulu. These others came seeking yellow pebbles and departed. Let no more come. You lie when you say you seek news of the other man. Those who went out will have said that he was dead."

"Tell him there is no limit to the white man's friendship," said Mitchell to Lipako. "Tell him we want to know just how this man died and if any of his men were with him when that happened. That we white men like to bury our dead in their own place."

Lipako got through comprehensively with the aid of signs, and the swollen figure that seemed incapable of self-movement grinned derisively.

"How can one bury that which is eaten?" he asked. "As for the head, what shall be offered for it?"

Mitchell took a long breath. Somehow he had held a last faint hope. Now it was gone. The dropsied wizard was looking at them mockingly. Then his mood changed.

"Why should I not take what you have, and gain more heads, more meat?"

"Tell him why, Lipako," Mitchell answered quietly when this was translated. "Tell him that, if we came in anger, we could kill all here as they stand, with him the first to go. Tell him to remember what the men who brought us here must have already told him. But tell him again we come in friendship as friends of Morimori. That Morimori will not be pleased if we do not return with what we wish.

"He's faking," Ned added in an undertone to Whittingham. "The drums have told him all about us. He just wants to emphasize his importance."

"He's got something up his sleeve, or would have, if he wore one," answered Whittingham in the same low voice, as Lipako struggled with his talk. "The old beggar's lying about something. I don't believe they ate poor Somers. White man's meat is distasteful to them, anyway."

Lipako ended, and there was a little silence while Taangi meditated and glowered, evidently torn between greed and policy. These white men were dangerous, but their goods were greatly to be desired. Was it going to pay to get them by fair means, or foul?

"Morimori can speak with me," he said finally. "And I with him, if I choose. But if I do not, how shall he know whether you ever came here in safety—or that you never left?"

This was practically an open threat. Mitchell's wrath began to mount. But Taangi all unconsciously had given him a perfect opening. Rummaging among the stores at Port Moresby for gifts, for things that might prove useful, he had come across some fireworks, rockets and signal candles. He had brought them along, and now they were suddenly of tremendous value.

"Tell him," he said again to Lipako, and his voice rang out with assurance, "that we too can talk with Morimori. To-night we will talk with the stars. We will send a star to Morimori, and he shall know how Taangi, whom he thinks his friend, treats us. For Morimori is a master of the stars, as the Mafulus perhaps know. When it is dark, in a little while, we will talk with Morimori."

Ned studied the wizard closely.

For the first time the misshapen bulk moved of its own volition, shifting uneasily on the throne. The mention of stars was not at all to his liking. There was a stir among the naked savages throughout the room.

"I will talk with some of my people," Taangi said huskily. "Perhaps I can tell you what you want to know."

"He'll lie to us," whispered Whittingham. "He's an artful old dodger. He'd give anything to rifle our loads and put our heads in those racks."

"We will eat," said the wizard.

It was a sign at least of truce, and the visitors left the clubhouse for the time after two stalls had been assigned to them, one for the carriers and their loads, the other for the two white men and their interpreter, who was also the nephew of Morimori. It was certain that that fact was not being overlooked. The three moved in, careful not to show open suspicion. They were making some progress.

Darkness came before the meal was really over. Mitchell had his fireworks ready, and he and Whittingham set them up with mysterious passes and much muttering of words.

"Now we can talk with Morimori," said Ned, and Lipako passed on the words to the big mass of flesh that had been carried out to the feast and now sat in the shadows.

With a rush a rocket flared, sending a flaming stream of fire to the south and breaking out into a shower of stars. It looked as if they might indeed be raining down over Mekeo. And the flaring trail was quite sufficiently like a comet to set the Mafulus gasping in awe. Here was a man who created and commanded comets. There went another.

Three rockets went whizzing over the ridges before Mitchell set off his great signal candles, larger than those Chance had himself used before Morimori. The exploding balls of fire shot up high into the night, and with every one there was a great sigh from the crowd.

Then came a stroke of luck, a not unusual but timely phenomenon. In the southern sky a falling star swooped in a long curve, and Mitchell seized the occasion.

"Morimori hears and answers," he asserted.

Taangi had no reply. He sat discomfited. There was no dance that night, for which the white men were duly grateful. The savages went in silence to the clubhouse, and the visitors followed. Again, in the darkness, Mitchell set out his tacks, he and Whittingham arranging to stay awake on alternate watches with an electric flash and gun ready.

The place settled down to silence. At the far end they could hear the thing in the cage rustling and whimpering. Mitchell fancied it some big ape. It was not wise to inquire too much into Taangi's mysteries but to make the most of their own. Ned fancied that Taangi was fairly well tamed. At the last the trip was going more smoothly than he had expected. The Mafulus were so savage and primitive that they were easily impressed. And the rockets had been a great stroke.

During the second watch there came a sharp cry and Ned moved swiftly to the opening of his stall, switching on the flashlight. Two tribesmen stood each on one foot, confused by the dazzling beam, caught in the attempted act of pilfering, a sturdy thumb tack well through the calluses of each of their soles. They limped away, muttering, and there was no more trouble that night, save the snoring of wild, overfed men and the reek of unclean savages.

A man came to the visitors' stall in the morning while the carriers were eating food prepared for them by order of Taangi. Whittingham and Mitchell had already had their own self-prepared breakfast. Lipako told them that the man had found the body of Somers and would show them the place. Also that if they wanted the yellow pebbles, they could take as much as they wanted, that Taangi wanted to prove his friendship and would give them carriers to the beginning of the mission road.

They lost no time following their guide, whom Lipako interpreted as best he could. It seemed the man had been one of several men loaned Chance by Taangi. Taangi was angry with Chance because he had been stingy with his parting gifts, but he had been afraid to openly antagonize him, because of a drum message from Morimori.

Little by little the true story came out. Somers had not fallen from the cliff. He had quarreled with Chance, so the man thought, and he had actually seen Chance push him over the edge of the precipice but had kept his counsel. This was on the last day when they had all the gold they could carry. And Chance had left the body to lie there.

Asked if the body was buried the man would not answer but looked at them slyly.

"That fella mean all same eat," was Lipako's grim verdict.

Now Mitchell was set to return. First he meant to secure Somers' skull, which he felt sure was in the possession of Taangi. He thought a bribe of rockets and the showing how to use them might turn the deal. Without doubt a white man's head was a great trophy for the tribe, but to be able to talk with stars would be even a greater thing—for Taangi.

But first the expedition, aided by a number of Mafulus, set to work to get the gold from the big pool below the falls. If the thing was engineered properly, the fall diverted, it would be possible to get an almost incalculable treasure from the deeper ledges. Even the gravelly shores were thickly seeded with "colors," pellets and an occasional nugget. The sand bars downstream yielded more. Above the fall the source of the gold might be found, but here lay all that the party could carry off, pound upon pound of it, virgin gold, of no value to the Mafulus in whose estimation the white men lost much of their prestige by their efforts to glean the soft, unworkable stone.

Ten carriers were promised them, and these could doubtless be replaced at the mission. Seventeen in all, to carry what trade gifts could be saved from Taangi's cupidity and the white men's sadly diminished supply of food. Ned and Buck would have to fare as their men did on the way back.

The Mafulus were not used to loads. They were inexpert and unwilling at handling them, but the expedition took out almost two hundred and fifty pounds of gold, worth well over two hundred dollars a pound when assayed and refined.

On the last day Taangi gave his visitors audience, his eyes greedy and cunning. Mitchell laid an array of gifts before him that seemed to exhaust the supply and then talked of the relic he wanted, for a special purpose that had taken gradual shape in his mind.

Taangi did not deny having the skull but stated that he set great store by it, that it possessed big *mana*. This Mitchell granted and offered to supply still stronger magic. It took two hours of bargaining before the wizard grunted an assent. Then he was shown, in private, how to let loose the magic stars from the tubes of white man's sorcery. Then, calling to his attendants, he was wheeled behind the curtain. When he came out again, rolling toward them, he held in his sausage-like fingers a square casket of dark wood, carved with a rough design of a turtle on the four sides and the lid.

Mitchell opened it, less with reverence and regret than with the first taste of revenge. He took out the gleaming, unpainted skull, its strong jaw and high forehead proclaiming it that of a white man. For a moment it seemed to take on flesh; the eyes of Somers seemed to look out of the hollow sockets, and lips seemed to frame the perfect teeth. Then the phantasm faded to the grim reality.

"I carry this myself," Ned said to Whittingham, who looked at him curiously, hard put to it to understand his mood.

As they left the clubhouse they heard a chuckle from Taangi and the rustle and whimper of the thing he had captive in the big cage beside him.

"He thinks he's put one over on us," said Whittingham. "I hope one of those bally rockets backfires and blisters him till he squeals. I wouldn't object to a little blood poisoning to follow."

"I've got what I came after," said Mitchell. "Now I'm going after Chance."

"Good for you," said Whittingham. "But I'd like to know why Taangi chuckled. He's holding out something on us."

• • •

VII

THE TRAIL OF CHANCE

THE FATES WHO HAD FAVORED MITCHELL now seemed to spin their wheel against him. He made the mistake of tracing the schooner, rather than the man, and because it had so much the start of him and the trail led bafflingly to places where information was vague, it was four months before he discovered it trading in the Hebrides with a skipper by the name of Griffiths who had bought it from a man called Rawlings. He knew nothing of Chance and Rawlings had gone to Tahiti.

Mitchell took sailing vessel and steamer to Papeete, only to find Rawlings in the Tuamotus, pearling. He ran his man down at last and got little for his pains. Chance had sold the vessel cheaply. Rawlings thought, but was far from sure of it, that the former owner had said something about going to Sydney. Wang had been with him, but Tufu had disappeared, and Hansen had departed before Chance sold the vessel.

It was a long way back to Sydney, but Ned followed the faint scent in person. He had tried cables and found them useless. He had plenty of money—twenty-five thousand dollars from his share of the gold—but he lived cheaply, not knowing how long his trail might be nor how much cash he might need to carry out the plan that was now fairly clear in his mind. Beyond all question he was no longer normal. He carried always with him the square casket with the turtle carvings on it, never suffering another to touch it.

Once a startled landlady, peering through a keyhole, saw him communing with a skull and told a police sergeant of her discovery. It took time to clear himself of suspicion of being first, a murderous lunatic, and then merely a crazy man who should be detained. And the affair ended in publicity that Ned did not covet. It might reach the eyes of Chance. After that he was careful when he talked with all that was left of his pal.

Chance had been in Sydney, months before. He had alternately been taken up and dismissed by the people. He had given lectures on the "Beetles and Butterflies of the South Pacific," exhibiting and loaning his collection, which was admitted to be unique and a valuable contribution to science. Then he had gone on a debauch, been mixed up in a rotten scandal, and had narrowly escaped trial for attempting to kill a man. He had departed secretly after a warning that he was not desirable, and Mitchell spent much time and some money before he dug up these things and located his man booked in the steerage of a vessel bound for San Francisco.

Chance had spent money lavishly and boasted of his wealth; these habits gave the next clew. He had stopped off in Honolulu and, with a Chinaman, undoubtedly Wang, got into trouble in Honolulu's Chinese quarter.

In San Francisco he had lorded it at the Palace Hotel. Here an announced lecture had been spoiled by newspapermen who remembered his name in Sydney files. The Chinatown squad had run across him in a raid and he had been fined. Where he had gone none knew. The man had two sides—one of cruelty and debauchery, and another showing more than a smattering of science of which he was inordinately proud. But his latest San Francisco fiasco had been broadcast by the Associated Press and he seemed to have abandoned the idea of scientific fame. That he still had money was doubtful, until Mitchell, picking up false clews and abandoning them with a patience that was born of indefatigable resolve heard of him in Tia Juana. There had been more scandal there, but Chance had won a large amount on the races, and again Wang loomed on the scene.

There the scent faded. Week after week and month after month Mitchell kept seeking for news of him, doing the thing quietly, for it was part of his plan not to alarm Chance until he was ready to commence his campaign. He stayed in modest lodging houses and haunted places where reporters went for late lunches, growing skillful at leading up the talk toward a man of Chance's habits, who might have been in that town and again have got in the news.

Mitchell crisscrossed the continent. From El Paso to Denver, to Chicago, to St. Louis, according as he fancied he had found a clew. But he did not find Chance. The ex-skipper appeared to have dropped out of sight.

He was a man readily enough distinguishable with that Mephistophelian cast of countenance, apt to be remembered by his proneness for the lower type of revels. Mitchell visited many an evil-looking dive without avail. His fad for butterflies had seemed a ready means of tracing him at first but now it was useless. Still Ned held to his resolve.

At last he came to New York, living here and there, hoping always, without definite aim now, to hear or see something of his man. Once he thought he saw him in a subway express, sure he could not be mistaken. He himself wore a beard, for it was no part of his scheme that Chance should recognize him. On the subject of Jack Somers he was unavoidably morbid, but he had cultivated a knack for gossip, for making acquaintances which, with his willingness to treat, made him not unpopular. Generally, though, he was regarded as a "queer sort," a "bug" who asked curious questions about a man who collected beetles and looked like a picture of the devil.

Nights he went over his plan, communing with the skull. He meant to haunt Chance, to threaten him mysteriously, to gradually make him think that the ghost of the man he had wantonly made away with was pursuing him, to use the supernatural. That Chance might withstand such a process, make light of it, never occurred to him. The plan had come to him, as he now believed, from the promptings of Somers' spirit. And, in the end, he would kill him.

As the time passed and his money began to get low, Ned went to spiritualistic séances and sought communication with his dead friend. He became a prey to charlatans and was placed on the "sucker list." Yet eventually he found his final clew in such surroundings.

He made the acquaintance of a little dried-up man who believed that he was in intermittent communication with Shakespeare, commissioned by the poet to write a posthumous play that would shake the world, a drama based on Socialism. The man was mildly mad, of course, and Mitchell knew it, but he met him now and then and felt sorry for him, even listening to his attempts at blank verse and sympathizing with his wasted efforts to get a hearing from managers and agents.

Sometimes he paid the other's fee, sometimes he gave him a meal and once he went with him to his lodging where the deluded soul read him his incompleted third act.

"Can you deny—can any one deny—that this is the true touch of the bard of Avon?" asked the would-be playwright. "Listen to this. It is immortal. The woman of to-day, idle, spendthrift—

> "A gilded butterfly, with peacock wings,
> That idles all the shining hours away and so, at last,
> Passes before the winter's sudden blast,
> Unuseful, profligate, the place she filled a void.
> An airy wanton of the wayward winds."

"I've seen butterflies like that, with wings like peacocks," said Mitchell, off on his own quest. The old man was flattered.

"You have? That proves it. It takes a genius to describe things that are true but unknown to him. Where?"

"In the New Guinea bush. And in a collection made by a man named Chance. A man who looks like Mephistopheles. Did you ever run across him?"

He was always asking that question. He had asked it thousands of times. He hardly expected a favorable answer.

"No," said the man who thought he wore Shakespeare's mantle, fingering his manuscript, "but, if you're interested in that sort of thing, you should go to the Museum of Natural History. They've got cases of 'em. Beautiful—but none with peacock's wings," he added in a glow of fervor.

Mitchell went there the next day. Chance would have lived his lecturing failure down by this time, perhaps. He fancied that the man had a conceit that would bring him again to the surface of the platform. He might run across him in the museum. It was a slight chance, but he was used to slight chances by now.

He wandered beside the cases, looking at the gorgeous insects. Then he stopped dead before a specimen of a hawk moth, resplendent and huge almost beyond belief. It was mounted poised above a flower from which its long proboscis was sipping synthetic nectar. But it was the label that arrested Mitchell.

MACROGLOSA CHANCEII
ORDER *Sphingidæ*
HABITAT NEW GUINEA

He might have passed the name, thinking it some Latin appellation, but the New Guinea convinced him. He found the attendant, his eyes shining, his manner excited though he strove for control. He had never consciously given up hope, but failure had undermined him, and his reaction made the man look at him suspiciously.

"Where is the man in charge of these butterflies?" asked Ned.

"I am. What's the idea?"

But Mitchell knew a guard from a scientist.

"I don't mean you. I mean the man who understands them." He gave the attendant a dollar bill.

"Mebbe you mean Mr. Edwards, the curator. He's in his office. Over at the far end of the room."

Mitchell thanked him and hurried off.

"All them bug-hunters is cranks," muttered the guard, as he tucked away the tip.

Edwards, peering through a microscope, looked up curiously at the man who entered, deciding he was a sailor. He was used to all sorts of visitors. Sometimes men, like this one, had something worth while. Oftener not. He waited to see the other produce some crumpled specimen that he would classify only too readily.

"You've got a butterfly out there called *Chanceii*," said Mitchell, mispronouncing the final vowels. He had got himself in hand a little but he showed strain. "From New Guinea. I've seen them in the bush."

"You have! Day or night?" The curator was almost the more eager of the two.

"Why, daytimes."

"Fine. Fine! That settles it. Diurnal, not nocturnal. You've done me a favor, my friend. But it isn't a butterfly. It's a hawk moth. Some say lepidopterous, others hepidopterous, a suborder that includes the nocturnal lepidopters. But this is diurnal. Most interesting. And we have the only specimen. You've seen them, you say? You must tell me about it. Where, and on what were they feeding?"

Mitchell humored him. He had learned to do this, to restrain himself. The curator was in rare humor. Then Ned put the question that had been burning on his tongue.

"I knew a man named Chance out there. Is this named for him?"

"Surely. An important contribution. And Chance is quite an amateur. Not strictly scientific, but useful,"

"He gave it to you?"

"A month ago."

"Know where I can find him?"

"Why, yes. I haven't seen him lately but I've got his address. He's living—let me see—I'll have to look it up."

Mitchell followed him over to the files, feverish, exultant. Run to earth at last!

"Pittsfield, Massachusetts. Post Office Box 989. I believe he lives outside the town, collecting Berkshire insects just now. But the curator of the Berkshire Athenæum can undoubtedly tell you just where he lives."

Mitchell took down the tentative address, fearful of a mistake. He dropped off the omnibus at Forty-second Street and got a time-table at the information bureau in the Grand Central Depot. Then he went to his lodging and opened up the casket, after locking the door, and seeing that the key blocked observation.

"Jack," he said to the grinning relic, "I've run him down. Now we'll get him."

But he took counsel with himself. If Chance frequented the Athenæum at Pittsfield and knew the curator, as he surely would, the latter would probably tell him that some one was inquiring for him. It might put him on his guard. Ned had wandered far. He would go slowly and carefully—now that he was sure.

He could linger in the post office, sure of his own changed face, till Chance came in. Then he must keep his hands from the skipper's throat. He couldn't charge him with murder, here in America, with the only real witness a savage thousands of miles away. Of course, there was Whittingham, but Ned had got out of touch with him. He himself was the avenger. Chance might send Wang for his mail. He'd follow him. Have a cab waiting. Or he might find his man in the directory, or in the telephone book. He wanted to use the phone in his plan. But he'd go to Pittsfield. His mind seemed to work with exceeding clarity. Later he'd come back to New York. There was one man he wanted to look up. The medico of their company, Somers and his, over in France. A fine fellow. Practicing in New York. Ned had seen his name in the paper, mentioned in an article on facial surgery. He had fancied that an accident, seeing that name. But things didn't happen that way. Not that Doctor Hilton had anything to do with his plan. That was for Ned alone to conceive and carry out. But he meant to go and see the doctor. Talk over old times. He'd tell him about Jack's death. Jack and the medico had been friends. The "doc" had been too highbrow for Ned. Maybe he'd show him Jack's skull. He was not sure about that. He didn't much care what happened to him after he got through with Chance, but it seemed more complete if, after he'd killed him, he was in no way connected with it.

That was to be a mystery. He had the means of death. A poison he had seen Morimori administer to a woman who was said to have bewitched a man. He had some of it with him. Just a few drops of distillation from a strange herb. The woman had died instantly, hardly seemed to have swallowed a sip. Ned remembered seeing the calabash drop from her hand and its contents sucked up by the dry earth. He had asked Morimori about it. It left no traces. You could put it on the point of a needle and scratch a man. Or mix it with the gum off a postage stamp. That was his idea. To put the fear of death and a ghostly reprisal awaiting him into the head of Chance, then to write him a letter about butterflies with a stamp inclosed. That might not work—he would have to watch him. See if he employed a secretary. But somehow he would compass it.

He paid his room rent to date, packed his grip and caught his train, walking up the hill from the Pittsfield depot in a glow of exultation. He registered at a small hotel on West Street and got hold of a telephone directory. The name leaped at him, with the address.

There was a pay phone in the office, and Ned went into the booth and got the number. New Guinea had seemed ages and miles away. Now it all seemed as yesterday. He had his man!

A singsong voice answered. Wang!

Mitchell hadn't included Wang in his plan. Wang could go his way. It was Chance who had pushed Somers off the cliff.

He asked for Chance. There was no hesitation in Wang's answer. He did not remember Mitchell's voice. It had changed, no doubt. Mitchell himself had changed.

"He velly busy. No can talkee."

"It's important."

"Wha' name?"

Mitchell grinned in the dusk of the booth. Wang would be a good messenger.

"Tell him Jack Somers is calling. I'll call again."

He heard a smothered ejaculation in Chinese as he hung up. He wondered whether Wang would try and trace the message. Or Chance? Let them. He had registered under an assumed name. He was not sure that any one had seen him enter the booth. The clerk was busy as he slipped out. He took a South Street car and rode out of town, past the country club on the road to Lenox.

He got off at the conductor's nod, having given the man a wrong number. Then he walked on and found the house, an old-fashioned place with a neglected garden, sitting well back from the road. No other dwelling very near it. Mitchell chuckled as he thought of what consternation his call might have caused. One from the dead. Jack Somers! That was the start. All he wanted this trip was to know how to find the house later on. He'd have to stay in Pittsfield overnight, but he'd go back to New York in the morning. Every day there would be some message from Jack Somers. His man might take fright. He'd have to plan for that. He could go back and forth—a four-hour trip—and during the train ride he could work out the next message, the next move. Small bother after what he'd gone through.

Long distance messages would be the best. Wang was sure to get onto his voice in time. He'd put in a personal call through an operator. Get through to Chance.

He talked with the skull again that night, and once again it seemed to take on flesh, to smile at him.

He was back in New York at noon the next day and went to a public telephone booth in the terminal. The operator put him through after a twenty-minute delay. This time it was not Wang. It was a woman's voice.

"I want to speak personally to Mr. Chance," said Mitchell.

"This is Mr. Chance's housekeeper. Who is it talking?"

"Just tell him it's from Livoro?"

"Livoro? Spell it please."

"L-i-v-o-r-o. He'll know."

He'd know. He'd see the cliff and the falls. He'd see the body of the man he had killed lying on the rocks. There was an afternoon train back to Pittsfield. If his man fled, he'd follow him.

There was no answer when Ned called up that evening. The phone had been disconnected. Well, there were other ways. He went out to the house and sneaked into the garden. There was a light upstairs. Then a switch was turned on below, and he crept up to a window and peered in through the vines that straggled there. He saw a woman, a little past her prime, standing by a table. Wang came into the room with a tray and she took it upstairs. Chance was sick. In body or in mind? Ned hugged himself. He would have to find out how ill the scoundrel was.

Luck favored him there. As he still hovered near the house, a car drove up, and a man got out with a small bag. Beyond doubt, it was a doctor. He got the number of the coupé. It had come out from South Street. The next car took him back and he got off at its terminus where North, South, East and West Streets joined, waiting for the car to come along. It might stop or he could find out later whose it was. As it happened the coupé returned in half an hour, crossed West Street and halted in front of a big office building on the corner. Ned saw the physician get out and enter the building. The rest was easy. There was only one doctor on the registry board.

He called him up next morning, inquiring how Mr. Chance was.

A nurse answered and bade him wait a moment.

"There is nothing very serious. He'll have to stay in bed for a day or so, Doctor Field says."

"That's good. I'm an old friend of his. Just what is the trouble this time?"

"It's his heart. He's had an attack of carditis. But there is no immediate alarm."

Heart trouble? Could anything be better? Chance was safe for a few days. Then he'd have another attack. Ned didn't want to kill him too soon, or too easily. Debauchery in the tropics had taken its toll.

Back in New York once more, he sent a telegram.

> So sorry to hear of illness stop Hope there is no danger stop I want to see you soon but will wait.
>
> JACK SOMERS.

They'd open that. The good-looking secretary. And they wouldn't show it to him right away. But the woman would tell him, sooner or later.

Mitchell's next move was to send him the skull. That would have to lie over for a while. The carved casket from New Guinea would tell Chance whose bony presentation it was. He'd know. Jack Somers wanted to see him. Well, he would—face to face.

In New York Ned felt restless. He was checked for a time. He decided to call up Doctor Hilton and got a cordial reply.

"Mitchell? Of course, I remember. I want to see you. Talk over old times. What are you doing to-night? Come and have dinner with me. I'm living at my club—The Bachelors', 98 West Fifty-fifth Street. Six o'clock, so we can have some ginger ale first. Don't bother about what you wear. Where's Somers? What? Oh, I'm sorry! That's bad news. I'll be on the lookout for you. Six o'clock. You've got the address, haven't you? Fine."

At the last minute Ned did up the casket in a brown-paper parcel. He hardly knew what prompted him. Of course, he'd tell the medico all about it. All except his hunting down Chance and what he meant to do to him. The doctor was a fine chap, who had liked Somers. Ned wanted to talk to some one who wasn't a stranger. He felt the strain upon him. Even if the medico guessed, later, he'd keep dumb. He'd been a sort of father confessor to the chaps overseas. Fixed up their bodies and braced up their minds. Understood them as well as the padre.

Letting his mind wander over many things, Mitchell fell asleep on his bed.

As a result, he got to the club a little late. Doctor Hilton was sympathetic, but talked of other things, never mentioning Somers till he had Mitchell in his room.

"Now tell me about it," he said. He was an understanding chap, and Ned told him all the long story, except the latter part of it—his quest and its ending.

"A blackguard, that Chance," said the doctor. "But you've got no real proof. What have you got in the package?"

Mitchell took out the crudely carved box, and the doctor examined it interestedly.

"Totem marks," he said. "Curious how that custom prevails. I suppose the turtle is sacred to that tribe. They'd eat a man's flesh but not a turtle's."

"Open it. Jack's skull is there. I swapped it for half a dozen rockets."

Doctor Hilton took out the cranium and turned it about in his supple surgeon's hands.

"You say this is Jack Somers' skull?" he said with a curious intonation.

"No one else's. Got it from Taangi, the wizard. What's wrong with it?"

"Only this. I am not positive, mind you, but I'd make a good bet on it. This isn't the skull of an American. Not the head of Somers, I'm practically certain. Look here. Did Jack ever have any dentistry done?"

"One tooth filled, before we sailed. What are you driving at?"

"Know the dentist?"

"Sure! Wait. Yes. His name was Conklin. Attached to the service. Doctor George H. Conklin. Had an office somewhere uptown."

Hilton had picked up a directory and was turning the leaves.

"Here he is. Too late now. Go and see him to-morrow. I imagine he'll have his diaries. If he identifies these jaws, I'm an interne. Look at that skull, Mitchell. It's a white man's, but it's unmistakably, to a surgeon, Teutonic. That's a German skull, or I'm a wop."

Mitchell got up excitedly.

"What's that, doc? You don't mean what you're saying! Not Jack's skull? Then Taangi—Buck said he was holding something out on us. Jack—he may not be dead, after all! But they found him at the foot of the cliff. Chance shoved him off. Hell! Suppose he's alive?"

The room whirled. Ned was pushed back in his chair.

"Drink this," Hilton ordered. "Get a brace on yourself. Don't jump at conclusions. This wizard fooled you, that's all. Somers is dead, in all probability. But you can check up these teeth. Take it easy, Mitchell. Somers was a pal of mine, too. You've been through a lot. I can see that. You'd better stay here to-night. I can get you a room."

But Ned would not stay. The doctor sent him home in a cab, hugging the casket. The world rocked about him. He did not look at the skull again. A

Heinie's? Got by the Mafulus in some raid or taken from Germans trying to slip out of Kaiser Wilhelm's Land. He must go back! He'd get the right one. And Chance?

He'd see the dentist and make sure. And he'd send the skull to Chance, no matter to whom it belonged. Chance shouldn't get by. He wouldn't know the difference, in that casket. Ned groaned. He'd been packing this fake all round the world—talking to it. The mediums had used it and fooled him. Spiritualism was a fake.

The cold morning filtered into Mitchell's room. The skull grinned at him from his bureau. It seemed ages before he finally got an answer from Conklin's phone and took a cab to his office.

"I've got my records," said the dentist, "and I never did this work. It's European and a bum job at that. What is this—a murder case?"

"Nothing that the New York police would be interested in," said Mitchell. "Call up Doctor Hilton. Never mind your records, if you're sure." He knew himself that both the experts were right. Taangi had fooled him. But Chance might be fooled, too. The skipper had certainly murdered Jack.

Mitchell departed, bearing the skull. He did not look far into the future. He was too confused, too upset for that. The skull, the only relic of his dead friend, in whose ghostly presence he had renewed his friendship and made his vow of vengeance; in whose empty orbits he had fancied at times that the eyes of his chum gazed out at him with approval—this was a sham, a mockery that Taangi had foisted upon him.

The scene came back to him again, with Whittingham's puzzled whisper: "I'd like to know what he's holding out on us." He saw the smug look on the wizard's face, heard his half chuckle and the whimper of the beast in the screened cage at the far end of that unhallowed clubhouse—*ravi*, as they called it. Taangi had fooled them. He had handed over the skull of some German who had been killed in a native raid or ambushed on a trail, at the beginning of the Great War. It was probably the cranium of some inferior soldier or servant—not to be compared with the skull of one of the three men whom Morimori had declared all wizards.

Mitchell had forced Taangi's hand a bit with his sending of star signals, and Taangi had taken this way of playing even by giving them the wrong skull. Beyond doubt Jack's was there somewhere in the clubhouse and Taangi was laughing at them while he discounted their prestige, since they had been so easily misled.

Ned's wrath began to mount against the far-off, bloated wizard. Jack was dead, and nothing could bring him back again, but a cunning black man had got the best of him—had made a Mafulu joke out of his vengeance.

That vengeance was still in the making—still to be accomplished. Or was it? He had been taken in. How much of a phrenologist was Chance? Not much, he fancied. His superstition had already been aroused, if Ned figured out that heart attack properly. He was a killer, not only of Jack, but of other men. That was established beyond doubt.

Suddenly Ned determined to make the most of his endeavor—he would send Chance the skull, in its casket with its turtle carving, which no man who had been in the South Pacific for any length of time could fail to accept as genuine. The result of that grim message should lie upon the knees of the gods.

Ned still had the poison. But Hilton's pronouncement and the dentist's verification had shaken him more than he realized. The passing doubt of Jack's death had left a germ that was even now beginning to work its leaven in his subconsciousness. It was not going to allow him to commit actual physical reprisal upon Chance, murderer though he might be on more than one occasion. The communications that Ned thought had come to him from the spirit of Somers had registered upon a surface made sensitive by the circumstances of the latter's death. Below that was a sounder integument. The psychological side of Mitchell responded to some prompting that told him that, by sending the skull to Chance, he might best test the work of justice. The justice to be meted out by what might be described as a supernatural if not spiritual agency. Bodily, Chance was without remorse. Mentally he might be reached.

Mitchell went about the thing almost methodically. He determined on what train his "sending" would go up to Pittsfield, and the approximate hour of its delivery, if marked properly.

He packed the casket; wrapped it, labeled it. The last was cleverly contrived. He must arouse Chance's curiosity and also allay any suspicion as to the source of the parcel, which must not be connected with the message he meant to send, by wire, since the phone was temporarily disconnected. His plan meant delay and with it, he practically committed forgery, but this did not bother his conscience. It was Chance's conscience he was concerned with, if the fellow possessed one. And Mitchell thought he did.

He found a quick printing shop in a basement and had some labels run off in proper form with the heading:

FROM THE MUSEUM OF NATURAL HISTORY
NEW YORK CITY

When he had printed in Chance's name and address by hand, the package looked quite authentic. Chance would surely insist upon opening it. His vanity would prompt that. Mitchell used two labels and destroyed the rest. Then he took the package to a main express office in ample time and had it marked perishable and for immediate delivery, with a valuation of a hundred dollars. It was bait for a killer.

He waited within half an hour of the train's arrival at the parcel's destination and sent his telegram:

> I shall be with you by this evening.
> JACK SOMERS.

He felt fairly certain Chance would get the telegram. He was not too sick to lack insistent control over his household. They would not dare hide the arrival of a message. And, if luck was with him, the package would follow closely on its heels. It would make a stir. The museum might be communicated with, but Ned knew that Chance would have no doubt as to whose skull this was. That turtle totem was too prominent on Taangi's temple decorations to be forgotten.

Ned took an early morning train to Pittsfield and chafed at the delay after his arrival. He could not well go out to the house until nightfall and when he called up the doctor's office he was met with a curt statement that there was no news to be given out concerning the condition of Captain Chance. Yet something told him that there had been a happening beyond the normal. The air seemed charged with it.

There was a daily paper in Pittsfield, issued in the afternoon. Ned heard the newsboys calling it and went out of the hotel—a different one this time— to purchase a copy. He had spent the day since his phoning to the doctor in his room, smoking.

The headline smote him like a blow. But he recovered from it instantly before the urchin might notice his condition. He stared at the sheet, while a wild exultation rushed through him.

Chance was dead! The gods had spoken!

The account extolled Chance as a noted explorer and scientist. He had been treated by the local physician for heart trouble, and an acute attack of angina pectoris was the cause of a death which had come suddenly. His Chinese butler, who had been with him for years, sailing with him to far lands, had found him clutching at his heart, supported by pillows on the couch where he was resting.

Before the stimulant prescribed could be administered, he had collapsed, and the doctor's endeavor to restore animation had failed. There would be no autopsy. There were as yet no arrangements for the funeral.

And there was no mention of the skull.

But Mitchell was sure it had been delivered. This was Wang's work—the oriental concealment of the actual cause. Ned had no doubt that the message, followed by the package which, instead of some specimens from the museum, contained only the grinning, mocking relic of the man whose name had been signed to the telegram, had brought on the fatal attack. Probably there was some original weakness there, engendered by Chance's way of life. But the gods had spoken. Somers was revenged.

Mitchell took a train for Albany and thence back to New York again, mapping out a course of future action on the way. It materialized swiftly enough, almost without conscious effort. The tiny germ of doubt was developing. Suppose Jack were not really dead? That question was not yet vital but it helped to determine things. His money was nearly gone. Ned was at a loose end once more. Why not return to Papua? Go into Mafulu? He had enough left for that, now that he knew the ropes. He would force Taangi to produce the real skull, or the final truth of what had happened to Somers.

There was plenty of gold left in the big pool. If he handled Taangi properly he might dam the stream, empty the treasure-house.

And there was Whittingham. Mitchell considered him still an active partner in the mining end of it. He could get in touch with the Britisher through his uncle, whose term of office was still unexpired. If Whittingham was available to go in with him, so much the better. If not, he would see that Whittingham got a share of what he secured. A fair equivalent of a non-working partner. Ned had a keen and appreciative remembrance of his English friend and, now that he was alone again, without purpose, he longed to see him.

Taangi could be managed. Ned would see Morimori first and make him gifts. And there was Lipako. It would be a worth while trip. And—if Jack was alive, by any miracle? If—

He spared a thought for Wang. That astute unworthy would doubtless feather his own nest from what he could lay hands on of Chance's remaining wealth. The housekeeper-secretary would not stand much show against the Oriental's craft, he fancied.

There was a boat leaving, through the Panama Canal, on to San Francisco. Thence he would ship to Sydney and so to Port Moresby. Ned booked his passage and shipped, curiously light-hearted.

At San Francisco he sent a message through to Port Moresby, by radio, addressed, on a chance, to Whittingham. He could not well arrange for a reply, but the word might be delivered—it would at least pave the way for getting in communication with him. He looked forward to that. The message had been brief, merely an announcement that he was returning.

The death of Chance seemed to have laid the ghost of Somers—if there was a ghost. But it was Whittingham, not Ned, Somers' own chum, who was to see the light that was to lead them marching swiftly through the Papuan bush at last, bent on the final unraveling of a mystery that was still unsolved, that seemed to show a faint clew to its labyrinth, that held out a purpose far greater than the recovery of the gold in the pool at the foot of the falls where Somers had been flung by Chance, with Wang and Tufu looking on.

And Ned was to find out that he had not yet properly appraised the man with one eye blind but the other very wide open.

VIII

BACK TO THE JUNGLE

THERE WAS A RADIO MESSAGE FOR MITCHELL AT SYDNEY, waiting for him in the hands of the steamer company's agents—from Whittingham. It was characteristic and welcome. The brief words conjured up a lively image of the Britisher with his mannerisms. At the same time Mitchell wondered why his friend was sending a boat for him, rather than coming in one. "Sending" suggested that Buck had become a millionaire or possessed of sudden great authority. He might have invested his share of the gold in some prosperous venture, though it was hard, somehow, to connect Whittingham with successful commercialism.

> Good egg stop Sending boat stop Meet you Cardwell.
> BUCK.

Cardwell was the last port of call of the coasting steamers that ran north from Sydney and carried the commerce of Queensland and New South Wales. Ned had been uncertain of his means of transportation to Port Moresby from Sydney. Now all was rosy. Whittingham was on tap. For the first time since they had left the Mafulu country he felt cheerful. The death of his pal no longer seemed a shadow that darkened everything. This was no faithlessness to his memory; it was rather a condition of natural reaction.

The wonder grew when, reaching Cardwell, Ned saw a gunboat in the harbor from which a brassy, fussy launch came darting out to the steamer. A smart ensign was in charge, inquiring whether Mr. Edward Mitchell was aboard. Ned appeared, and the officer saluted.

"The compliments of Colonel Whittingham, sir, and we are at your service with the *Panther*. The colonel regrets that official duties prevented him meeting you in person and trusts that you will excuse him."

"Good egg!" said Mitchell and saw the ghost of a twitch pull at the corners of the ensign's mouth to match the twinkle in his eyes. "How come the official duties and since when is Buck Whittingham ranking colonel?"

"He came out of the war a major, sir. His present rank is that of chief aide to the lieutenant governor of New Guinea."

So Whittingham had been received into the bosom, official and otherwise, of his own family! This, after all, was the career for which he was really fitted. To adjudge and adjust colonial affairs and administer them with impartiality called for just such a temperament as Buck's.

They were good to him aboard the gunboat. Ex-corporal Mitchell hobnobbed with the members of the officers' mess and found them all good sports, evidently prepossessed in his favor. They begged him for yarns of the Papuan back country and bemoaned the fact that the rivers were not navigable for any great distance and that the services of the navy were ignored on expeditions of exploration or punishment.

"There's a trip brewing up Mafulu way, I gather," said the lieutenant commander. "I don't know much about the details but I understand there's a wizard been cutting up didoes who is due for a lambasting, and Colonel Whittingham is just the chap to give them a lesson. I suppose he'll take you along. I wish you could fix it for me. I'd have a shot at leave. But it's no go. The navy is not encouraged ashore. Ducks are ducks and chickens, chickens. Only the marines are hybrid. But I envy you, sir."

They did not know the name of the wizard or any details. Ned supposed it must be Taangi. Then what had happened to Morimori? It seemed as if he had arrived in the nick of time. He wondered just what Taangi had been up to. As chief aide to the governor, Whittingham would be stretching a point if he personally led the expedition, but Ned fancied that it would be hard to keep him away from it, uncle or no uncle. And Buck was essentially the man for the job. If Mitchell could be attached, it would just fit his own plans. He would have to arrange for his personal carriers and for staying in the country to settle the matter of Somers' skull, which he now meant to see had proper burial. Also he was determined to get out all the gold he could. Even a British colonel and an aide to a colonial governor could use gold. Some day Whittingham would go home and find some English girl with whom he would enter into all the dignity of British family life. Some day he would indubitably be knighted and write a ponderous book about British administration in Papua. He had already served his country well. When Ned thought of his having been the trail chum of a major he had to chuckle, a trifle abashed, the discipline of the old days reasserting itself, a little before he realized that rank after all, was only a stamp that might grow illegible.

Fighting the dysentery together, following cannibal trails, they had built up a real friendship, and Whittingham's radio message, with the sending of the *Panther*, proved that it still existed. As Buck Whittingham, the other did not give a hoot who Ned Mitchell was, what he had been, or where he came from.

Mitchell marveled how his friend had been able to make these arrangements. Chief aide though he was, he would still have required the signature of the governor on the request. Remembering that horse-faced official, with his creaking shirt bosom, emblem of his own unbending and starched authority, Ned knew that the governor must have considered the reason adequate and fit for registry in his official log or portfolio.

Mitchell's Yankee sense of humor looked upon much of the British executive program as a joke, though not without perception of his own country's fallibility, but he was bound to admit that it worked.

Whittingham was on the wharf to receive him, calm and cool and authoritative, receiving and returning salutes with an air that almost sent Mitchell's own hand to his forehead until Buck let his eyeglass fall and winked at him. The next moment he had Ned in a motor car, a two-seater which he drove himself, and they were on the way toward Government House. For a moment Mitchell feared he would be quartered under the official eyes, but Whittingham relieved him.

"You'll bunk and chow with me, Ned," he said. "I've got my own diggings in a little bungalow. Can't stand the old boy and my revered but rigid aunt all the time. Also the old boy is a bit under the weather. Nothing serious but he's been out here long enough—malaria's got into his system and needs working out. Liver's a bit spotty.

"He wants to see you. He's got quite a high opinion of you. I didn't tell him everything that happened on our trip to Mafululand, but it was your conduct on the plantation that he considers 'very meritorious,' for an American.

"The main point is that there will be no difficulty about your going on the trip we're getting up, to teach Taangi to be good. Morimori passed out. I saw Lipako about two months ago. He's a big bug amongst the Mekeo now and he's got the new wizard under his thumb.

"He don't amount to much, Lipako says. There will not be another Morimori in a hurry. He had his points, but he got *puri-puri'd*—bewitched— in the end like the rest of 'em. My private opinion is that is was dysentery, but they all consider it magic, and Taangi—our old elephantine pal, Taangi—gets all the credit, or discredit. He used those rockets to good effect. Gave it out that he could talk with the stars just as well as Morimori, and then Morimori got sick, and Taangi heard of it, so he shot off a rocket or two in Morimori's general direction, just as we did, and announced that Morimori was about to die. It was his luck that his prophecy turned out correct. Morimori's *mana* is supposed to have entered into him—and he's been getting mighty cocky. They killed a couple of miners—whites—six weeks ago. We've been collecting evidence and now we are going to spank Taangi hard. He's gone beyond the limit. Openly scoffs at the white man and says he is their master. There's some talk he holds white men prisoners and exhibits them to prove his power. We're going to jolly well look into that. Taangi's goose is in the oven. Soon as I got your message I took it to the governor and told him you were just the man to go along; in fact I stalled a bit with the preparations.

"It worked out fine. I wangled the gunboat out of the old boy when he began to fret and fuss over the delay. Some one wrote back home to the *Times* or something like that, asking why the governor of Papua was unable to properly preserve the lives of British subjects in his territory. They've been cabling us some hot grounders about it. But here we are. I've got fifty of the armed constabulary lined up for the trip. I'm in command. All natives except us. A good lot. Martini-Enfields—.303 cartridges—and a couple of portable machine guns.

"If Taangi wants to be militant, we'll oblige him. It seems he's got a native regiment of bow shooters who can hit the mark at two hundred yards, so we may have a bit of fun. Here we are. I've got a good cook; there's ice—club soda and Johnny Walker. We'll have a peg and a smoke before tiffin and you can tell me why you came back. After the gold? Pity to waste it. I'm not in on that now, of course. An official must not personally profit by the natural resources, or some Johnny would kick up no end of a row. The merry old job is not all beer and skittles, but I like it."

"You're my partner," said Mitchell. "I did come back after gold, for one thing, but that's not the main reason. It's a long yarn."

Whittingham poured out fresh highballs.

"Go ahead. First of all, you got Chance, of course?"

The tale ran into dinner and continued after it, Whittingham keenly interested.

"By Jove! I'll have to spin that to the governor," he said. "Expurged, of course. He'd never approve of your chasing Chance with a skull. Highly unethical. But efficient. The old villain funked it at the last and got fooled, just as Taangi fooled us. We'll clean up his clubhouse properly this trip.

"He probably knows by this time that we are coming. Bound to have leaked out. We've got men from all over the country in the armed constabulary and they know where they're bound for. They'll talk, and talk soon gets back in the bush. That may be an advantage or a disadvantage. Taangi won't know you're along—not yet. And he's all puffed up in his mind as well as his body nowadays. Thinks he owns all Papua. Thinks he's invincible. We'll show him. I suppose he calls himself mighty since palming off that Boche skull."

"That's what he was holding out on us," said Mitchell. "Remember you said there was something?"

Whittingham nodded. He had relapsed into his official shell, Ned thought. Buck's face was very grave, his eyes serious, thoughtful.

"I remember," he said, "but I'm not so sure. I've heard things since then. It's hard to sift out the talk that comes in, and I don't want to raise false hopes in you, Ned, but—" He sucked at his pipe, sending out puffs of smoke and regarding them judicially.

"I'm taking a bit of time over it," he went on, "because it's only just come to me, since you told me you had the wrong head, joining that up with the rumors. You see, Ned, I don't believe Taangi was so smug over just the substitution of the skull. I've learned quite a bit about the beggar lately! Port Moresby is the headquarters of the central court and, though they've got a sort of circuit, there are any amount of cases tried here, from plantation labor troubles up to murder. The judges visit at Government House and we talk over the things that come up. Then there are three or four men in the constabulary, one of 'em a sergeant, who are from the Big Rivers neighborhood, next door to Taangi.

"I believe Taangi didn't hand you over Somers' skull, because he didn't have it. Giving you a head was a good way to get rid of us and get the rockets. But I don't think he'd rate one white skull particularly high over another. He'd have given you the right one if he could have produced it."

"Just what are you driving at? That they didn't eat him—that he wasn't dead?"

"Hold on. Easy on the curb for a jiffy. Suppose Somers wasn't killed by that fall over the cliff? Chance thought he was, but he wouldn't bother much to monkey with any life that might be left in your chum. He left him there, knowing the natives would handle the body in their own way—dead or alive.

"Now, I don't know why they wouldn't have killed him, meaning the Mafulus, and made long pig of him except—" Buck checked off his reasons on his fingers:

"First, they are not crazy over white flesh, though they would have liked his head.

"Second, if he was alive at all he may have been knocked silly. That may have protected him. They're like your Indians; they leave crazy folks alone.

"Third, they may have wanted—Taangi may have had a whim—to use him as an exhibit."

"You mean—in that cage in the clubhouse?" Mitchell leaned forward excitedly, but Whittingham was unruffled.

"Exactly. It was a big cage, screened in, you remember. And there was something alive in it, whimpering and crying. What was it?"

"I thought it was some sort of a big ape. I remember hearing it that night, fancying it was wisest not to get too nosey about it. I was satisfied that Jack was dead. When I got the skull I forgot the cage."

"Same here. But—there are no big apes in Papua. No animals bigger than a wallaby. And they wouldn't keep a wallaby in a cage. There's this recent talk about Taangi having white captives. It would give him a lot of prestige if he did have one. Keep it, something as you or I would keep a tame bear, only he wouldn't treat it as decently. If Somers is out of his head, Taangi wouldn't mind that.

"It doesn't quite seem a sufficient reason for having spared him in the first place, but there may be something else that will come out. In the meantime, Ned, I think there's a good show that your chum was in that cage the night we stayed in the *ravi*—is there now. And, if he is, by jingo, we'll bring him back with us! We'll do better than that. The surgeon at the government hospital has been pestering for a chance to go along with us. The governor didn't see it at first, but now he will. Ned, I've got one of your hunches. We're going to find your pal alive—and, by George, old top, we'll bring him round!"

He swung a hand into Mitchell's with an infectious enthusiasm that communicated itself to Ned in a firm conviction coupled with self blame. His first hunch—that Chance had made away with Jack—had been correct. Chance had done his worst. Now he felt a hope that was almost an assurance, as he remembered the creature that had shuffled and whimpered round that great cage while the enormous wizard smiled smugly at them. It was the mental picture of that mocking smile that bolstered Ned's belief that Somers might not be dead. The more the two discussed it the more plausible seemed the theory that they built up.

They spoke of Chance's death. Perhaps after all he had not been an actual murderer, but he thought he was—and there had been other cases.

"No need for you to feel any remorse over that rotter, Ned," said Whittingham.

"I don't."

"Look here. What about Wang?"

"I imagine he got hold of all he could and beat it. I didn't bother my head about him. Why?"

Whittingham frowned.

"I was wondering. There have been quite a lot of Chinamen trailing into town lately. Most of 'em have been working as cooks and house boys, but some of 'em are running trading stores. We've rounded 'em up and they all seem to belong. It's bothered us a bit. Wang's no fool, from all accounts. He knows about the gold. He may be going back after the rest of it. Wouldn't trouble about a license. The Chinese have got pluck enough. The natives have killed a lot of 'em, but they stick to it. They're natural gold hunters. This may be all nonsense, but Wang wouldn't be worried much about a skull, and it's quite on the cards he'd slope out here and get a gang together. He knows the way in. Chinese are considered white men by the tribesmen. I'm going to find out if a one-eyed chink has been seen about Moresby. I'll look around a bit myself. If he sees you he'll be onto us, but he doesn't know I was with you on the trip. Doesn't know that there was a trip, perhaps, though he'll have found out about it all by now.

"If we run across Mr. Wang and he hasn't got a permit we'll trim his sails. I'll tip off the constabulary to try and find out what all the chinks are up to."

Mitchell was not deeply interested. Wang's possible interference was secondary, as were all other things, to the chance of finding Jack. The expedition was to start in three days. The governor was anxious to be able to report Taangi subdued. Preparations were already in hand, the carriers arranged for, government stores handy. Mitchell was not to take any carriers at the start after all. He could get some men from Lipako's people, possibly Lipako himself, and Whittingham promised to leave him enough trade goods to carry on with his gold mining. But Ned took some dynamite, fuses and caps, with a few necessary tools to work at his proposed diverting dam—if he stayed. For these supplies, five extra carriers were commandeered by Whittingham.

If they found Somers, and he was in need of immediate surgical attention, Ned meant to come back at once. The gold could wait, even if Wang got to it. Jack was paramount.

And, if Wang was in Papua, there was no sign of it. But the Chinese who had been drifting into Port Moresby suddenly disappeared overnight in a sloop owned by one of their countrymen who was trading in sea slugs. Word of them came from Hall Sound where they had vanished into the bush. Yule Island lay in Hall Sound, and the St. Joseph's River emptied into it. Though not particularly concerned with the yellow men, the official party made the first stage of their journey in a launch to this point. They found no trace of the Chinamen.

The expedition was well organized, and the constabulary in their blue jumpers and sulu kilts, edged with red, their scarlet sashes under belt and cartridge pouch, were used to the work and efficient. The interior villages received them with a certain reserve, but food was furnished promptly as well as relays of carriers.

They found Lipako, who welcomed them with great ceremony and a turnout of the village, painted and ornamented with feather headdresses. The girl he had once coveted was now one of his wives, of which, by right of chiefhood, he had three.

"I am extremely fond of her," he told Mitchell, "but I do not show it. I make her do most of the work and she behaves very nicely. Her old husband was not much good."

Lipako was glad to hear that Taangi was to be taken in hand. Some of his tribesmen were missing and he had no doubt that Taangi had taken them, killed and eaten them. But he did not volunteer to come along until he heard of the possibility of Somers being a captive in the *ravi*. That excited him.

"I have heard of such a thing," he said. "But I thought it was the boasting of Taangi. If you want me I will go with you and help to take Taangi. If he has done this thing you will surely hang him?" he asked Whittingham. "It will take a strong rope, for he is a very heavy man. And none will wish to eat his flesh," he added.

• • •

They made forced marches to the Big Rivers and once again Mitchell's tidal pontoons were constructed to cross the bridgeless current, though this time Ned did not have to swim. Two of the constabulary, beach men and experts in the water, made the passage. Each carried a light line, and one was left stretched to aid a swimmer on the return trip.

Lipako had sent out a drum message forbidding others to be sent for two weeks but he did not doubt but that Taangi would find a way to know of their arrival. There were natives in the Mekeo district who would cater to him out of fear of his wizardry, and there was a method of smoke signaling that could be used.

Traveling was terrific work at the pace they maintained. The ridges that had to be crossed were thick with almost impenetrable brush. The moist tropical heat was exhausting even to the natives, and all those who wore clothing might have been traveling in a vapor bath. There were myriads of mosquitoes and flies, with ants that crawled and flew, that leaped and ran and jumped, biting and worrying day and night. Huge spiders lurked in sticky webs and the tiny pests of the scrub itch covered the feet and legs of the men working their way through all clothing. There were great snakes and centipedes and mountain cockroaches, all of which were perhaps minor matters but wrought up every one to intense irritation, bodily and mental. Whittingham took all as a part of the day's work and he seldom lacked a jest at the right moment. The surgeon backed him. Ned frequently strode in the lead, climbing rocks, swinging down cliffs by vine handholds, and attacking all obstacles viciously. He felt it was his own stupidity that had condemned Somers to his horrible prison cage—if Jack was still alive—and he feared that Taangi, unless the wizard was confident of beating off the constabulary, might kill his captive and get rid of evidence that might hang him.

At last the party came to the sharp ridge on top of which was the *ravi* and village of Taangi. As before, they had met no sign of life nor had they been ambushed, though opportunity was plentiful for blow-gun work. They struggled up the steep pitch, tripping over tangled rattan and thorny lawyers' vines—traps that crept along the ground or looped a little off it, hidden by the thick vegetation through which they forced their way. The Mekeo carriers had left part of their loads cached at the foot of the ridge, in order to assist with the machine guns and lighter packs. They climbed like apes, but even they were held up now and then by barriers of natural ropes covered with lacerating thorns. And sharp-edged, serrated leaves grew on almost every bush.

There were great trunks of fallen trees, sometimes visible, usually masked by undergrowth. These rapped and bruised the shins, and often the rotten timber gave way in a sort of vegetable smoke, when a man attempted to climb over the obstructions.

They never saw the sun, or even the sky, and all about them was the stifling reek of vegetation that had decayed or was constantly decaying, as the jungle life forced itself through its swift period of fighting life and death. Then the ridge was split with a deep and narrow crevasse down which the expedition made its slow and perilous way, never knowing whether the next step would be on ground or in midair, to send them crashing downward. At the bottom of the gorge was a morass where leeches attacked the travelers voraciously, and the guides wandered for two hours before they could find a way up the opposing precipice. It was nightfall when they emerged, bleeding and bruised, on top of the ridge and found the village deserted!

The great clubhouse was empty, its skulls and images gone, its decorations removed. The men made camp and lit a fire. But it was no sooner started than the rain came down in torrents and drove them into the *ravi* where, with sentinels set, they passed the night, listening to the *boom boom* of drums that seemed to be sounding all about them as if Taangi was calling his warriors to arms.

There was no fear of a night attack in that weather. The rain ceased abruptly a little before the dawn, which came in a savage burst of splendor. The men bivouacked outside, while the leaders cooked their breakfast on the big firestone at the end of the *ravi*. The cage was gone and the fate of its occupant was heavy upon them.

Their position was sound, but they were undoubtedly surrounded. The bush, shining with moisture that was beginning to turn swiftly into a mist, might be filled with their enemies. It was possible that the Mafulus, instead of waiting to be attacked, would rush them. They could not stay there long. The question of food was a serious one.

Whittingham took it coolly, keeping his men together near the clubhouse, cautioning all not to wander into the fog. The constabulary, well-drilled, muscular men, stood by their arms, the two machine guns arranged to sweep the ridge now covered thick with mist that would pass in an hour but which for the moment offered a great opportunity for covering evidence of a concerted rush.

They talked the matter over with the native sergeants, discussing Mafulu methods. The Mafulu bowmen carried weapons only half the length of their arrows. The latter often measured eight feet and could be discharged with terrific force and effect; they were dangerous up to two hundred yards, flint-tipped, and likely to be poisoned with fish gall. At close work there would be stone clubs, spears, axes of flint and knives.

No one showed any signs of fear, unless it was the Mekeo carriers and Lipako set them a good example, telling of the valor and magic of Whittingham and Mitchell. The constabulary seemed a trifle nervous but they were picked men who had fought cannibals before—knew what defeat meant and could be trusted not to waste their shots.

It was as if they were on an island surrounded by enormous waves of verdure, ridges that showed now and then as the sun and wind began to thin the fog in patches. But the vapor was still too heavy for comfort. The air was cold and a fire was kept going. There was no need for concealment. The three white men conversed in low tones, smoking as if they were on a hunting trip, waiting for the beaters to drive the game out of the forests. The birds were silent and it grew very quiet.

Suddenly—the direction was hard to determine—there broke out somewhere below them a hideous howling, a beating of drums, mingled with yells in savage babble. Then the bark of guns echoed through the jungle.

Mitchell, Whittingham and the doctor looked at each other. The Mafulus had no rifles. It meant that white men were near, were being ferociously attacked. Whites, or men esteemed as such.

"It's Wang," said Whittingham. "The Mafulus have got his chinks hemmed in. We could never find them. It'll be our turn next. Thank the gods the mist is clearing off. Listen to that, will you? They've downed the poor beggars."

The gunfire was getting intermittent, drowned out by yell after yell of unmistakable triumph. The drums ceased. There came one shot, then another—and silence. It was a situation to test the nerves. Taangi's warriors, excited and heartened by their victory, sure of Taangi's supremacy, would soon come on in an exultant horde. Ned and Buck stood by, preparing to hold the *ravi* as a last resort if the attack was too fierce to check, or the numbers overwhelming. Lipako thought that the Mafulus might muster five hundred warriors. If so, the odds were nearly eight to one.

The day wore on and there was no rush, no signs of one. It grew unbearably hot and the tension on their courage was tremendous.

Whittingham inspected the food supply and his eyes were grave.

"We'll have to get out of this by tomorrow," he said. "Get that stuff we cached, if they haven't run across it or the white ants got at it. If they have, we'll have to go find a village. Get hold of pigs and yams. And we'll have to go soft and pretty. What are you fixing up, Ned?"

"I toted the dynamite myself," said Mitchell. "If the machine guns go out of commission—I've known 'em to in rapid work," he added, with a lively recollection of the trenches—"a few half sticks may be demoralizing."

"Good egg!"

Buck walked off and Mitchell went on splitting his half sticks, inserting primers and fuses, binding them in, splitting the short fuses in turn and putting match heads in them for swift ignition. He had to do something, thinking of Jack and the vanished cage. If Taangi's men had killed Wang and his men they would hardly spare Somers now.

The birds began to call and screech. The life of the jungle, halted first by the mist, then by the savage fight that had ended so suddenly, with such ominous abruptness, asserted itself. But there was no sign from the Mafulus. Scouting in the mat of bush was impossible. Lipako proposed one method of observation that he said would not be available until nightfall. He pointed out a towering tree, fully two hundred feet in height. From there, at twilight, he would look for smoke. He did not have to suggest to them what kind of food would be prepared at those fires, but he mentioned it briefly, relapsing into beach English, to the three whites.

"Too much they *kai-kai*, those fella Chinamen," he said.

The blistering heat grew greater, and the men sought what shade they could. The interior of the clubhouse was foul with all kinds of refuse. They had stood it at night because of the pelting rain; now, under the frightful glare of the sun it was insupportable. There was water enough in rocky pools beneath the trees and, if they cared to venture down the farther ravine, in the creek that ran to the great fall whose voice was plain to their ears.

"I don't believe they'll tackle us till dawn," said Whittingham. "They'll eat long pig to-night and make themselves strong. If they eat too much they'll sleep perhaps through another day. And we'll have to go hungry or get out. They know where we are all right. And I'd rather have them come to us than chance going through the jungle."

As the sunset came, promising relief, Lipako climbed the tall tree, putting a rattan twist about himself and the trunk and hitching his body up until he reached the boughs through which he scrambled swiftly.

He stayed there several minutes and came back with a face that was not reassuring.

"Five smoke, I see," he announced, holding up his right hand, open, and then pointing about the sweep of the horizon to five fixed points.

It meant that the Mafulus were divided into five villages, each of which was feasting separately. To-morrow they would join in attack or, if Taangi possessed real strategy, come separately in a rush from all sides.

Darkness came, bringing cold that the party fought with fires. Great stars came out, and the mosquitoes clouded through the smudge which had been raised for protection. All night the drums called with a barbaric rhythm that seemed to boast of what had been done and what would be repeated. It did not rain. There was no morning mist. And there were no Mafulus.

The rations for breakfast were short ones. A white man, any man, fights best on a full stomach, and a native does not fight at all well on an empty one. There was a little grumbling, which the sergeant suppressed. Whittingham ordered a drill and then—they waited.

Waited until the heat of the day drove the birds to silence, waited while they imagined the gorged cannibals awakening, then creeping on, up through the pathless jungle, yet choosing the easiest ways that they alone knew, understanding the contours that lay hidden beneath the high undergrowth that reached up to join the foliage of the trees, knowing of ravines and gorges that would check the stranger, hold him where they, unseen themselves, might shoot him down.

"We'll have to get out of here before nightfall," Whittingham announced finally. "We'll cut out lunch—we may need what we've got. Funny we don't hear any drums. Either they're asleep or they've made all their plans."

They parked one machine gun close to the ladder of the clubhouse platform where it could be quickly taken up, and Mitchell arranged his dynamite bombs there on the veranda, setting them out handy for flinging.

The best of it was with the Mafulus, if they had brains enough to know it. They could hold the white men here until they were forced to forage and then, ranging through the trees, slaughter them with arrows or with the short-ranged but deadly blowguns. But there was always the mystery of the white man's *mana*. Experience had taught them that the white men fought hardest in an emergency, that his brains were apt to turn the tables when the day seemed won.

Mitchell suggested that they might herald their way back to where they had left their supplies, through to the river, by flinging short quarter sticks of dynamite ahead of them. It did not seem impracticable, but Whittingham shook his head.

"We've got to whip Taangi, not frighten him," he said. "And there's Somers to clear up."

It had cost Mitchell no little effort to even suggest leaving his pal's mystery unsolved, yet he felt that the others must not be sacrificed for an uncertainty. Now he was glad when his plan was vetoed.

The sun rose to its zenith, the shadows retreating, while the heat sapped the energy out of the waiting men. Only the whites, and Lipako, were vigilant.

Whittingham consulted his wrist watch, loath to give the order to march. Somehow he had to circumvent Taangi, teach him a lesson, not allow him an abnormal victory by his, Buck's failure to do what he had set out to do. There might be a village on the next ridge. Lipako had seen no smoke rising there at sunset the night before, but Taangi might have been smart enough not to have lit fires where their vapor could be seen so easily against the sky line. Once more the young chief climbed the tree, coming back bathed in sweat from the effort. There was no smoke visible anywhere, he said. The ovens had been closed.

There was no breath of air on the ridge, nor any that stirred the trees.

Then, with a sudden and rising series of howls, the painted, naked savages, clad many of them in wicker cuirasses, with headdresses fluttering, charged out of the forest in four companies, to right and left, shook their weapons in defiance, and leaped back into the fringing trees downhill, while scores of flinted shafts came winging, whizzing, toward the defenders. The open space atop the ridge was in places less than eighty yards wide, nowhere much over a hundred and twenty. The arrows were well aimed, well placed, and three men went down. Meanwhile the rifles of the constabulary showed no such reprisal, and the tribesmen vanished in the brush, shouting in triumph. There were some two hundred of them, Buck calculated; the full forces were not yet in the field.

The surgeon attended to the wounded, who were taken under the *ravi* platform for first aid. One was dead, pierced through the breast by a long shaft, bright with white and scarlet feathers.

"We'll have to coax 'em out," said Whittingham. "Can't stay in the open. Get up on the platform. We'll run this gun a while."

He stepped to the machine gun and squatted on the saddle, peering through its little shield.

"I'll feed," said Mitchell. "I've done it before."

The native police went up the ladder in fair order, the carriers scrambling more eagerly, and a howl came from the hidden foe. A drum started booming messages, and the Mafulu warriors came bounding out after a flight of arrows, stopping clear of the brush to notch more shafts. These found no victims, though they stuck quivering in the timbers and heavy wickerwork of the clubhouse while Martini rifles barked back at them.

The insistent drum urged them on and the savages came with a rush, in great leaps, making for the platform.

"Magnificent, but it's not war!" said Whittingham to Mitchell. "Here's where they learn something."

The machine gun sent out a spray of lead, as it coughed its *rat-tat* at the door of death. The charging natives fell pell-mell but seemed not to notice it, so swift was their rush, so fierce their temper and so confident their belief in their invincibility. They had the flesh of white men in their bellies, the *mana* of white men eaten was mingled with their own. Reserves now followed from the jungle. The open place was black with them, coming on with their plumes fluttering.

A nest of five machine guns could not have stopped them. It was a matter of seconds before they were up to the spouting muzzle, springing high to surmount it, howling like devils loose from the pit.

Ned and Buck were forced to abandon it, under cover of their own pistol fire and that of the gun mounted on the porch, which broke into action in a short-range barrage and gave them a chance to scramble up the ladder.

Warrior after warrior went down but the rest swarmed like angry bees, scaling the scaffolding and the crude steps in the face of rifle fire, of Whittingham's and the surgeon's revolvers and Mitchell's automatic. It was not until Ned got to his dynamite and flung two sticks whizzing into the thick of them that they showed the first sign of wavering. Then the devastating blast, the yellow fumes, the sight of broken bodies that spattered blood from headless trunks and flying limbs, got home to them. Here was white man's magic, showing itself at the last moment.

The insistent drumbeats that had directed them changed. Some one was overseeing the fight. They fell back in confusion, raced for cover and gained it, leaving their maimed and dead behind them. But for the silent or writhing bodies, the square was deserted, almost as if a slide had been shifted from a screen.

There was a different rhythm now in the pounding—an order. Arrows came hurtling across the open space. Whittingham's men lay down, firing back, without visible targets, afraid to expose themselves. There might be no more rushes but they were beleaguered. The wounded men had been lifted to the platform where there were more to join them now. Seven in all, and the one dead man below.

"We've stopped 'em," said Whittingham grimly. "Your dynamite did the trick, Mitchell, but they've got us about where they want us. There are all of four hundred, outside of those we dropped, and half of them have got bows. With the bush to cover them those weapons are as good as rifles—better."

The drum was still sending. It seemed to come from the next ridge and Whittingham trained his glasses there, searching every foot of it.

He gave an exclamation.

"By George!" he said. "Come here, Mitchell. Take the glass. Look next to that big tree with the white trunk, to the right of it. What do you see? Isn't that our old pal?"

The focus suited Mitchell's vision, and the lenses were powerful. Irised slightly by the sunlight he saw a mammoth figure seated in a chair that had poles on either side for bearers. It was Taangi, the elephantine. Back of him a man swung a club at a great log drum suspended from a bough. Beside him were perhaps half a dozen warriors—the "staff" of the Mafulu army.

Taangi could see them in the clearing. Native sight was phenomenal. But he would not think himself visible to their eyes as he sat in the dense shadow.

"Look at the bloated old he-wolf," said Whittingham. "Thinks himself Napoleon. Well, he's not such a bad imitation, but here's where he meets his Waterloo. I had orders not to fire unless I was attacked. After that I was to use my own discretion. I'm going to and, if they don't like it at home, they can have my job. We've got one dead man and seven casualties. The medico says two of them are going to pass out. We're in a hole and we've got to get out. Old Taangi is the brains of this investment. We're out of grub and we're hemmed in. I don't figure that's our fault. It's Taangi's, and he's going to pay for it. Where's my gun bearer?"

His manner was grim, as a man crawled up to him and handed over the case in which was the German rifle that Howell had given him. He assembled it, slipped in a clip and raised the sights, checking the range by observations with the binoculars and his naked vision.

"I'd call it all of eight hundred yards to that ridge," said Buck. "What would you say, Mitchell?"

"I should guess around that."

"Then Heaven bless Howell! Here's where Taangi goes over the range. I'll try a sighting shot. He can't get out of that chair in a hurry nor they pick him up. I was mistaken—there *is* big game in Papua and I'm going to pot it."

He lay down, resting the barrel on the low platform rail and cuddling the stock against his cheek. The sweat ran down from his forehead, and he coolly wiped it off with a cambric handkerchief.

"Taangi is the head and front of their offensive," he said. "I was runner-up for the Queen's Prize at Wimbledon once and there was a nasty wind blowing. None here. Just a matter of trajectory, if I've got the distance right. It's deceptive up here in the mountains. Get Taangi, and we got them on the run. He's big magic; we've got to show bigger. They'll quit if he snuffs out. There he goes again with his damned drum."

Mitchell, through the glass, saw Taangi make a ponderous gesture and the drummer raise his club to strike the hollow log.

"It's another charge," he said, as the beats quickened to the rhythm that had prefaced the first rush.

"Righto. You attend to that. I'll attend to Taangi. And I'll plug the drummer next, for luck. Give 'em some dynamite, Mitchell. They don't like it. They're not half so brash as they were about coming out."

But they came at last and Mitchell stooped for his bombs, seeing Whittingham squeeze the trigger.

A spurt of dirt came just below Taangi's chair. Whittingham grunted, swiftly lifted the hind sight a notch and fired again. The swollen figure fairly stood up, then collapsed. A second shot sent the drummer back as if he had been struck by a catapulted rock. The drum ceased. The Martinis roared, Mitchell's dynamite crashed, and the forest sent back the echoes of the explosion. The machine gun spat out its venom, and their volley of arrows sped, the Mafulus slowed up.

"Come on, Ned!" cried Whittingham. "Taangi's done for. Let's man the other Lewis."

With the two machine guns raking them, the Mafulus dived into the bush. The open space held half a hundred corpses, some frightfully mutilated by the explosive. The leaden bullets clipped the leaves where the rest had vanished, panic-stricken. The constabulary charged, sending volley after volley through the tangle, hearing the flying natives crashing down to the ravine. Mitchell hurled dynamite after them for good measure and there was a geysering of boughs, then only the sounds of the routed savages.

A wail went up from the opposing ridge, the death song for Taangi.

"That's that," said Whittingham, "thanks to Howell. We'll cross the stream and make that ridge. I've a notion we'll find a village up there. If not we'll locate one somewhere. I'm hungry. Ned, I've got a flask of Johnny Walker left. Medico, let's have a drink. We'll rig litters for your wounded. We'll have to bury our chap that got killed. Here's hoping we find some sort of a trail."

Lipako found at last what might pass for a path after they got down to the stream that flowed from the basin below the falls. Everywhere were strewn the weapons of the discomfited Mafulus. With Taangi slain there was an end of their rebellion. There would be mourning in the villages. The white man was again dominant. Lipako and the native sergeants were sure there would be no more trouble. The Mafulus would disperse to their villages in fear of more reprisal.

A guard was left to tend the wounded until the party made the ridge. There they found Taangi's chair and the enormous form of the dead wizard. Ants were acrawl on his corpse. In a few hours he would be only skeleton, with the bodies left in front of the *ravi*. He had been too big to carry off, even if his staff had not been too terror struck at the magic of the death that had brought him down from such a distance, to move him.

Marching along the ridge toward the falls that ever sounded closer, they found a straggling village. The clubhouse was half the size of the deserted one and there were fewer houses. About them a few men and women were hurriedly gathering together their household goods. They fled at sight of the conquerors and Whittingham forbade more firing.

But, as they neared the huts, one man, rushed with a flaming torch and scrambled up the ladder of the *ravi*, thrusting the burning stick at the dry wattling, flinging it into the thatch, which caught instantly. Flames showed pale under the sun and smoke began to roll upward.

The man was burning their trophies, doubtless borne there from the main village, so that they might not fall into the hands of the whites. This had been Taangi's headquarters. And Mitchell guessed what else might be inside—the cage, with Somers in it, if they had not killed him.

Ned glanced at Whittingham and saw that the Britisher shared his idea. The two of them raced for the *ravi*. The front was a mass of fire. It was burning like a heap of straw. The thatch and the woven sides, dried by the sun to the quality of tinder, were crackling and flinging off great sparks and flakes and gouts of flame that caught in the roofs of the village. House after house began to flare like great torches.

The pair ran side by side.

"At the back!" gasped Mitchell. It was their only chance of entry, and

Ned remembered the cage's former position. At the rear, standing downhill, the posts and scaffolding that held up the *ravi* were high, but they climbed up them, guns in their belts, and then halted, calling for knives. Constables came running, bringing blades, tossing them up to be caught, clambering after them.

Desperately Ned and Buck hewed at the tough wattling while the flames roared and devoured the big structure. At last they made a gap and forged through. The interior showed bright with the burning of the roof. Lumps of burning stuff dripped down and ignited the flooring, revealing the wicker gods, racks of skulls, shields—and *the cage*. Something inside was beating at the screens, shaking the bars of bamboo, rocking the structure.

"Jack!" shouted Ned. "Jack!"

He held no hope of an intelligent answer, but the call came spontaneously from the prisoner's throat:

"Ned! Ned!"

Mitchell tore down a screen, Whittingham beside him. A wild figure crouched within. They hacked at the flinty bamboo while the fire bellowed and ate its way toward them. The floor was alight. The sides were burning. Flames spouted and smoke rolled thick through the place. Fire licked at them, blistering, but they did not heed it. Ned slashed at a bamboo bar and then Whittingham and he tugged at its splintering toughness till it bowed and the figure squeezed free, dropped to the ground.

Swiftly the three ran to the rear. The opening Ned and Buck had made was masked now in snapping flames. There might be some other exit—the wizard's private one perhaps. They tore down mats, hurled aside the wicker figures and found a barred door. This they struggled with, half suffocated, the fire crisping their clothes and hair, and burst through at last, finding a rough ladder down which they slid—to safety.

Somers was nearly naked, filthy, covered with sores and scarcely recognizable in his heavy beard. But he was sane, though he was sobbing with emotion, as Whittingham and Mitchell picked him up and, in a chair made of their locked wrists, bore him to safety.

"Close call, what?" said Whittingham. His uniform, smirched by the trip and tattered, was black with soot and scorched with flame. Mitchell was in no better shape. "But we've got him. Now for some grub. There must be pigs and yams about."

He left the two friends together. Already the constables were chasing and slaughtering grunting hogs, heedless of the burning village that sent its dense smoke rolling skyward. They sought for yams and fruit and brought them in to where Whittingham, monocle in place, imperturbably directed activities.

• • •

Somers' story came later. He was incoherent at first, exhausted and emaciated, unable to credit his rescue, unmanned by it, and his long incarceration.

Yet he had not been too cruelly treated beyond filth and neglect and the loss of hope. He had been a show, a living witness to the greatness of Taangi. His fall had stunned him, left him with a wound in his head that had slowly healed. For months, weeks at least, he had been out of his senses. But it had slowly healed at last, thanks to his clean blood.

"I kept on playing crazy," he told them. "I figured that was my safety though I think *this* was what really kept me from the pot." And he showed them, half obliterated by dirt, the tattooed emblem on his right forearm, a tortoise that he had had put there on a whim that must have been an inspiration.

Lipako, looking wisely on, nodded.

The turtle was the totem of the Mafulus. They would not kill one under any circumstances, nor eat its flesh. It was, they believed, their ancestor and therefore sacred. It was the badge of their clan, a stimulus to artistic effort and, while they could not understand why a white man should use it, it pointed to some common plane of origin that, to their crude minds, savored of mystic things.

"I've been through hell," said Somers, his speech halting, but more glib with the last of Whittingham's Johnny Walker. "I was their side show— trotted out whenever they wanted to show off or when Taangi pulled a séance. You say you came here before, Ned? I was crazy then. They thought I was going to die and they doctored me up with some sort of herb poultices. Not much humanity in it. But they wanted their freak kept alive. I gave up hope lots of times, or thought I did, but it must have stuck. When I heard the firing I knew whites were near. They wanted to kill me, some of them, but I was a tribal fetish by then and Taangi wouldn't stand for it. They rushed me out of the village, and I heard them planning to surround you. I've caught on to their lingo, you see. They ran into a gang that had some Chinamen with them. Last night they showed me the heads, with the cues on. They had a feast—"

He covered his head with his hands and cowered, with Ned's hand about his shoulders. The surgeon gave him a reviving dose and he shuddered and got a grip on himself.

"I've been through hell, Ned, living with devils, since Chance—damn him!—pushed me over the cliff! But I'm all right now. And, if it's the last thing I do, I'm going to get Chance."

"You don't need to," said Mitchell. "Chance has paid. I'll tell you all about that later, Jack. Try and eat something."

"Jolly good spare ribs," said Whittingham. "And the yams aren't half bad."

The surgeon pronounced that the wounded men ought not to be moved for a few days. He had antitoxin with him, which he injected to guard against blood poisoning and tetanus, and they set up a hospital by the side of the stream. Somers, clothed again as a white man, recuperated marvelously.

"As long as we've got to say here," said Whittingham, "I'll loan you my men to help you go gold mining, Mitchell. I can stretch a point. I've a notion some of our Mafulu friends will come in and say they'll be good. And it is part of the government schedule, whenever a new field is opened, to see that the proper royalty is paid the crown. So go to your dam."

Mitchell insisted that a third of it should go to Whittingham on the merits of their old partnership which was not dissolved. Another third was for Somers, and Ned determined that the surgeon, government regulations notwithstanding, should have a share.

They went above the fall. Somers was feeble at first, but soon he was able to help direct the engineering. The rest of the dynamite helped create the dam and, in a week, with the aid of the constabulary, employed on a private understanding at wages that made them work like beavers, the water was diverted and the great pool lowered itself.

It showed a series of roughly concentric ledges, and these revealed themselves like the sides of a churn, yellow with the precious metal. A fortune was in sight, and it was swiftly gathered, while the chastened natives came in and offered themselves for immediate hanging or such forms of fealty as Whittingham decreed. Some of them he arranged with to take to Port Moresby. There imprisonment waited them, which was actually to be for them a treat, while giving them an object lesson of the white man's power to take back to their villages when their terms were up.

"I'll fill them up properly," said Whittingham. "I'll put the fear of the British Empire in their hearts and show them magic they'll talk about while they live. They'll be celebrities, but they'll manifest the might of Great Britain, and that's the game."

The expedition came marching into Port Moresby at last, Lipako still with them. He had provided ample bearers, who had gone back for packs of gold dust and nuggets too heavy for their caravan to handle. And he departed, laden down with gifts, fixed for life with an income from a sum deposited by Mitchell and Somers. Proudly he wore a decoration that the governor himself had bestowed upon him with due ceremony, a medal with a magnificent ribbon edged with bullion fringe.

There was difficulty over Whittingham's accepting any share. He vowed that he had had a "bully" time, but Mitchell had a talk with the governor, after making a fitting present to his lady, which was graciously accepted. And Buck succumbed.

It was easier with the surgeon. His pay was none too large, and the governor made a special dispensation.

All was well that ended well. Somers and Mitchell retained a lease on the Mafulu mine, going back to America in state, as befitted potential millionaires.

"What are you going to do with your money, Jack?" asked Mitchell. "Marry some girl and ask me up week-ends?"

Somers grinned.

"First find the girl," he said. "Let's you and me pick out a couple of cute ones and buy places on Long Island, adjoining. You can grow roses. As for me—"

"What?"

"I'm going to start a turtle pond. Feed 'em chopped liver. And I'll call the place 'Turtle Lodge.' "

OUTDOOR STORIES

| Vol. II | AUGUST, 1928 | No. 6 |

RAMA, THE ROGUE
by J. Allan Dunn

I

AN ELEPHANT HUNT

"ELEPHANTS, OF COURSE! That's what I wanted to see you about," Leveson said to Cartwright as they sat in the comfortable lounge of the Trophy Room in the Empire Club at Cawnpur. "They tell me you know all about them."

"I've seen a good deal of 'em," the American replied to the big blond Englishman as he sent a ring of smoke from his fragrant cheroot into the air. "I've hunted elephants in Africa for ivory, and I've been in charge of drives in Burma, Ceylon, and here in India. I know something about them. There are no more open drives in Ceylon. Some of the Kandian princes put on a show once in a while for distinguished visitors, but that's all."

"No ivory in Ceylon anyway. What?"

"Most of them are tuskless. But you know there's no more shooting in India except to save life—and you have to prove that—unless you go after some elephant officially pronounced a rogue. Five hundred rupees fine and the ivory confiscated for breaking the rule."

"We don't want to break any rules," said Leveson—whose name was pronounced Lawson. "I haven't been over here long enough to know much about the game. Just the same, tusks are what I'm after—plus the finest live bull elephant that was ever captured."

He looked about the big room. On the walls were heads and horns and skins, with more skins on the floor, all trophies of the chase, provided by members. His glance rested on the trophy of which the club was proudest, a pair of great tusks, evenly matched, that thrust out from their setting above a big buffet. Overhead a punkah swept back and forth, stirring the sultry air. Cartwright followed the other's gaze.

"You want to beat those?" he asked. "Nice pair. And you want to bag a live *koomerich*?"

"Whatever a *koomerich* is, old chap," said Leveson, "is probably what I'm after."

He was placing a lot of personal confidence in this man his friends had so cordially recommended. The American was quiet spoken, efficient looking, keen, lean, bronzed, broad of shoulder and flat of loin—essentially aquiline as opposed to Leveson's stockiness. The Englishman was sure Cartwright knew his business and was a mighty decent chap besides. If he could get him he would be well satisfied.

"There are three grades of Indian elephants," Cartwright said. "Top grades are *koomerichs*, the thoroughbreds—ten feet or more at the shoulder, usually with piebald patches about the base of the trunk. Not too many of 'em left. Worth five to ten thousand dollars for tuskers; cows about a thousand dollars, on the hoof, by which I mean untrained. *Durasalas* come next, and make up about seventy per cent of the herds, wild and tame. *Meergas* are weedy, with small heads and tusks—runts, in a way, piggy brutes, but they've got long legs and they're rangy and fast. Good for chasing down elephants and roping them on the run."

"By Jove, Cartwright, that sounds sporting! We'll have to try that. Elephant punching, what? But I'll tell you why I'm after the *koomerich* and the tusks.

"There was a chap up at Oxford with me named Rawalpindi. Rajah of a petty little princedom, under British control nominally, of course, but actually independent. He was a mighty decent sort. Played a fine bat at cricket. He and I were in together when we beat Cambridge eight-nine runs in four innings. Rawalpindi was seventy-one, not out. He was a rattling good shot, too. I took him home to my place, and he wiped the eyes of most of us over pheasants.

"When he heard I was out here, nothing must do but for me to visit him and get my tiger.

"Old Pindy—we used to call him 'Pindy' at Oxford—lives in style as far as his income permits. Family is as old as the hills and he's haughty as they make 'em. Gave me quite a shock when I saw old Pindy togged up, jewels, turban, throne, guard of honor with tulwars, and all the rest of it.

"But the old family fortune has deteriorated. He only owned one elephant called Moti, for all purposes. Pindy is a good scout, remits taxes and all that sort of thing, so he can only afford the one—or could. He put a hunting howda on it for me.

"They beat a tiger out of the bamboo for me, and I got a line shot at the brute. Might as well have missed. Better. Didn't even cripple him, but made him raging mad. He broke through the line, swiped a beater, and landed on Moti's head in one gorgeous leap. I just saw a streak of black-and-yellow lightning, and there he was, front claws digging into the base of Moti's trunk, while Moti trumpeted and almost chucked the mahout off his pad.

"The mahout came scrambling for the howdah, eyes sticking out of his head, and his skin the color of those cheroot ashes of yours, from fright. My shikari handed me the spare rifle. The scared mahout was in the way. All this time Stripes was trying to get at me, with his hind claws tearing at Moti's trunk lower down. Pindy waited for me to fire, like the ripping sport he is. The howdah was rocking like a coracle in a gale. I got Stripes through the head, but poor Moti was in bad shape, squealing about his lacerated trunk. It was a mess.

"Pindy made light of it. Said his head shikari would heal it up in no time. I was chump enough to believe it. I plastered the wounded beater with some rupee notes and he recovered, but—well, Pindy didn't show at the last durbar. Sent his regrets and made some excuse. I found out here at the club that he didn't have any elephant. The wounds had got infected and Moti had gone must. They had to kill him.

"Staggered me, no end. My fault, you see. Shouldn't have tried that running line shot. Pindy was embarrassed. And—a rajah without an elephant—they tell me he might as well abdicate. Almost as bad as losing caste."

Cartwright nodded understandingly. He was beginning to like Leveson.

"So, old chap," the Englishman went on, "it's up to me to repair ship. I couldn't send Pindy an elephant I'd bought, with my compliments, because he's prouder than Lucifer. But—if I went in for a drive and we bagged a herd of them, it wouldn't mean much more than if I sent a pal a brace of pheasants. Same idea. Save Pindy's face. What?"

"You'll find it a bit more expensive than pheasants, I imagine."

"I'm not so sure. You've no idea how much it costs to keep up the birds. Anyway, the expense be hanged. I'm well fixed, as you Americans put it."

"It's a long job," warned Cartwright. "The government leases out the drive privilege to the highest bidder, for one year. You've got to send between three and four hundred coolies and headmen out into the jungle to build fence and the keddah, months ahead. They've got to be fed and paid. The elephants come down to the salt licks about October. That's a good time for them to get into big herds.

"You've got to hire shikaris and mahouts and a herd of tame elephants—*kionkis*, they call 'em. To get the most profit you should train your catch. That pays, but it takes time. Your *koomerich*—a thoroughbred elephant—for the rajah, if you're lucky enough to get one, will have to be properly trained for a gift."

Leveson dropped his monocle and repolished it silently before replacing it.

"Righto!" he said. "We'll do all that. We're going to *have* luck. Whatever profit there is, you're in on half of it, plus your figure for the whole job. That's settled. Now, about the tusks.

"I want to be what they call a 'Trophy Member' of this club. That means you have to trot out skin or head, horns or ivory, to beat the existing record. Gets harder right along, of course. Limits the memberships and makes 'em worth while.

"Major Gillespie bagged those tusks. Eight feet, two inches. I've heard of longer ones and, with your help, I'm going to land a pair.

"As for landing the lease, you can tell me the usual bid and I'll top it enough to make sure of it. I'd like to get the Chila privilege. There's a rogue posted there who used to belong to the maharajah. Went on a rampage and broke loose. I heard they changed his keeper and he didn't like it so he killed the new one. Went about bowling over the watch towers in the paddy fields. Lives in the jungle back of Chila. Comes out once in a while and helps himself to cane and rice. Up to all sorts of tricks.

"Now, they say his ivories were eight feet, five and a half inches. He was the maharajah's finest brute, though he has no use for it since it killed one of his retainers. Name of the beast is Rama. He's a proscribed outlaw. If we get the Chila privilege we ought to be able to round him up. We'd be regarded as public benefactors if we bagged him. How about it, Cartwright?"

Cartwright puffed at his cheroot. He was thinking about Rama, with a price on his head. He had a notion that Rama was more sinned against than sinning—if he could believe the tale of his head shikari, who was a cousin of the man who had originally taken charge of Rama.

Cartwright had seen Rama on more than one occasion, splendidly caparisoned, with the maharajah riding in state on his back. Rama's ears had been gilded and his head and trunk frescoed in fantastic designs; silks and brocades upon his back glittered with bits of glass and shining metal. He had looked very stately, and not at all happy. It was Rama who had once delayed a procession by deliberately squirting dust over his newly decorated hide.

Cartwright knew how an Indian elephant hated the sun under which Rama had to parade and stand. He was more mischievous than wicked, Cartwright believed, though he had killed his keeper and then, as if he knew punishment, perhaps death, awaited him, he had butted out the back of his stall and made his escape. If Cartwright went with Leveson and they saw Rama, the latter would certainly be sacrificed for his tusks, and Cartwright would assist in the operation. It was his business. Still, he had a certain sympathy for Rama.

"I imagine we can come to an agreement," he said. "You are liberal with your profits. I'll do my best to see you don't lose on the proposition. Elephants are high. There's the circus market for top specimens and odds and ends. Burma will always buy for work in lumber. Over here there is the same use for the beasts, together with their usefulness to the government in hauling mountain batteries and siege guns. Native princes will purchase a few. Elephants are not hard to sell. They are useful as well as ornamental."

"Fine," said Leveson. "We'll have a couple of fruit punches and talk over the details."

II

LORD OF THE JUNGLE

RAMA LOUNGED THROUGH THE JUNGLE, LORD OF IT. His immense bulk drifted silently under the trees as he sought to find a certain grove of wild figs from which he meant to strip the milky bark. It made good eating.

He was a big bull, well over ten feet at the shoulders, with long ivory tusks tipped with brass knobs that aggravated him but were hard to get rid of. He went alone, but he did not know that he had been proclaimed an outlaw and a rogue. He had his cause for leaving the service of the maharajah and he had no conscience to sit in judgment on the matter.

He did not review the affair. He had an excellent memory, but it reacted only to emotions aroused by his senses. His sensatory nerve centers were part of his brain. Scent, especially, would bring up anger, fear, hatred or pleasure. There were few living things that he feared—certain creeping and crawling creatures most, or small animals that lived in grass or hay and might injure the end of his proboscis. A centipede, for instance, or a mouse.

His confidence in men had been shaken, and a mischievous rather than malicious side of his nature had been aroused against the two-legged humans. He bore no especial ill will toward any one but the man who had insulted and hurt him. He had flattened him out like a chupatty, or wheat-cake.

This was the tale of Rama's trouble. He had been taken in a drive when he was a bull calf, hairy as a young mammoth, three feet high, weighing three hundred pounds, still suckling from his mother's udder that swung full and vitalizing between her front legs, which also protected him.

From then on humans had taken charge of him, trained him, fed him. After he had grown up he got a maund of rice a day—twenty-four pounds of the cooked grain made up into balls the size of a man's head. His diet also included chupatties, with goor—balls of crystallized sugar—rolled in the midst of each cake. Hay was provided for roughage.

Rama missed that diet now, but he was fast learning how to forage for himself with the revival of natural appetites and instincts. Occasionally he helped himself to man-grown crops because they furnished succulent food, conveniently massed.

In the jungle he found many good things, The shoots of soft-wooded trees—peepul, banyan, rubber and fig. Bamboos, reeds, plantain, and grass he pulled up with his trunk and beat free of dirt against his forefoot. Then there were bananas, fruits, sappy vines. He no longer had to bathe in a tank or be sluiced down. There was a river where he, mightiest of all four-legged swimmers, could revel to his heart's content, trumpeting, flinging water in spray over his back and shoulders, or swimming submerged, save for his trunk, which he carried like a curving snake, the tip clear. He could swim for hours at a stretch without tiring.

He made his own toilet when he felt like it; he was no longer scrubbed with a brick and guided with a hook. He took care of his own feet through constant exercise; he plastered himself with mud to get rid of the irritating ticks, and there were birds that acted voluntarily in that capacity.

His time was his own. He was sagacious, and what he learned he did not forget. Nothing bothered him but the ticks, and they were minor evils. A few days before, a tiger, snarling over its kill, and resenting the approach of Rama, whom it knew to be purely a vegetarian, had challenged him. Whereupon Rama, who turned out of his way for nothing that crawled or flew or went on four legs, curled up his trunk out of harm's way and left the tiger looking like a misused rug. He had not even lost his temper over that little affair.

All in all, he was like a schoolboy out of bounds, but far better able to take care of himself. His memories of the herd were dim, and, so far, he preferred his solitude. He saw other elephants, in troops of six to twice that number, led always by an elderly cow. He was not sure of a welcome, fancying they were not anxious to make his acquaintance. He was shy, and there were so many strange and delightful things to be tried out that he was content to live alone for the present. The mating instinct had not touched him since his freedom.

Occasionally he did miss the man who had first taken care of him. Rama was twenty now, full grown almost, with a long life normally ahead of him. The keeper had been mature when Rama was a calf. He had been ill, and the new maharajah had favored a younger man. Rama resented the change. Gray-haired Sibi had understood him, talked to him soothingly and flatteringly, fed him dainties, looked out for his comfort in every way possible.

The younger man was tricky. He had stolen Rama's rations. Once, when Rama had shown rebellion, the man had put ground pepper and ginger in his rice balls and then denied him water. The elephant had asked for it, and the man had mocked him. With his throat raw, his body feverish, Rama had protested, and the man had struck at his trunk. Then Rama had killed him and broken loose.

He had no mental balance of good and evil, he felt no remorse, but he had a sense of satisfaction that almost amounted to a realization of just reprisal. After that the scent of men annoyed him, automatically. He had bowled over some watch towers, he had robbed fields of mealies and rice and cane, and he had chased one man who had fired stinging pellets into his trunk, treed the fellow, and held him there until his cries brought his friends and Rama sensed capture. If the tree had been a little less stout Rama would probably have killed that man also. But he was not voluntarily vicious.

Then he was a stray, knowing nothing of the jungle, long dependent upon men for food. Now he had achieved freedom. But he had still some things to learn.

He came to a nullah—a dry gully with steep sides. Rama had his limitations. He could neither trot, run, canter, nor gallop. When he was in a hurry he quickened his one gait, which was almost, but not quite a pace, the fore and hind legs moving together on either side in not quite perfect coordination. He could shuffle along at about fifteen miles an hour, faster than the ordinary man could run for any distance. A seven-foot ditch would have halted him, since his stride was six and a half feet. But he slid down this nullah on his tail and went up the far side like an enormous cat.

His eyes twinkled as he saw a young banana, and he plucked the sweet, soft heart from it, munching it avidly as he went along, chewing and spitting out husks. Then his trunk curled, swung to one side, and he stood stock-still. He smelled honey A delicious sensation vibrated through him. He followed the scent to a bee tree where the insects worked busily over a dead bough they had selected for their treasury. More bees flew back and forth, but Rama, greedy for this dainty, remembering the balls of goor and the honey-smeared cakes that Sibi had brought him, did not bother about them. Boring insects were his grievances. He did not know yet that the honey was the property of the bees.

He wrapped his trunk about the bough and tested it. Then he got his tusks under it and heaved. It cracked and he butted at it, bringing it down. He gave a pig-like half grunt, half squeak and munched the comb and decayed wood. He saw a pool of honey forming and set his trunk in it, drawing it up by suction. It did not squirt readily into his mouth, but the taste intoxicated him and he went after more. This time a bee stung him on the finger-like process with which he could pick up the smallest twig. Others had been doing their best on his hide and now they seemed to have discovered the most vulnerable point for attack. They swarmed on his trunk and another sank its scimitar into the tender end. It began to swell immediately.

Rama trumpeted, enraged, helpless. His trunk burned—it was closing up, he feared. He forgot all about the honey, and the wild figs, and made for the river. He thrust his trunk into soft mud and found it allayed the scald of the sting. The bees had followed him and he waded out into deep water, swimming, with his trunk under at intervals. At length the bees left him, and he floated on with the current under the shady trees, forgetting his trouble as the fire of the stings burned out.

The river shallowed around a bend. Rama grounded on the edge of a pool and was about to wade out when he saw a herd of his fellows come to the bank. It was the largest one he had seen. A cow lunged into the water first. In all there were nine cows, four calves, and three bulls. None of them were as large as Rama, and they appeared not to notice him. They were in a hurry. More than that, they were afraid. Rama scented their fear and wondered at it. The wind blew, at that point, from him to them.

The calves were young, they did not yet know how to swim. One of them mounted like a jockey on the back of a young bull and balanced there, looking as if it were standing on top of the water. Another followed suit. The biggest bull had two of them. They went fast across the river, paying not the slightest attention to Rama, and plunged into the jungle on the far side.

Rama did not follow them. Their fear had not passed to him. His reaction was that of courage mingled with caution. He wanted to know what had caused this flight, and he went out where the other elephants had come in, following their trail.

Now the wind was ahead of him, what there was of it. He had not gone far before he checked himself suddenly. The air was charged with man scent. It was heavy and obnoxious. Man scent he had been taught not to mind, even in sweating crowds, but it had never appealed to him and, of late, its associations were fraught with disagreeable memories.

But he was curious as well as brave. He went on, his gray shape blending with the shadows. Rama was a *koomerich*—his long tail, which did not quite reach the ground, was well feathered, and there were creamy blotches on his face and at the base of his trunk, but he could not have been distinguished ten feet away.

He heard voices, and the smell was stronger. There was also the odor of wood smoke and the sound of chopping. The last two were fairly familiar to Rama, though smoke always made him uneasy.

There were hundreds of men, brown skinned, white clad, half naked many of them, making a clearing, setting up tents, building fires.

Rama watched, calculating, if not actually thinking. Instincts and memories worked together for discretion. Automatically he tapped with the tip of his trunk on the ground, blowing at the same time, making a curiously metallic noise. It was a signal of warning and displeasure. Then he wheeled and vanished in the dense growth, making for the higher ground up the river.

III
SETTING THE TRAP

CARTWRIGHT LEFT LEVESON BEHIND when he made his first preparations. The Englishman was being entertained extensively, and there was no sense in his going into the jungle for preliminaries that were uninteresting and arduous. Cartwright wired for two white shikaris, who correspond to guides or professional hunters in America. He had his own native headman, and it did not take him long to gather his little army of coolies, most of whom had been used for the same sort of work before. He knew where to go and what he wanted. Leveson placed money in the bank, and two weeks later Cartwright was at Chila, on the River Ganges, which he had made a meeting place for his headmen.

The scene was familiar to him but always interesting, with the crowds on the streets in all their variety of colored garments, the sights of the bazaars—not to mention their smells—the flat-topped roofs, the narrow streets, the mosques and minarets, and the Sacred Stairs of Vishnu leading to the Holy Water, where saffron-robed priests fed the sacred fish while the sacred monkeys jabbered and raced along the temple walls and swung from the boughs of sacred trees. A very holy place, and also a very busy one.

His two white aids had arrived respectively from Patna and Benares, eager to take the field. The coolies were gathering, the equipment being collected.

As Cartwright stood looking on at the river, his native headman, Hissar, came up to him with another Hindu, who was older, a little bowed, but still vigorous. The man was respectful, with a dignity in his manner that was neither arrogant nor offensive. His turban proclaimed him a Nepalese. Hissar also came from that province. Both were hillmen, short of stature, but swift of manner. Their native town was Khatmandu, not far from Gorkha, on the lower slopes of the Himalayas. They were born, as the saying ran, under the beneficent shadow of Gaurisankar—native name of Mount Everest—towering twenty-nine thousand feet between Hindustan and Tibet.

They had been to the temple, and the same caste marks were fresh upon the foreheads of both of them. Cartwright would have known them anywhere for "elephant men." They were of a fighting race and they had served their regimental terms. Their heads were erect, their eyes bold, their nostrils finely cut. Men quick in emergency or quarrel, men without fear, men of fealty, whose word was their bond.

"Sahib," said Hissar, "this is my cousin, who seeks service with thee. He is a good man."

"If you say so, Hissar, that suffices. A good man is like a jewel."

Hissar's dark eyes sparkled with pride and pleasure. He looked at his kinsman with the glance meaning, "Did I not say so?"

"His father and mother were elephants," he went on in vernacular phrase. "Their tusks were his cradle. He will serve the sahib faithfully."

"I doubt it not. He is engaged. It is an order."

"*Hai!*" The two came to the salute.

"Your name?" asked Cartwright.

"Sibi, sahib."

It did not surprise Cartwright. He had suspected something of the sort from the moment Hissar had said the man was his cousin. Here was the old-time keeper of Rama. And Rama was the outlaw whose tusks Leveson wanted to place in the Trophy Room of the Empire Club at Benares.

Cartwright knew the affection that often existed between a mahout and his charge, not often merely one sided. He knew that an elephant might be dangerous with a stranger, but never harmed the man who was truly his friend. And Sibi had been the friend of Rama. The American did not mention the matter nor foresee any complications that could not be smoothed out. Sibi was a servitor, first and last. He knew that Rama had transgressed the law of the land. Cartwright did not doubt that one of the main reasons Sibi wanted to go on the drive was because he hoped to see Rama. Hissar had talked it over with him, had probably sent for him. The ties of kinship were close in India, never closer than among the hillmen. Beyond that, Hissar knew that Cartwright realized the situation. He had pledged Sibi's fealty with his own.

Among themselves, according to their caste, they would gossip. No white household or organization in Hindustan holds secrets from its servants long, unless it is on matters the servant cannot comprehend. Cartwright had no doubt but that Leveson's desires were known. If the Englishman did not get Rama, some one else would. It was the law.

Jungle law made some elephants rogues. The inexorable law of Nature made some mad. Man's law had outlawed Rama.

Two weeks later the little army went into base camp in the jungle. There was much to do, and Cartwright soon had his organization in full swing, mapping out the extent of the outer ring of fencing, which was to inclose an enormous area that included the saline springs and rocky pools to which the herds always repaired at regular periods.

This fence was not intended or expected to hold back elephants by its construction. There were places where it consisted of nothing more than heaps of chopped wood. It was the evidence of men's work that would prevent the beasts from breaking through when the drive came; the dreaded scent of the drivers who would manifest themselves in many obnoxious ways when the time was ripe. The keddah, a strong inclosure, would be a much more elaborate affair, the labor of weeks.

Vows were made and petitions sent up to many gods by the native workers. Important among the deities was Ganesha, the elephant-headed, pot-bellied god of Good Luck. The coolies ate apart, cooking according to caste, great pots of rice, which they ate with ghee—melted butter, usually rancid—and with preserves, wheatcakes, and corn. The whites had their own camp with their personal servants, known as wallahs. Later on, when the keddah stockade was finished, the tame elephants—the *kionkis*—would come with their mahouts to cut out the imprisoned animals and commence their taming.

Hissar was a foreman and Sibi a deputy, the latter principally because a hillman has natural authority and can enforce it. Axes rang, men called to each other, there was the noise of mallets, and the herds went farther back into the foothills. But they had been seen. They would come back to the salt licks.

"This is good elephant country, sahib," said Hissar in the afternoon of the first day of the establishment of the base camp. There are *koomerichs* among them."

Cartwright went with Hissar and Sibi to where Rama had left his imprints in soft dirt. The marks told their own story. Sibi knelt and smelled them. He showed excitement, but said nothing. Neither did Cartwright, knowing that the man was obsessed with the thought of Rama. The tracks were those of a great bull, beyond all question. But Sibi's interest was born of his imagination.

At night there was great talk about the fires of other drives. Of one at Chittagong where a hundred and fifty elephants had been taken in the Coimbatore district. Drives northwest of Meerut, among the saline forests in the swamps of Azufghur; in the Western Ghats, at Belaspur, Mandla, and in the hills of Mysore, all along the foot of the Himalayas to the valley of Dehra Din.

There was talk of well-known *koomerichs*, boasts of those who had known them, of Silver Star, of Bijli Prasad, the Lord of Lightning, of Narram Gaj Prasad, the Peerless Lord. There were lies as to their height and weight and the length of their tusks. Tales of hunts, of chasing and roping, passed around.

Only Sibi said nothing. He could not mention Rama. He was certain that he had seen his tracks, sure that Rama would come down to the salt licks, and he was sad at heart. He did not listen to the tales or the chanting, or the throb of drums and music of pipes and stringed instruments.

He knew that Rama might have merited death under the law, but he knew elephants and he was sure that Rama had been given cause. Never had there been a wiser, a more chiefly and courteous beast. Rama was a king, a pearl, and now he, Sibi, was with the men who wanted his tusks, with the knobs on them that Sibi had so often polished until they shone like gold.

"*Bismillah!*" sighed Sibi, accepting Fate's decree.

There was a long, V-shaped space that led to the main corral of the keddah, that in Ceylon was called a kraal. The mouth of this V was a mile across. Here the fence was stouter as it neared the corral, built of braced logs hidden by trees and brush. Trees and undergrowth were left growing between, so that the moving herd would not be too easily alarmed in the beginning.

The logs of the corral were twelve feet high. They were interwoven with tough vine cordage. A ditch seven feet wide was dug as a discouragement to charging tuskers. A platform was built along the top of the stockade on the outside for men to stand on and help to hold back the herd. The great gate was made like a portcullis, suspended ready to fall at any moment.

The platform extended outward for some distance along the wings. Wooden clackers were set up, which could be pulled with strings to add to the din when the drive was on.

The corral would be the only quiet place for the harassed brutes—if they came down. There was always a hazard that, after all the work and expense, a drive might fail. Elephants were uncertain brutes. A moody or suspicious leader, generally a strong-minded female, might lead them far afield at the last moment. It was all very uncertain.

Cartwright had his trackers out and went with them frequently to assure himself that the herd was still in the neighborhood. The visit to the salt licks was an annual event with them—a necessity. They would not easily relinquish such a favorite haunt.

The work went on expeditiously. At last Cartwright left all in charge of his white shikaris, Swain and Russell, both Americans and Westerners, and went back to order the tame herd to advance and to advise Leveson that everything was in readiness. Cartwright was well satisfied.

Sibi sought audience with him the evening before he left. The hillman was agitated, and Cartwright took pains to put him at ease. He salaamed thrice before he spoke what was on his mind.

"Sahib, is it true that the Feringi lord who comes back with you seeks the tusks of Rama?"—Feringi being the native name for a European.

"That is his intention, Sibi."

"Sahib, Rama has been called a rogue. It is not right. There has never been a more high-born elephant than Rama. I, Sibi, who have known many elephants, who are to be as my brother and sister, swear this is the truth. If I had not been found too old in the eyes of the young maharajah, Rama would have not done this thing."

"He has killed, Sibi. It is the law."

"Sahib," said the old mahout, his eyes fiery, his voice low but firm and eager, "the law of the Feringi is just. Rama was condemned unjustly. He could not speak his defense and others would not. The sahib knows how grooms will avoid trouble. Rama was as my right eye, he was as the core of my heart, and I of his. If the sahib had seen him—"

"I have," said Cartwright. "Many times. A fine beast that did not like to walk in the sun. He has been happier in the jungle."

"Then why take away his happiness, sahib? I have heard talk—it has traveled far, but it is true talk—that the Feringi lord desires a *koomerich* as a gift to a friend. By Ganesha, he must be wealthy!

"It will take months to train a wild beast for a proper gift, sahib. And there are not many like Rama. None with his wisdom. Sahib, I have slept between his feet, and once he saved my life."

Cartwright was interested. He knew that an elephant, ordered by one it is accustomed and willing to obey, will show bravery and do almost anything within its power, but it will not, like a dog, voluntarily go to the rescue of a man. He saw that Sibi was a fanatic on the subject of Rama, but the hillman was not a liar. He was pleading for Rama in a hopeless cause, already lost, but he would not tell a falsehood lest the gods might make his plea fruitless because of it.

"There was fire, sahib—fire and smoke—and I was heavy with sleep."

Arrack or opium might have had something to do with that, Cartwright fancied.

"Sahib, Rama awakened me. His trunk was about me and he lifted me to the hollow of his head. We were the first to arouse the rest, to save the stable and get out the elephants. Rama might have fled. Elephants fear fire. But he waited to awaken me and then he did his duty. Is that the act of a rogue?"

"It is not, Sibi." It was idle to point out that Rama, reared by man, might have been dependent enough, sagacious enough, to link Sibi with safety. "Go on," said Cartwright.

"What are the tusks of an elephant but a memory of what he was in life, stately and beautiful, strong and faithful? Better for Rama that he should walk sometimes in the sun, under fine housings, bearing a prince, than that he should die and his body rot while the carrion beasts and birds tear at it and the ants polish his bones at the last."

Sibi was eloquent. His heart was in his glance. They both spoke in Sibi's language. It was a part of Cartwright's training to learn dialects and not trust to self-serving interpreters.

"What is in your mind that can change the law, Sibi?"

"Sahib! Never have I forgotten Rama with whom I lived twenty years. Nor has Rama forgotten Sibi, who slept between his feet. It is true that I may not be able to prove what I am going to tell you, for the witnesses are scattered and they might not bear out what they have said in private—words which were brought to me by those on whom I can depend. Also, it would cost many rupees. But Rama's mahout was the rogue, not Rama. He fed him crushed ginger and peppers in his rice. He sold his rations. He denied him water when his throat burned like fire. He mocked him. Sahib, you know that an elephant can tell the mood of a man by his voice, that he can smell those who mean him evil.

"This is the word of an old man, sahib, but I swear by Ganesha, by Vishnu, by Siva, that I speak the truth!"

"It would have to be proved, Sibi, before the commissioners," said Cartwright. "I doubt if it would suffice, even if they listened, even if the witnesses could be gathered. There would have to be much more than that if the ban is to be removed from Rama. Such a thing has never been done."

The American spoke kindly. Sibi was a crank, but it was in a kindly cause. The thing was impossible. Leveson wanted the tusks; he had bought the right to them, if Rama was found in the district. He could not be expected to be sympathetic to the plea of Sibi. Rama was a condemned fugitive, a murderer. It might, Cartwright fancied, with a half smile which he suppressed, be justifiable homicide rather than a first-degree offense; but poor Sibi's fevered vision, that even he must know was fantastic, of a rogue being pardoned by law, was an idle dream.

"I will speak to Leveson, Sibi," Cartwright said.

Sibi, dismissed, salaamed again. The light had gone out of his eyes. Cartwright's held a suspicious trace of moisture.

IV

RIVALRY

THE PRESENCE OF THE HUMANS DISTURBED RAMA. He slept naturally only a few hours out of the twenty-four, and all the time he was awake he was conscious of them, of danger that aroused him to a strange admixture of fear, curiosity and daring. While he did not like men, he was used to them, and he wanted to see what they were about. There was hardly a day that he did not drift back silently to where he could at least hear them at work. At night he would watch the fires from afar. There was a warning deep within him, that suggested he might be involved somehow in all these endless preparations, but he stayed on. It was not just elephant stubbornness. He had come to feel that the jungle was his heritage and he resented visitors who were not beasts of the jungle.

Other changes were taking place in him, instincts that his captivity had inhibited. Among the elephants the bulls were the warriors but the cows constituted the council. At any time a bull would allow a cow to take from him some dainty morsel he had found. The protective instinct was strong with the males. They quarreled only among themselves, for the possession of a mate or the masculine supremacy of the herd. While the females led, in times of stress there was one bull who took charge, usually but not always, the biggest and strongest.

When this leader was dethroned, a rogue was often made. There were times when a male elephant went love mad or must—when tarlike stuff oozed copiously from two orifices in his head and he became a sullen, murderous brute, venting his wrath on everything that in any way opposed, or seemed to oppose him, from living animals to thickets of bamboo or thorny growth through which he would stamp, trumpeting, thrashing, and tearing up and down with his trunk.

There was nothing of this sort the matter with Rama. His, when it came, was a gentler passion, though it was to have its inevitable moments of despondency and jealousy.

The noises in the lower forest had largely ceased. There was little chopping or hammering compared to the clamor that had been going on. Swain and Russell scouted for continued assurance of elephants in the neighborhood, but contented themselves with tracking, anxious not to disturb the herds. What work was done consisted principally in finishing the keddah corral by interweaving the logs with the vines until they were bound together in a pliant basketry. Some stout trees had been left standing for snubbing posts and these were stripped of their bark so that when captive elephants strained against the ropes that would presently hold them, the cords could get no purchase on the bark but would slip on the smooth surface and destroy leverage with their shifting.

The work of the coolies was over for the present. A few were paid off and these returned to their homes. Sibi remained. Cartwright considered that he would be useful later on in training the prisoners and he had not the heart to dismiss him, aside from being willing to please Hissar. He believed that he had seen in Sibi's attitude resignation to the inevitable. This was largely true. Sibi's flame of hope had been a feeble one at best. It had died down now to ashes that would not readily arise to kindling heat unless circumstances brought about the miracle for which he prayed constantly to Ganesha.

Little man scent now came from the base camp. It was the sweat of labor that intensified it. Jungle odors nullified the hated odor, and there was little wind at that time of year. Twice Rama slid into the river and floated down with the current, after drinking at the usual hour of sunset. His protruding proboscis looked like a snag; his great bulk, almost motionless, produced no telltale ripples.

He saw fires, far down through the maze of jungle, a bright spark here and there that both warned and, somehow, attracted him. For one thing, the sight stimulated his appetite for chupatties and goor, for rice balls and mealies.

Rama had a sweet tooth. He had not touched honey since his battle with the bees. He had gained a wholesome respect for those winged fighters.

To the rest of the jungle life, outside his own kind, he gave slight heed. The chattering troops of monkeys, the night prowlers, from tigers down, the deer that was beginning to troop in to the salt licks, the brilliant birds, the screaming peacocks—which were sacred, protected from shooting under penalty of a heavy fine—the crows and vultures that soared down from the high peaks in search of carrion—they were all subjects of his realm.

In the restored quietness the jungle went back to normal. Once more Rama saw small herds of elephants, and now his shyness was wearing off. He was lonely—more than just that. The novelty of his solitude had worn off, and he felt the need of a mate.

Koomerichs come from natural selection; Rama would choose only his equal. Their offspring would be a *koomerich*, too, a native thoroughbred.

He had seen his chosen one twice—once, at the twilight drinking hour and, once, emerging from a crossing of the river. Both times he was conscious that she had observed him, though she gave no sign. The herd she was with was a small one but it was notable. An old cow led it invariably. A calf was always at her side, trotting along and making a rumbling sound which signified hunger. The mother sometimes stroked it and sometimes struck it lightly with her trunk when it strayed or annoyed her. There was an old tusker, a young bull, two more cows, without calves and she. Then there was one other—a bull that came close to matching Rama in bulk, in height and the length of its tusks. It lacked only the cream-colored patches that marked the true aristocrat. *She* had them—blotches at the base of her trunk and on one cheek. She was a *koomerich*. The bull was better than a *durasala*, and it was very evident that he regarded the cow as his own exclusive property—or about to be.

They would probably have mated if she had not seen Rama. Nature's instinctive eugenics worked in her. She saw Rama's piebald distinctions as he saw hers. She knew there was nothing of the rogue about him. His scent was pleasant to her, flattering.

She was not averse to flirtation. She knew the value of a rival. She liked the stranger, but she meant to take the better elephant and knew how best to determine that. The bull with her noted that she paused as she came out of the water, twisting her trunk about a feathery tip of bamboo while she glanced back, both to see and be seen.

He saw the tall form of Rama, shadowy but magnificent, and knew at once why Rama was there. Later the cow dropped her tuft of bamboo without mouthing it, and the bull reacted to his aroused fighting instincts. He would have to fight to win her, to dispose of this newcomer. He saw the brass knobs on Rama's tusks, weapons otherwise even with his own. He did not reason that the knobs might give him a great advantage in an encounter, though he sensed that the tusks were blunted—and his own were sharp. But these brass additions made him feel still more that Rama was strange, an interloper.

An elephant's processes of resolution move slowly when not stimulated by action that whips up his rage. When Rama was out of sight, the bull grew almost content. However, the cow, who previously had not demurred at his advances, became capricious. The image of Rama was with her, the memory of his pleasing scent still lingered. She looked forward to seeing him again.

Sibi saw Rama, from afar. He had vague dreams of greeting him, reviving their friendship, riding with him into some strange province where they might find service together under some prince. But he knew that such thoughts were impractical. Also, he saw that Rama was attracted by the *koomerich* cow. He would not respond to any overtures that man might make him at present. And there were certain preparations Sibi must devise, even when the time was propitious. Also, there was his fealty to Cartwright and to Hissar, his kinsman. At times he was almost distraught, wandering in the jungle, thinking of Rama, miscalled a rogue. Rama, who was the fruit of his eyes, the core of his heart. Rama, the regal!

When he came back to the camp he sat morose and silent. Hissar said nothing. By and by there would be work for his cousin and he would forget. Hissar did not believe Rama would ever be taken in the keddah. He was wise in the ways of men. The main device of the initial drive lay in the fact that there was always *one* place left open, one avenue of escape that tricked the elephants on to the corral. Rama did not like men or their scent, but he was used to them—he had once overcome one of them. He would go through where the rest would shrink back. After the drive there would be a hunt for Rama, with Sahib Leveson holding the rifle that would bring him the coveted tusks. It must not take place before the drive, or they might lose the herds. So Hissar bided his time and humored Sibi.

Soon the tame *kionkis* would be coming up, and Sibi would be assigned to duty.

It was noon and Rama stood in the deepest shade, half leaning against a tree, his ears flapping automatically and lazily as he drowsed. The tick birds were busy on his back. The heavy fragrance of the jungle filled the silent forest. It was the hour of siesta. His trunk hung pendulously. Now and then his body twitched, and the birds flew off only to return again. Deep rumblings of digestion came from within his bulk. He stood thus for nearly two hours and then gave a deep sigh and opened his small eyes.

Sight did not warn him of the event that was coming. Smell or hearing— it is hard to say which—first aroused him. He remained stock-still among the root stems of a big banyan, waiting.

The herd came on, marching in open order, now and then stopping to browse. The air was still. Only the *koomerich* cow seemed to notice Rama, to suspect his proximity. The bull who was her admirer was butting at a wild tamarind to bring it down and reach the fruit pods, meaning to offer them to her. The trunk was tough and elastic and resisted his efforts. The cow wandered off, apparently aimlessly, but moving ever closer to Rama, who surveyed her with admiration. In his eyes she was beautiful, graceful, perfectly symmetrical. To her he was superb.

Slowly he came out, mighty and powerful, his trunk curling upward. A low, pleasant trumpet sound issued from him, and the cow turned. Rama went toward her, and she affected not to see him, not to feel the gentle stroke of his trunk.

But the other bull heard and then saw. He shrilled a challenge and came on at a swift shuffle, head lowered, trunk curled, gleaming tusks threatening.

The cow squealed, then went aside and prepared to watch the tournament. The rest of the herd gazed at the rivals.

They came together like two battering-rams, butting with their heads, striving for an advantage, for a chance to thrust a tusk into a vital spot. Rama had the weight. Slowly, because of his immense power, he forced the other back into a clump of growth that masked a nullah.

The bull squealed as he felt himself sliding down, and Rama charged. He saw his opponent's side, his flank, the slack space ahead of the pelvic bones.

They slid down together, the herd bull off his balance, Rama on top of him. The thick growth wavered, as, with a roar, Rama drove his right tusk to its target. If it had not been for the brass knob, that tusk would have gone deep into the other's vitals. As it was, hide, flesh and muscle were indented, and the force of the blow sent Rama's rival to the bottom of the ravine, off balance, trumpeting and crashing on his side and back. The herd bull lay there with legs upright like posts, and belly exposed.

There is a code to the fights of elephants, when they are not must. Quarter is given, a temporary defeat accepted, a fight not necessarily renewed. The victor of the first skirmish may follow the vanquished in his retreat, but he is not vindictive if the other has "enough." He gives him that chance, and Rama was content to see if his rival would give up his claims to the cow. He disdained to thrust again, to trample him, but went around the recumbent form and mounted the far side of the nullah, while the herd bull struggled to regain his feet, badly bruised where the knobbed tusk had hit him, truly shamed in his defeat.

When he was upright he went on down the nullah. The cow was not won. Rama was favorite, but supremacy had yet to be established. She sucked some dust up into her twin tubes and flung it over her back as she went off to the herd and stayed close by the cow with the calf.

Rama sensed that his blunted weapon had failed him. He had tried often enough to get rid of the brass ornaments since he had been in the jungle. He watched the little company march off, his rival already out of sight.

When they had all vanished he went to the tamarind tree that the other had failed to uproot and set his own strength against it. It came crashing down, and he plucked off the pods and ate the raisin-like fruit, astringent but sweet and medicinal. For an hour he amused himself by testing his own strength, tearing off branches and tossing them aside with mighty heaves. Rama was not satisfied with the fight. It had gone his own way at the start, but he had lost the mastery when it came to inflicting the thrust.

A ray of sun glinted on those brass knobs. They annoyed him. His anger began to mount, and he charged at a stout tree and snapped it off. Then he tried another—which would not budge. In a quieter moment he would not have attempted to demolish it. Now his eyes rolled in rage that anything should resist him.

Rama backed off and charged, full tilt. The main trunk had forked into three parts that grew close together for some distance up. Vines clung about the base and climbed to the higher branches, hiding the fissures between the three main stems of the bole. Rama's right tusk drove through, wedged there. He blared a call of anger. He was right-tusked, favoring this one, as others favored their left. Now he was mad clear through and heaved and butted, twisting his head and striving to withdraw the ivory. It came away suddenly, and he sat back, on his haunches. But the knob was gone. He could not reason out the process. He was still confused. One tusk was still capped, but the right was free. The end was like a lance-head. It was lucky for the rival bull that this had not happened before the fight.

The base of Rama's tusk was sore from the impact and the twisting wrench of delivery. He went away grumbling to himself.

Meanwhile the lead cow of the little herd took the elephants far away. She was not interested in Rama, save as he caused trouble in her jurisdiction, and she meant to correct this. The young cow, now more flirtatious and coquettish than ever, was in high spirits.

Soon they came to a branch of the river where the stream gathered in shallow pools, with connecting lanes of water. The dry season was approaching. The lead cow went into one of the great puddles; the others followed and soon they were all clowning together, from the old bull, who had lately feared dispossession, to the young calf.

They squirted mud over themselves and each other, wallowing, rolling in their sport, their eyes twinkling with real fun. When they came out they were coated with mud, slimy and dripping, looking like moving mounds of the sticky stuff. All about the pool the trees and bushes were coated with it.

Later, when it dried and caked, they would wash it off in their swim. Now it was cooling, soothing plaster that was discouraging to the boring ticks.

Sibi, perched in a tree, saw Rama roaming through the forest and put up another petition to Ganesha. Rama did not wind him, but went on to higher ground. Twilight was falling, and Sibi slid down and returned to camp.

A runner had come in. The sahibs were, coming—the *kionkis* were on their way.

V

COUNCIL

A DOUBLE MARQUEE TENT, with a connecting platform, had been set up for the use of Leveson. Toward the end of the afternoon of the day on which he arrived, a council of war was held there on the stage between the two shelters. The marquee was comfortably furnished with easy-chairs of bamboo, other furniture, and many rugs; lanterns had been hung up, and a punkah-wallah tugged automatically at the contrivance which kept the air stirring. Other wallahs stood around, clad in immaculate white pantaloons and tunics, ready to serve refreshments.

The council consisted of Leveson, Cartwright, Swain, Russell, and Hissar. Cartwright had looked out for Leveson's comfort in every detail, even to an ice machine and charged water. Ice tinkled in long punch glasses, and the fragrance of choice cheroots was in the air, the smoke drifting in the punkah's draft. Nets kept out all insects.

"You've done me jolly well, Cartwright," said Leveson. "Now what's the situation?"

Swain was the senior of the two white shikaris and he made his report. Night sounds and scents came in from the jungle. The herd of tame elephants, the *kionkis* hired from the Nepalese government, were quartered some distance away. The mahouts were crooning to their charges.

Swain began.

"It looks good. The herds are still here. They have quieted down considerably. They are beginning to band together and they will be down to the salt licks any day. We estimate that there are between a hundred and fifty and two hundred elephants in the neighborhood. It's hard to be sure. Hissar thinks the last number is not too high.

"There are a few *koomerichs*. One of them is Rama. He's been sighted and seems to be behaving himself. I'd hardly call him a real rogue. There's one bull that is almost his size, and Hissar says its tusks are just as long. It lacks light markings but, outside of that, it is in the *koomerich* class. In the same herd there is a likely looking cow—nicely marked and thoroughbred. Must stand close to nine feet. Worth a thousand dollars of any man's money untrained. Good breeder. Ought to fetch a fancy price if it's handled right."

"That's great!" said Leveson. "I'd have liked to have a marked *koomerich* for the rajah, but this one sounds good and we mustn't grouch over luck like this. With him, and Rama's tusks, it looks as if I'm jolly well favored. If we get anything like the majority of the herd, you ought to come out all right for all your work, Cartwright. I hope so, I'm sure."

"Thanks," said Cartwright. "Things do look good." He had been observing Hissar, while Leveson was speaking of Rama's tusks. The hillman's dark face was impassive, revealed nothing.

"We'll inspect to-morrow," continued Cartwright. "I'm sure we'll find all in good shape. No better team than Swain and Russell here, with Hissar. Then we're all set for them to come inside the ring fence.

"It's not altogether a fence," he went on to Leveson and explained to him the method to be used in the drive. "But it'll hold 'em," he ended the description.

Russell made a supplementary report, and then Cartwright turned to Hissar, who spoke English fairly well.

"Tell us what you saw," he said.

He doubted if Hissar would tell everything. He felt sure that Sibi had been keeping in touch with Rama, but he did not mean to press that. Hissar would not hold back anything that would be of importance to the drive. Hissar was not personally interested in the fate of Rama.

The hillman gave a detailed account of the elephants he had seen. Rama had been sighted only once.

"Swain Sahib is right," he said deferentially. "Rama does not act like a rogue. He is not must. He is content in the jungle. I do not think that he will come into the corral. *Koomerichs* are wiser than the rest, more fearless. They might lead a stampede. It will be better if they do not come."

"We can trail Rama," said Leveson. "Track him down and shoot him in the open. My first elephant! But how about the big chap for Rawalpindi?"

"We may be able to show you some sport there," said Cartwright. "There are two ways. We have some good noosers with the *kionkis*.

"You take four cow elephants with their mahouts and have extra mahouts along for relief. When the men are riding they stay hidden under blankets, as much as possible. As soon as you get in touch with your bull, the cows entice him out—they're trained for that sort of thing. These koomkies, as we call 'em, seem to get delight out of roping the wild elephants. They may have a secret pleasure in landing a male of the species.

"Anyway, they keep him interested, in two relays. They lavish blandishments on him, and he gets so fussed up and conceited he forgets to eat. They don't give him a chance to sleep. The mahouts, of course, take turns. About the third day the bull is tired. He'll drowse off. They get hobbles about his front legs, sometimes all of 'em. The koomkie cows stay with him, one on each side, coaxing him along, and then the mahouts start to make friends with him. They win him through the cows and his stomach. It's tolerably simple."

"It don't sound sporting to me," said Leveson. "Treacherous, what? Get the old boy all fagged out and then snag him. Delilah-and-Samson sort of process. It don't appeal to me, particularly."

"I didn't fancy it would," said Cartwright. "I mentioned the other way. We call it 'chasing.' You pick out four cow *meergas*, long-legged and fast—we've got some along. They each carry three men, the mahout in the usual place, a 'nooser' on a pad in the middle of the back, over a girth to which his rope is fastened and a driver near the tail.

"When you sight your elephants you give chase, throw running loops over his head, and there you are—sometimes! It's a sporty game. I've seen a whole outfit wrecked, if the chase is a big fellow and you don't get your ropes on fast enough."

"Sounds bully to me," said Leveson. "I don't suppose I'd qualify as one of the riders; that's the only trouble. I hope we get a chance at it."

The meeting broke up. Cartwright stayed behind with Leveson. He had promised Sibi to speak about Rama and he meant to keep his word. It was up to the Englishman. It was his drive, and his money had made it possible. Leveson listened without comment, smoking his cheroot and sipping his iced pawnee.

"They tell me," he said finally, "that the owner of an elephant never rates very high with the beast. He pays attention only to the man who looks out for him. Natural enough. This Sibi seems a bit dotty on the subject. But I can appreciate his attitude. After all, Rama killed a man. He's under the ban. If we didn't get him, somebody else would. He's carrying the tusks I want. I've got a sporting wager with Major Gillespie that I'm going to bring back a pair to beat his.

"I suppose we must figure Sibi prejudiced in Rama's favor, but it would be a rotten trick if the elephant had been treated that way. How are you going to prove it? Or get him a pardon? Damned interesting, Cartwright. Thanks for telling me."

Cartwright looked at him curiously. He had not imagined that the Englishman would forgo those coveted tusks because of a mahout's tale. Beyond question Sibi *was* a little cracked in the matter. He might have imagined most of his evidence. Tusks were tusks.

"You say it will take time to train that big bull decently," Leveson said, as he finished his glass and set it down. "How long?"

"You can tame him in a week or two. Might take months to bring him to where he knows the whole routine," said Cartwright. "There's more to it than just kneeling down. Depends upon the kind of brain he has. It's a matter of repetition and memory. That's why a circus man will pay high for one who has been taught all the ropes."

"I see. Well, you've got everything in fine shape, as I knew you would. I'm going to give Swain and Russell a share in the profits off my end. And Hissar, too. I think I'll turn in. Bit tired. See you in the morning, Cartwright. And, thanks again."

Cartwright smoked another cigar before he went to his cot. Leveson, he decided, was a mighty decent sort.

VI

THE DRIVE

THE SMALL HERDS HAD JOINED TOGETHER. They came down to the salt licks, a little timorous and on their guard. They appeared easier after Cartwright left them alone for the first day. The licks were in the middle of the outer ring of the drive fence. Inspection had shown everything in top shape.

Scouting revealed that Rama was not with the herd. Nor were the big bull and the *koomerich* cow. This did not bother Cartwright. They might be able to chase the cow and noose it, as well as the bull. And the hunter did not think Rama would be far away. He knew elephants. He had an idea that the bull and the cow were interested in each other and that Rama, also, was attracted. Rama seemed peaceable. There was the danger of a fight, of course, but that was a hazard of the game.

At dusk, the army of coolies took up their stations along the outer fence. The elephants would start browsing during the night, and then the drive would begin.

An hour before midnight a prearranged pandemonium broke out. The elephants had separated into three herds of about sixty each. These units did not stray far from each other, for the beasts were still a trifle uneasy.

A lead cow approached the outer ring, going toward the river. Suddenly the quiet jungle awoke to an indescribable racket. The startled beasts caught confused glimpses of dancing, shouting figures. They heard noises that were hideous and terrifying.

Strings were pulled that manipulated wooden clackers in the trees. Some men bore torches. Others pounded on drums and clanging tom-toms. All of them yelled at the top of their lungs, defending their territory.

The elephants swerved and passed on. Wherever they came near the ring the same uproar greeted them. Flaming brands stopped them, sometimes at the last minute. Slowly they retreated, seeking quiet and found it at last in the center of the place. Upset and uncertain, the herd was glad to be left alone in the silence that followed. The headmen made sure the beasts were headed properly, and the coolies closed across their rear, some sleeping, some on watch; the shikaris remained watchful, and Cartwright oversaw it all.

"They've jolly well cracked my eardrums," said Leveson, as the leaders finally got back to his marquee for refreshments. "But it's a ripping sight! Wouldn't have missed it for the world. How are you going to prevent them bolting back? If they once got going, they might barge through everything."

"They instinctively prefer moving toward the hills," said Cartwright. "Accidents do happen, of course, but I'll show you a trick to-morrow or the next day, or maybe the day after that, that will wind up the show as far as the climax. There'll be excitement enough in the corral, I promise you. Swain used to be a cow-puncher and he says keddah driving has got that beaten a mile.

"The whole thing is a sort of jujutsu method. We never block them— leave one way open all the time—and the corral is the one quiet spot left at the last. Then some of them are apt to turn nasty or sulk."

"I would myself," said Leveson. "Bully time I'm having!"

All the next day the herd, assembled in one body for mutual comfort and protection, was deftly urged forward. Blank cartridges took the place of the torches; otherwise, the procedure was the same.

In the hills, Rama wondered what had broken loose. He was seeking the *koomerich* cow, looking for the big bull. He knew they were not far away. The lady was playing hide and seek with them. Her love of salt had been submerged in the mating instinct. So with the bull. Rama had always had his regular rations of salt; now he did not particularly miss it, for he, too, preferred the joys of courtship. There were men down there, of course, but he was away from them, intent upon winning his cow and the prospect of combat with a rival.

It was mid-afternoon when the herd got within the mile-wide entrance of the V that led to the corral gate at its apex. The coolies were lined up on both sides of the palisade, mounted on the platforms.

The herd began to mill. Cartwright saw the danger sign and gave his order.

"Here's the trick," he called to Leveson. "You'll recognize it. It's borrowed."

Leveson was flushed with excitement and exercise, his face bright pink under his cork helmet, his monocle in place, his stocky figure encased in white shirt and riding breeches. He was having what he called a "topping" time.

"Bring on your show," he called back. Then he gasped a little at what he saw.

The drivers along the stockade were silent now. The milling elephants were surrounded by a circle of about a dozen of their number—three bulls, the rest cows, all waving their trunks in the air. Other cows herded the calves. Rumblings and quavering trumpetings went on continually.

The circle broke up. An old cow with one broken tusk, her hide hanging slack, like a misfit garment, wheeled with the rest of the council to the rear and started determinedly forward. If they got going they would reach the bank of the outer ring long before enough coolies could intercept them. If they once got stampeded nothing could stop them and they would undoubtedly head for the river.

But Cartwright played his trump. The old cow wavered, halted, stared with the rest, her trunk swinging, her little eyes worried.

The forest was advancing. A hundred coolies moved forward, each bearing a big bush or a well-branched sapling in front of him. The jungle had turned upon the herd! The trees marched on, nearer and nearer. The world was upside down. Nature had betrayed them.

The old cow straightened her trunk and let out a trumpet of terror. Her ears fanned out, and then she turned tail and bolted, straight up the V. The rest trailed her, pell-mell. Fire was bad and noise was confusing; but this was something they had never seen or heard.

Leveson slapped his boot with the *wanghae* cane he carried.

"Jove, but that was smart!" he exclaimed. "Slick, you Yankee, slick! Like a scene from *Macbeth*. 'When Birnham woods shall come to Dunsinane.' What? We've bagged the whole herd."

"Looks like it," Cartwright answered. "Let's go and see."

The great gate slammed down behind the rearmost elephant and was swiftly braced with slanting supports, set deep in the earth.

They were in, milling, charging in short dashes, shrinking back from the seven-foot ditch and squealing at the sight of the stout fence. Then the din broke loose again, and the elephants began to circle the corral. It was a critical moment.

Great wooden clackers thwacked overhead. Tom-toms clanged and drums boomed. Blank cartridges and firecrackers exploded, while the excited, triumphant drivers thronged the platforms and let out ear-splitting yells. Some of them carried long bamboo poles with which to strike the trunks of any elephants that might come too close.

They were in—a hundred and sixty-seven elephants, not counting calves. Not a dozen *meergas* in the lot. *Durasalas*, all of them. The expense had been great, the hire of the *kionkis* alone a big item. Training would cost more, but there was a good profit in sight.

"Ripping!" exclaimed Leveson. Cartwright grinned; Swain and Russell wiped the sweat off their faces, and Hissar's grave features were wreathed in a smile.

There was yet much to be done. The potentiality of the imprisoned herd was enormous. If they knew their own strength in combination they could make light of the ditch, the stockade, and the howling drivers. Just now they were more frightened than anything else. The ditch held them back for the time, but if they revolted they would attempt it, crossing over the bodies of those who fell, smashing down the heavy posts of the platform with its living load, trampling and charging their way to liberty. It had been done before. It might happen again. All the beasts needed was a determined leader.

It looked for a while as if they had found one. The old cow who had already asserted herself, and who had been going steadily round and found the corral, examining its defenses, decided that the gate was the most vulnerable point of attack, in which she was quite correct. She brought another cow and a bull to her side, and the three of them halted while the rest milled on, covering the trio's actions for the time.

Their trunk fingers worked busily at the end of the flexible proboscides, feeling, testing. They butted slowly but vigorously at the gate and found that they could move one side of the barrier where it had slid down between the double posts acting as grooves to hold it. They had it swaying when Hissar discovered what they were about.

Coolies dropped down from the platforms and tried to drive them back, but the elephants did not seem to fear them so much when they were on the ground. The humans were no longer mysterious figures in the night, with flaming lights, but just men, out in open daylight.

The old cow sounded her bugling call, and now half the herd was facing the gate in solid phalanx, the leaders butting steadily at the gate where, since it was the entrance, there had been no ditch placed. The heavy timbers creaked and groaned. The wooden barrier could not hold out much longer against a combined force like this. The herd was gaining confidence. They faced the spit and sting of blank cartridges. It looked serious. A support gave way; a stout bar broke. It was beginning to grow dusk. The sun was just over the treetops. A few minutes more and the swift tropic twilight would blossom and fade into night.

Once out, charging through the darkness to the river, the elephants would never be stopped. They would not come back to the salt licks that season. Probably they would leave the district, pass beyond the jurisdiction of the lease. They could never be redriven.

Another bar cracked. The weight of the rearmost animals seemed to be pressing on the front ranks. The sun, crimson in the mists, sank like a falling fire balloon. The jungle darkened; color went out of it. Torches were lit and served only to show the great forms of the herd, which now appeared to sense escape. The flares lit up their eyes, their tusks. The mob of coolies in front of the gate outdid themselves in their shouting and efforts; those on the platforms kept up the noise of tom-toms and clackers until Cartwright's order reached them to remain quiet. They might only urge on the frantic herd. Cartwright hastily set men to strengthening the supports, but the bars themselves were giving way before these living rams who could smash through solid walls and bend stout steel once they put out their strength. There was no time to erect a secondary barrier. It was going to be a matter of moments. Leveson's money, all the efforts of weeks and months, might vanish like the going out of a dam.

"What about shootin' the ones in front?" suggested Leveson. "Might discourage the rest. What? We can afford to lose a few."

Cartwright shook his head. He knew, as Swain and Russell and Hissar knew, that one never could be sure how death would affect surviving elephants. In Africa Cartwright had known cases where carcasses from which the tusks had been taken were visited in the night by the returning herd. He had sometimes found putrid bodies which the elephants had moved about. To kill the leaders now might enrage them; he doubted strongly if it would stop them. They would surge forward as the front rank fell, and that very impetus might crash down the gate. Then there would be death among the coolies. A stampeding herd could no more be checked or turned than a torrent swollen from a cloud-burst.

Something had to be done, and done quickly. The regular contrivances were about to fail.

Suddenly Cartwright turned and started to run back to the place where they had camped the night before, shouting to Swain and Russell as he sprinted off.

"Hold 'em! Start a fire outside the gate!"

The command was not the easiest thing in the world to obey. There was any amount of wood about but it was green, most of it sappy. The torches had been specially selected and brought in from a distance. But the two white shikaris did the best they could.

They dared not set their fire too close lest the gate itself should catch, or the slanting supports which they had set up. The windless days were followed after dark by more or less of a breeze, as the sun's heat was withdrawn. What there was of this blew toward the gate and made the hazard greater.

Cartwright ran at top speed through the dusk. There were fires burning at the temporary camp in preparation for supper; small tents had been set up for the sahibs. Leveson's was green, with a fly, and Cartwright dived into it. The Englishman had his photographic outfit along, which he meant to use to register the keddah performance, and he also hoped to get some night shots of jungle beasts by means of a flash light worked by a trigger and a line attached to the bait which would attract the subject.

He had not thought of this, but Cartwright had. He snatched up a lantern and rummaged through Leveson's equipment, finding the tin box of magnesium powder. He went tearing back with it, leaping the obstacles that lay in his direct route. He could hear the trumpeting of the herd above the cries of the coolies and he saw a line of fire burning in front of the gate.

The front rank of elephants feared it, but there was too much weight behind for them to retreat. The bars of the gate were giving way when Cartwright arrived in long jumps, ordering the rest aside. He raced along the fire, flinging into it small quantities of the flash powder, which ignited with a roar and a dazzling glare. The flames scorched his clothes and singed his eyebrows as he turned and came back down the line, throwing in the box with the last of its contents as he sprang back, blinded by the brilliance.

It was too much for the elephants—a demonstration that all could witness as the black jungle seemed to leap out of the darkness. With one accord they backed, turned, bolted for the far end of the corral, stumbling clumsily, their eyes temporarily out of commission. Some rolled into the ditch, but their retreat was scattered, and they were cowed so that the platform men kept them away from any serious attack on the stockade.

"By George, you use your head!" said Leveson.

"You lose your night pictures," said Cartwright, blinking.

"I'd have lost all the elephants if it hadn't been for you. The jolly old gate was going when you raced up."

They set to work at repairs, leaving the gate stronger than it had been. The clamor went on all through the night. The herd got no sleep, the coolies little, except in short snatches. Weariness and hunger would overcome the elephants at last and make them ready to respond to advances of food, water and soft words. In their dispositions lay their prime weakness—their willingness to surrender to kind treatment. Not all of them. Cartwright noticed several who were going to turn out sulkers. They would be the first chosen for handling.

The third morning after the closing of the corral dawned. The sky flamed above the jungle. Birds awakened, screaming, whirling above the treetops. Peacocks shrieked. Monkeys chattered, swinging among the boughs, seating themselves to watch the proceedings. Tired coolies rubbed their eyes. Their work was over, but they did not want to miss the finale—the great excitement of the taming.

In the corral elephants stood wearily with closed eyes and drooping trunks. Some weaved to and fro. Occasionally one trumpeted hoarsely. Only the cows with calves had been fed. Grass had been flung down to them, and they had eaten sparingly. The rest would not touch it. There was not enough for all, and their jungle code left it for the females and their young.

The mahouts who managed the koomkies (cow elephants trained especially for this work) gathered outside the gate, sounding solemn chants to their gods, kneeling in prayer. They had caste marks on their foreheads, newly painted; some were smeared with turmeric. They were engaged in hazardous service. A wild bronco can send a group of cowboys scattering, but here were mammoth brutes, weakened by hunger and lack of sleep, yet with plenty of force still in them. Some of them were sullen, ready for trouble.

The gate was hoisted. A few of the prisoners raised their heads, and one bull lowered his but made no other movement as the tame koomkies entered in close ranks. They were all cows. The chivalry of the bulls, the sympathy of the wild females for their sisters, all contributed to their submission.

Cartwright pointed out the beasts to be tackled first.

The process was simple but dangerous. Two koomkies sidled up, one on either side of the elephant selected. Their presence was soothing. They caressed him with their trunks and uttered soft sounds. It was a species of treachery. They were obeying orders, acting as they had been trained to do; but they took pleasure in it. They pushed the captured one gently until he moved. A roper slid to the ground and deftly noosed one foot, then another. A loop settled over his head, and the ropes were quickly fastened to one of the stripped trees. Each roper caught at an ear of his koomkie and, barefooted, climbed nimbly back to his place. The tame cows moved on.

The wild brutes took the treatment according to their natures. Some plunged, straining against the ropes that slipped on the barked trunks, fearing their displeasure. Swain and Russell watched, with Hissar, for chafed spots that might develop into ulcerous sores, treating them with strong disinfectants and shifting the bonds. The majority submitted apathetically. The presence of the koomkies bewildered their tired brains.

Great quantities of water were brought up, hundreds of maunds of rice prepared, with wheatcakes centered with balls of goor. The tamers, moved among the fettered beasts, coaxing them, making noises that were elephant "pidgin," used the world over among trainers and keepers. Once food was accepted the task was almost over.

The beasts could not resist it. Only three bulls held out, sulking, ready to starve. Cartwright set koomkies to stay with them. The others sank their trunks in the water tubs, sucking up the needed liquid for a distance of eighteen inches in their tubes and squirting it gratefully into their parched throats. They did the same with the loose grain spread before them, blowing it into their mouths. The rice balls were set on mats before them, and following the example of the tame cows, they permitted themselves to be fed by hand, opening their maws as the tamers deftly tossed in the molded rice.

Empty stomachs rumbled like distant thunder. The great creatures uttered contented grunts. At last they used the water to squirt on their shoulders, winding up with a second bath of dust. The cows were taken out first, roped between koomkies, and taken off to the preliminary training grounds. The two sulkers gave in the next day; the third one Cartwright ordered turned loose in the jungle after he had been escorted there by two koomkies.

"His kind would die in captivity," he told Leveson. "Partly from weakness, partly from grieving."

"Good luck to him," said the Englishman. "The poor devil was crying. I didn't know elephants could weep. We've got enough."

"We haven't got yet what you want most," said Cartwright. "There's the *koomerich* for your friend and the tusks that are going to discount Major Gillespie's. We'll get after them right away. I'll send trackers out to-morrow. That *koomerich* cow ought to be worth going after."

"I never saw such a beggar for work," Leveson answered. "I don't believe you've been off your feet for ten hours since we started the drive."

"I'll soon catch up. They may not get on the trail of any of them right away. Can't tell what the racket we've been making has done to them. But I don't believe they've left the district. They'll hang round for the salt."

Cartwright did not notice Sibi close by, screened behind a bush, listening intently. He did not think of him as he went back to camp and turned in, dog tired, to sleep round the clock.

When he awakened, Hissar was seeking audience.

"Sahib," he said with a salaam, "Sibi has gone. Is it the sahib's wish that I go after him?"

"Sibi is not a child," said Cartwright. "He has worked well during the drive. We shall probably see him soon. Is there any news from the trackers?"

He saw relief expressed in Hissar's face, as if it had suddenly been cleared of shadow. Hissar had pledged his kinsman's fealty. The hillman did not doubt that Sibi's absence was connected with Rama, nor that Cartwright Sahib thought as he did. Personally he thought his cousin mad.

"They have sighted the big, almost-*koomerich* bull," he reported. "The one that is not spotted but has the great tusks. A runner came in ten minutes ago. They will keep close to him."

"Bully! We'll show Leveson Sahib some sport. Go to the *kionki* camp, Hissar, and arrange for four cows and twelve men early in the morning. We're chasing him. I'll want an elephant for Leveson Sahib and myself. You, if you wish, can come, Hissar."

Hissar salaamed again. Cartwright Sahib was not displeased with him. To be invited on this chase was a privilege. Swain and Russell would be envious.

"It is an order, sahib," he said, and vanished.

Sibi was missing. So was almost a maund of rice and a stack of wheat chupatties with balls of goor, taken from the abundance provided for the herd in the corral.

Hissar was right. Sibi was a little mad, obsessed. He did not know exactly
what he was going to do, save that he meant to find Rama and renew their
friendship, somehow to save Rama from the fate of a rogue.

He believed that the romantic episode between Rama and the *koomerich*
cow was completed. He had only to find fresh, or fairly fresh spoor of a bull
and a cow to trace Rama. There was the other big bull, of course, but Sibi
was certain that Rama must have been the winner, in love or war.

He had performed faithfully for Cartwright Sahib during the drive. There
was no work for him now. He did not mean to steal Rama. He had given
up that idea as chimerical. But he meant to plead for him, and he was not
without hope of doing so, if he could prevent Rama from being shot. He
had some proof to present to the sahibs, and he had meant to develop his
evidence immediately, until Cartwright's talk made him realize the necessity
of finding Rama.

VII

MUST

WHILE THE GREAT DRAMA OF THE DRIVE had been going on about the salt licks,
romance was developing in the higher hills.

The great herd bull had lost favor in the sight of the *koomerich* cow. He
made a mistake as human as it was elephantine. He sulked. Rama showed
his devotion, if not his wisdom, by following his lady and revealing himself.
Perhaps he was not unconscious of the picture of mammoth majesty which
he made as he stood in the shadows, sometimes with a filtered beam of light
revealing his tusks, the great dome of his forehead and the creamy spots that
proclaimed him of royal blood.

The wild bull was not yet willing to renew the fight. He had been made
ridiculous in the last one, and he knew and resented it. Also, his side still hurt
where Rama had tilted at him with his blunted lance of ivory. Muscles, inner
layers and linings, had been badly bruised, and he walked a little stiffly. No
animal is more sensitive to laughter at its own expense than the elephant—
the dog excepted. The bull sensed that the cow was laughing at him and he
grew moodier; then he tried to be masterful—and was rebuffed.

The next time Rama appeared the cow let him know that he was favored.
She fell behind the herd and sauntered toward him. She let him stroke her
back and entwined her trunk with his before she left him. He knew that he
was accepted. That night the herd started for the salt licks, but the cow did
not go with them. She had found her mate. The wild bull stayed also; rather,
he returned when he found the cow was not with the herd as it joined another
one bound likewise for the licks.

He was too late. The pair had made for a glen which the cow knew, a secluded spot, high up. Here a waterfall tumbled into a deep pool, from which a stream emerged, to disappear again in an underground channel. There were succulent grasses, bamboos and other browsing. It was a little paradise shut in by mountain walls, the entrance so narrow that the pair had to enter single file, the cow leading.

They had loitered by the way, as lovers will, and the herd bull came up just as Rama started to follow his mate. Rama felt the other bull coming by the vibrations of the ground, and smelled him at the same instant. He backed out, wheeled and stood in the gorge, his flanks almost touching the rock, enormous, stately, belligerent. He preferred not to fight, with the cow waiting for him, but at the same time her presence made him eager to repel his rival's attack.

The wild bull surveyed the situation and found it far from his liking. He had already discovered that he could not out-butt Rama, who looked as solid as the mountainside itself; he could not get at his flanks except by strategy, and his mood prevented him from planning such device. He trumpeted a defiance, and Rama let out a savage roar that echoed back from the cliffs. Then the bull turned and went off, solitary and remote from all his kind.

His defeat now turned in upon itself and worked evil in his brain. A tarlike fluid began to secrete itself and ooze from orifices in his forehead. He was going must! For three days he neither ate nor drank. The fourth day he spent in the river, swimming violently from shore to shore. Then he lost all control and raged through the jungle, trampling and tearing down everything he came across. He was mad, surcharged with misdirected energies that gave him surplus strength.

The fifth day he slept, leaning against a tree. The next saw a cessation, or an intermission, of his must fever, though the dark flow had not stopped and the red light of malice remained in his eyes. He was worse the following day, when Cartwright's trackers glimpsed him, thrashing through a thicket of bamboo, taking violent delight in fighting the great, pliant stems that swung back and lashed him as he passed. He spent the night there, only feeding in the early morning. He was there when the shikaris saw the bamboos waving as he made his way out, intent upon going back to the highlands.

His rival and the cow would be out of their glen by now, and he had turned killer, bent upon fight, charged with the desire to murder. He was intent upon goring Rama, heedless of odds, and trampling him into shapelessness. He meant to kill the cow also. He was now a mere machine primed for destruction.

The hunting party sighted him. The drivers on the four fleet *meergas* plied their spiked mallets, and the elephants increased their speed. Cartwright, with Leveson and Hissar, were on a fast beast, riding in a light hunting howdah of wicker. A mahout was seated on a head pad, goading his mount. The great beast's gait was smooth on level ground, and while they fell behind the *meergas*, they kept the chase in sight and all gained on the bull.

The mad monster did not seem to heed them, but kept going up a slope of grassland, intersected by numerous nullahs formed by storm water. These gullies were overgrown now by bush and vines. The bull crossed them with great agility, and the *meergas* followed. They were piggy brutes, save for their long legs, and there was some spirit in them that reveled in the hunt. One showed its heels to the rest and began to close up on the insane bull.

"Hope we'll be in at the finish," said Leveson, clinging to the side of the howdah as they slid down a gulch and clambered out of it. "He's a beauty. Look at those tusks! Too bad we can't take those and not spoil him."

They had their rifles along—expresses, carrying heavy loads—in case of trouble. The bull might charge. It was the uncertainty of this that spiced the adventure. He could down one of the *meergas* easily enough and squash the men on it. The drivers were filled with daring, buoyed with excitement and the promise of rewards that Leveson had made, with an extra prize for the crew that got the first rope on the big bull. They urged on their beasts and made their nooses ready.

Cartwright had given Leveson instructions as to where to shoot if it became necessary. The Englishman was cool, and Cartwright imagined he was a good enough shot, though he had failed to cripple his first tiger. That was excusable, considering the elusive target. The flash of Stripes through bamboo is not an easy mark.

"There are only four places to be sure of bringing him down," the American said. "He can take a lot of lead, even when you use explosive bullets—which I don't, myself."

"Nor I," said Leveson. "Not sporting."

"I'm not keen on the shoulder shot," said Cartwright. "Back of the ear, or through the temple, are better. For a head-on charge you aim three inches above the line of the eyes. If he curls his trunk—an African elephant doesn't—make it lower, at the base of the trunk. You've got to get through to the brain."

"I hope we don't have to shoot, Cartwright. He'll make a fine gift for good old Pindy. By jingo, they've *got* him!"

The leading nooser, kneeling for better aim, sent his great loop circling out ahead just as his *meerga's* head came up with the big bull's flank. The rope fell true, back of the ears. It was hard to know just what happened then. The spiked mallets were being plied, the drivers and mahouts yelling to their charges, anxious to get the other ropes on the bull. They were on a bare stretch of land, strewn with ant hills. Dust rose like a cloud, and it was difficult to see clearly from the howdah where the white men watched.

The touch of the rope seemed to bring a sense of danger to the mad bull for the first time. His shuffling stride quickened and lengthened, just as the *meerga* stumbled, or hesitated, on the brink of a nullah. Down this the bull charged to the limit of the rope, which was tied to the tame beast's girth. Another rope settled as the next *meerga* hauled alongside and paused to negotiate the gully.

The bull was plowing down the slope. The first rope went taut, and the leading *meerga* was hauled sidewise by the captive's weight and strength. The bull charged on up the farther slope, and the scrubby cow, losing its balance, was dragged down, with the second falling on top as both ropes twanged like bowstrings, broken by the mad fury of the giant bull.

One man was flung wide, the rest went down with the two *meergas*. The bull kept straight on. Another time he might have turned to gore and trample—now he was obsessed with one idea—to get at Rama and his cow. He plunged into a bamboo thicket, with the broken ropes trailing, bamboos shaking like grass before the wind as he forged on.

The other two *meergas* pulled up, their men sliding to the ground to help their comrades as Cartwright's elephant arrived on the scene. The chase was over for that day. One *meerga* was shrilly proclaiming that she was hurt, a hind leg strained. One mahout was unconscious, badly bruised, but not crushed. Two more were studded with thorns, and one man lay with his face all crimson, where a frantic trunk had broken his nose.

By the time they got the *meergas* out and had examined and repaired injuries as best they could, thankful for no greater disaster, the great bull was gone. They heard him trumpeting far away. The mahout of the *meerga* that had stumbled came up to Cartwright and Leveson, salaaming, apologetic.

"We did not see until it was too late, sahib," he said. "He was too strong for us. Also, he was must."

"Must?" That would account for the ease with which the stout ropes had snapped. "How do you know?" Cartwright asked him.

"Sahib, I saw the flow from his head when he hauled us sideways."

Cartwright translated to Leveson.

"You don't want him," he said. "I'm sorry, but there is no telling if he will get over it. It seems to rot the brain. Must elephants are never to be trusted, and it would be next to impossible to train him."

"Well, that's the luck of it," said the Englishman. "It was great while it lasted. Good thing nobody's badly hurt. Tell that chap his crew gets the reward. They got the rope on first. We'll have to give Pindy the pick of the *durasalas*, I suppose. Might buy him a *koomerich*, put it in with the herd, and give him his pick. He wouldn't choose the best though. Can't be helped. We'll take these chaps back to camp and then, to-morrow, we can get after Rama. What?"

VIII
BATTLE OF THE TITANS

THE LOVE TRYST WAS OVER. Rama and the *koomerich* cow emerged from the glen. He still showed her great affection, waiting for her to choose her food before he ate, or finding tempting selections for her. And she took them, less as her right than as an appreciation of his chivalry.

Presently, in nature's course, they would part company. Now they caressed each other with their trunks and squirted water and dust upon each other. They were heading toward the big river while the wild bull was in the bamboos, so they saw and heard nothing of the chase. But after their swim the cow climbed out on the far side and Rama did not.

Instead, he made for his favorite grove of wild figs. Here Sibi had found his tracks and was waiting to greet him in hope of his speedy arrival. The old mahout was careful not to let Rama wind him and when he saw his former charge start feeding he rejoiced, knowing he had plenty of time. He had already dug a pit, gathered dracæna leaves and lined the hole with dry wood over stones. Now he made fire in this crude oven, well away from Rama. When the ashes were glowing he wrapped rice and cakes in the leaves and put them in to steam, covered with banana fronds and a mound of dirt in which he left vents.

Stealthily he made his way toward the big *koomerich*, his friend, the core of his heart. Rama was eating slowly now, plucking ripe figs for dessert after he had filled his stomach with the milky pulp of the shoots and bark. He was in friendly mood, ruminative. His ears lifted as he heard the sound of a pipe. He knew the tune. The keeper he had loved had often played it to him—Sibi, whose name Rama knew as he knew and understood many things that Sibi said to him.

He turned his head, his big body motionless, his trunk lifted a curve sniffing the air. There was an odor in it that made his mouth water. It was long since he had raided a paddy field or stolen maize. The jungle had satisfied him. But now an odor—

Steamed rice with ghee! Chupatties and sugar! Then Sibi spoke:

"Listen to me, O Rama! This is Sibi, who has slept between thy feet. Sibi, who was always good to thee, O Rama! Rama, the Mighty One, whose tread is like thunder and whose strength is only matched by his beauty!

"This is Sibi, who has fed thee—Sibi, who has groomed and bathed thee, tended thy feet. O Rama, Sibi brings thee food such as thou love! He comes in friendship, Rama, to save thee from a fate thou deserveth not. Be friendly to thy friend, who brings thee offerings."

Sibi's low-pitched voice was pleasant. Pleasant recollections came with the sound of it. Rama saw his old keeper coming through the trees, bearing a big basket.

Sibi advanced slowly, but without hesitation. He felt that Rama knew him, was not hostile, and he spread a mat which he had plaited of reeds and laid upon it the balls of rice, warm and fragrant. Then came piles of chupatties in which he set the goor.

As he served he kept talking soothingly, praising Rama.

The big elephant let out a curious squeak, a sign of pleasure, and curled his trunk, opening his mouth, into which Sibi placed a chupatty cake.

Rama had eaten already but this was different. The rice vanished; also the cakes. Sibi scratched the big beast back of the ears with a stick, standing close beside him.

"We must hide, Rama," he said. "We must go to a secret place where thou wilt be safe from those who think falsely that thou art a rogue—who would kill thee for thy matchless tusks, unless I can persuade them against it. You have taken life, Rama, but I will give thee mine. Shall I go with thee?"

He took hold of one pendulous ear, and Rama swung his trunk gently toward him and curled it about his waist, lifting him. He did not reason that this might be a return to servitude. It had its compensations. The taste of the old, good food was still relishing to the elephant's palate, and he loved Sibi—Sibi, who had known him since he was a hairy, mischievous calf. His emotions were amicable.

Sibi had no goad but he had shaped a forked branch, and Rama responded to his prods as Sibi sat, padless but secure, in the hollow space that the Indian elephant possesses as if designed to hold a rider.

Slowly they moved off and up. Sibi did not as yet attempt to guide his brute friend down to the camp. Of course, the white sahibs would not shoot on sight if they saw *him* placed as mahout on Rama's back, but his plans were as yet confused. He knew a place in a little valley he had found on his trip. There was a pool there where Rama could drink at sunset. Then, heavy with food, Rama would rest and sleep. Sibi also needed sleep. His head was not clear, and he was very tired. He had eaten some of the food he had brought. He did not consider the great wild bull or the *koomerich* cow. He had found Rama, and Rama was once more his friend. That was enough.

The gentle wind blew up the mountain and then stilled. This was hours later. The moon rose over rocky gorges and showed Rama standing under a great tree, motionless, with Sibi between his feet.

Close by, a cleverly built fire burned against a back log. Rama did not mind it. It was made by Sibi, whom he trusted. It might mean more rice and cakes and goor. Once he sighed and then slept, snoring now and then, his stomach rumbling.

On the valley's slope the insane bull stood uncertain. His must fever was intermittent; it no longer controlled his senses. He saw the fire and knew it meant man. A vagrant puff brought man smell. He moved off, a moody brute.

• • •

Once more the day flamed, and Sibi stirred, feeling for Rama's great foot. It was not there. Rama had gone while he slept. He had found him only to lose him.

It had been light for some time. The high crests had lost their rose color, and the sunshine was well on its way down the mountain. The valley was still in shadow, but all objects were plainly visible. Sibi reviled himself for oversleeping. It had been the inevitable result of his troubled mind, the hard work during the drive, in which he had not spared himself to make good his pledge of fealty with his cousin and Cartwright Sahib, and the relief following his meeting with Rama.

He saw where the elephant had stepped over him and followed the tracks that showed so plainly in the dewy herbage. Rama had been careful not to disturb him, but Sibi read the trail that showed Rama breaking into his fastest shuffle, his stride lengthened to the limit. Sibi did not believe that the elephant was deliberately running away from him. Something had happened. Sibi's head no longer ached; his brain was clear. Before he discovered other tracks he guessed much of what had occurred.

Monkeys mocked him as he hurried along the trail. At the mouth of the valley he found that Rama had swung to the right, following the imprints of two other elephants, traveling at top speed. One set was smaller than the other—a cow's. The other tracks might have been Rama's from the size of the marks.

The *koomerich* cow had passed a lonely night. When the moon rose she had re-crossed the river, not seeking Rama so much as searching for her own herd—or any herd at all. Gradually she became panicky, finding that all her fellows had mysteriously vanished. She had not been averse to meeting Rama again. There had been no violent reaction after their brief honeymoon, but the mating urge was over. Now she craved the company of others of her own sex.

In the first gray light of dawn she was close to the valley where Sibi had taken Rama. She would eventually have turned in there had it not been for the must bull. His fit of madness had returned strongly again, and mind and body were poisoned by the mischief it wrought. The thick fluid flowed freely from his head, but it gave him no relief. His senses were functioning badly; his nervous system was short-circuited. Neither sight nor smell registered as it should. He saw phantoms—images filed long ago in his memory—leaping out at random, like a badly assembled movie film. They confused themselves with actual objects of external vision.

Sane, he would never have attacked a female. His instincts were all against it. But they were sidetracked now, running wild, without orders; his cerebral ganglia were congested; the one emotion governing all was hate.

He saw the cow as he stood in a grove of deodars. His head was down, eyes bloodshot, trunk swinging, with the tip twitching back and forth, while he shifted the weight of his enormous bulk from one side to the other.

As she passed, a quarter of a mile away, he sighted her in a reddish haze born of his madness. Her size was uncertain; her scent no longer registered with him, and aroused no emotion of respect. It was a part of his mood, part of his madness, that sought to kill.

He came out of the tree, lunging down hill at a shuffling singlefoot, trumpeting harshly. There was no mistaking that note of menace. The cow heard it and saw him charging her with tusks shining dimly in the dawn and trunk upcurled. She squealed in fright and fled.

She had not his stride, but she was young and agile and she kept ahead. Fear matched the bull's madness in sending extra strength into the fibers of her muscles.

After her the crazy brute came lurching, sounding again and again his wild call. After her first cry the cow was silent.

Sibi, deep sunk in exhausted sleep, heard nothing, but Rama did. He stepped over Sibi and saw his mate racing past the opening of the valley.

He saw the bull behind her, a little closer now, and he swung into his pacing shuffle in pursuit. He did not trumpet. He saved his breath and concentrated on overtaking the bull, set on battle.

The cow fled on, unconscious of a rescuer, all her energies intent on escape. She could feel the ground shake with the tread of the raging bull. He, too, was silent now. There was less than a hundred yards between them— eighty—seventy—sixty—fifty!

He let out one snorting sound like the exhaust of an engine and his trunk extended, as if feeling for his victim. He meant to bowl her over, to thrust his trunks into the quivering body and trample it. Elephant chivalry was forgotten. As long as his must fits were dominant, the mad beast would charge every elephant he came across.

Rage, bred of protection for the mate he had selected and taken, rather than sheer jealousy, spurred Rama. Now the insane bull was conscious of him, coming on behind. So was the cow. They had come far down the slopes. A thicket of giant bamboo stretched across their path, the stems bright in the early sun. Birds flitted through the lacy tufts that waved gently in the morning wind.

The cow was only twenty yards ahead when the bull trumpeted. Rama, too, let out a shrill call like the blare of a bugle. The cow swung to one side just as they reached the edge of the bamboos. The mad bull lurched on. His quarry had disappeared too swiftly for him to make the turn. His foe was at his flank, and he had to turn somehow and face him. The heavy growth of cane gave him the best chance for that. It would interfere with charging, as the stout stems were swinging back and forth. He was not running away, but his cunning prompted him to the only thing to do—maneuver so that he could make his stand and meet Rama head to head.

The cow stood watching the lane they had made, already closing in, but leaving a plain sign of their leviathan progress.

Soon she saw Sibi coming and drifted back between the root pillars of a banyan. His presence made her uneasy. Nature, which had prompted her mating, now issued orders for her to protect herself. A month before she would have stayed to watch and know the result of the combat. But another phase of her life had come. Some time between eighteen and twenty-two months from then, there would be a calf shuffling beside her, hairy as a young mammoth for the first few months, butting and nuzzling at her, a *koomerich* of the first class, blotched with cream markings, even as Rama had been when Sibi first knew him. Her maternal instincts were strong. She watched the old mahout, who had neither eyes nor ears for anything but the bowing bamboos which told him of the whereabouts of the two bulls. Sibi listened to the trumpet calls of anger as Rama, constantly baffled by the thick bamboos from charging, taunted his enemy; and the other, ready enough for slaughter, sidled and circled.

Silently, slowly, the cow moved off. Sibi kneeled and salaamed until his brow touched the ground, invoking the aid of Ganesha, the elephant god. Rama would win, but this other bull must be must to have attacked a cow—his bellows told the hillman what his evil purpose had been toward her. Rama would need all his strength and the protection of Ganesha to offset the influence of the devils that had entered into the other elephant.

Now there was crashing deep inside the grove. There were roars and hoarse gruntings. The bamboos clicked against each other with their silica-hardened stems as the jungle titans thrashed back and forth. The birds had fled. A wild sow and her litter rushed out. Gibbering monkeys, seeking birds' eggs, came helter-skelter, making for the trees and perching there in excitement over the battle royal.

The two bulls were head on at last. They came together with the shock of locomotives, neither yielding, straining their mighty sinews, thrusting with all their strength and weight to gain the advantage. Their trunks were upcurled; vapor formed in the still cool morning air from their bursts of hot breath, sounding their anger.

Their mouths were agape, their rugged teeth exposed as the lower lips curled back and froth dripped from them. The wild bull had turned in a place where the soil had been less fertile and the growth correspondingly less dense. Now the gladiators had trampled down an amphitheater of their own.

They twisted their heads from side to side as their tusks ground together. These weapons were evenly matched, save that Rama's left tusk was still blunted. Again and again the two bulls met, butting and digging deep into the ground with their feet. Their tails were held rigid above the sloping hind quarters, which were braced against bamboo stems or the sides of holes they had gouged out in their struggle.

The loose skin of their flanks swelled like bellows, inflating and deflating. The sun rose as they fought on.

Sibi still besought Ganesha for victory, for the ultimate safety of Rama.

"Thou knowest, O Ganesha," he petitioned, "that Rama is not a rogue—that he was persecuted and wrongly judged. It was but justice which he meted out to the thief that stole his food and tortured him. Now, therefore, do justice to him, Ganesha! And thy servant shall sound thy praises and make votive offerings to thee as long as he lives."

IX

RAMA'S RETURN

ACROSS THE GROVE, HISSAR POINTED OUT THE DISTURBANCE to Cartwright and Leveson. Scouting ahead, he had glimpsed the battle and hurried back to tell the sahibs.

They were out after Leveson's tusks—after Rama, the rogue. Hissar was their shikari. Swain and Russell were superintending the final taming of the captured herd before sending them to the training grounds and elephant markets. It would take two weeks of kindness and special feeding to establish confidence enough to commence the march.

Both the white men were on foot. Four natives attended them, two bearing extra weapons. The Englishman wanted to make his kill from the ground. Cartwright meant to cover him, knowing that buck fever is mild compared to the sight of one's first elephant, where the actual target is so small that the deviation of an inch brings a wild monster charging and towering over the marksman.

"Sahibs, there are two bulls fighting in the bamboos!" Hissar cried.

As the hunters halted they could hear them—the thrashing, the snorts and roars, the trumpeting.

Leveson dropped the monocle from his right eye and slipped it into the pocket of his hunting shirt. He looked to his rifle, holding it at port.

"Do we go in?" he asked.

His nerve was greater than his wisdom. Cartwright shook his head.

"Too risky," he said. "You might get a clean shot, but it's doubtful. Probably have to try back of the shoulder. Anyway, by the time we get halfway through that thicket the whole thing may be over. They can't keep that sort of thing up long. No telling how long they've been at it now. It will quit when one of them gets badly hurt. Both bulls may come out, or the winner may stay there for a while. It's too much of a gamble. You couldn't get a decent sight through the canes, ten chances to one. If either of them charged you'd have a hard time dodging."

"You think it's that mad bull and the rogue?" asked Leveson.

"Not much doubt of it—with the *koomerich* cow the cause of it."

"Gad! If we could only see it! My tusks are in there, Cartwright, whichever wins."

"One wins now," said Hissar.

Out of the bamboos there came a roar of triumph, followed by a shrill trumpet of pain. The thrashing of the canes died down. Then it commenced again. One of the elephants was coming out, heading straight for the waiting party.

"Here are your tusks," said Cartwright, stepping back and a little aside of Leveson. "He'll be head on. Aim just above the line of the eyes, or at the base of the trunk if his head is lowered. Good luck!"

Leveson stood with his lips firmly compressed, his eyes narrowed, the express rifle ready. Outwardly he was as cool as a shooter at clay-pigeon traps. But Cartwright knew the Englishman's pulses were beating fast and hard. No man's could be otherwise, facing, for the first time, a charging elephant that would not be seen until it broke cover thirty yards away. There would be only seconds to choose one's mark, aim, align the sights, and squeeze trigger. The American thrilled to it himself, as he always did, for all his experience. His own blood tingled, but his pulse was normal and his nerves were steady.

It was the wild bull that was coming out.

Rama had forced him to his knees at last and, as he swayed, Rama had set the brass knob of his left tusk to the shoulder and surged forward with the sudden vigor of anticipated victory. The wild bull strove to rise, but Rama shoved again and made him lurch. Then, with a roar, Rama swept forward, raking his ribs, thrusting his right tusk deep into the other's side where it brought up with a *skreel* against the hip bone. As Rama withdrew it the wild bull, shrilling in pain, almost toppled before he regained his feet and fled.

He was still must. It vented its wrath in flailing at the bamboos with its trunk, blundering through while Rama watched, winded, ready to follow slowly. Through the dying tumult of the wounded bull's headlong rush out of the grove Rama heard the clear, thin notes of Sibi's pipe. If Rama had won, Sibi believed he would come out to him. If not, he would go and seek him. He knew that one of the bulls had fled. Then he heard a distant shot, another, and all was silent.

The wild bull, spouting blood from the deep stab, burst into the open. He was running wildly, barely seeing the white figures in his path, the foremost of which raised a shining tube. His head was lowered and he was moaning from pain in his lanced vitals, his trunk twisting like a wounded snake. It made aim and judgment difficult.

Leveson pulled the trigger and his rifle spouted flame, while its heavy recoil set him back a step as he reached for his spare rifle. The bullet struck too high, plowing a deep groove in the bull's skull but not piercing it. The shock of the impact of lead and bone was tremendous, but it failed to check the bull. The animal came on like an express train, stupendous, deadly.

The man with the Englishman's spare gun hesitated. Cartwright Sahib would shoot. Leveson Sahib must leap.

And Leveson started to spring aside as Cartwright's rifle came up and snuggled to his shoulder. He glanced along the barrel at the frenzied bull, then fired.

The steel-jacketed missile went fairly in at the base of the trunk. Leveson, his foot caught in the loop of a ground vine, fell on one elbow. The bull lurched on under the impetus of his last effort. Then the great body shuddered, swayed, and toppled, as Hissar dragged Leveson away.

The big brute, dead in its tracks, its brain shattered, dropped on its knees and then over on its side where, a split tenth of a second before, Leveson had crouched.

He got up, his ruddy face patchy, fumbling for his monocle.

"Lucky for me you were along," he said to Cartwright. "You saved my life," he added to Hissar. "I'll not forget it. It's quite valuable—to me." He paused to fix his glass and, after shaking hands with Cartwright, gave grip in turn to Hissar.

The American admired Leveson's coolness. The latter had already taken a steel tape measure from his pocket and proceeded to gauge the tusks.

"They're really yours," he said to Cartwright. "I can't claim them as my bag. Just the same I'd like to give them to the club. My bet with the major was that I'd bring back a bigger pair than his, but, of course, that meant off my own gun."

"You got in the first shot," said Cartwright. "This is your drive. It's your ivory."

The tusks were eight feet, five inches, perfectly matched.

"There's still Rama," said Leveson. "I might wipe your eye yet, Cartwright."

Hissar came forward.

"Sahib—" he said hesitatingly, then was silent.

"What is it, Hissar?"

"It is nothing, sahib. Unless—"

"There'll be no 'unless' about anything you want from me," said Leveson.

"Remember that, Hissar. Anything Cartwright Sahib or you want from me is yours for the asking. It isn't every day a chap gets his life saved twice inside of two watch ticks. What?"

They were busy getting out the tusks when Hissar straightened up, pointing.

A big elephant, regal and lofty, a *koomerich* of *koomerichs*, with creamy blotches on face and trunk, one tusk tipped with brass, the other stained red, was advancing toward them. On its head, holding a forked stick for goad, was the missing Sibi, sitting cross-legged in the hollow of its skull.

"By Jove!" exclaimed Leveson. "I say, you know, this is most extraordinary. What? Must be the rogue. Can't shoot with Sibi there."

Sibi was calling to them, calling in Hindustani to Cartwright.

"Sahib! This is Rama. He has fought the must bull. Do not shoot, sahibs. I can prove that Rama is no rogue."

He made his plea from where he sat. His voice rang with conviction. Cartwright listened gravely.

"Salute the sahibs, O Rama!" Sibi concluded. "Give them salaam, for they are just men."

Rama curved his trunk in salute. He lifted one foreleg, bent it, and made a salaam. Leveson stared in growing astonishment.

"Don't look as if there was much rogue about him," he said. "What was the mahout saying, Cartwright?"

"If what he says is true, there's a chance that you've got your *koomerich* for the rajah and your tusks on the same day. I'm not sure that it can be arranged, but Sibi says there is a mahout with the koomkies who served in the maharajah's stables and who knows the truth of the matter concerning the treatment that made Rama revolt. He's certainly under control now."

"He won from the crazy bull and chased him out for us," said Leveson. "He deserves consideration. Tell the beggar to bring his pal back to camp. We'll talk it over."

Mirdi Lal, once in the maharajah's service, questioned by Cartwright, assured by Hissar that the sahibs wanted the truth, the whole truth, and nothing but the truth, gave testimony. Moreover, he said that he could produce others who would swear that Rama had been mistreated, deprived of food and water by a thief whom he had justly killed, under due provocation according to elephant law.

They had not spoken before because of the rage of the maharajah at the loss of his best elephant and of his servant. Besides, the head groom had been an uncle of the dead man. Silence was a golden gift of the gods upon such occasions.

Hissar took his stand before the white men at their table on the platform of Leveson's marquee.

"Sahib," he said to Leveson, "this is the thing I would have asked, concerning a reward for me—that Rama be not killed. In this matter I thought my kinsman mad until I saw him on the head of Rama. Now I know that all this is a sending of the gods, whose judgment will be pronounced through thee."

"I'm afraid I don't look much like a mouthpiece for the gods," said Leveson. "What do you think about the matter, Cartwright?"

"There's the government first to consider," returned the American. "The maharajah has a claim, of course, though I doubt if he'd want Rama back. If the district commissioner could be persuaded to revoke the ban, why, it looks as if it *was* a 'sending.' Your friend, Rawalpindi, could hardly hope for a finer elephant than this."

"He has forgotten nothing," Hissar put in. "Sibi has tested him. And he is gentle."

"Pindy will give him a good home," said Leveson. "Whole park to himself. The big chap is evidently happy with Sibi. I've got a certain amount of influence. That is, I can exert what you'd call a 'pull' with the government end of it. Two or three strings I can jerk, I fancy. It happens that the maharajah is a bit embroiled just now. Nothing serious, you know, but I wouldn't be surprised if he'd be nice about Rama. It would be a gracious move on his part and he wouldn't lose anything by it. And, as I have said already, I have a friend or two at court on the British side—relatives. Hissar, send for Sibi.

"Tell him I think we can work the thing out, will you, Cartwright? There's a good chap. Evidently Rama needs no training, but we have to get housings for him and Sibi can deliver him. Look here, Cartwright, why don't you come up with me to Rawalpindi's? Any friend of mine is welcome. He's a good scout, no end."

"I'd like to," Cartwright answered, "but I've got a lot to attend to yet. We've got the herd, but they aren't sold."

"I suppose so. Sorry. I'd forgotten all about the commercial end of it. Leaving that to you, old chap. We'll work out the shares for Swain and Russell and Hissar. Hope yours will satisfy you. I'll go in to-morrow or the next day and get busy with the powers that be. When is a rogue not a rogue? What?"

Cartwright strolled down to the tame-elephant quarters at sunset.

Rama was apart from the rest. Sibi was spreading a mat before him. The handsome *koomerich* had just been watered and now he looked on expectantly at the preparations for his meal. These were fleshpots. The jungle was losing its charm. With Sibi there were many compensations. The food smelled good and there were no stinging furies with the goor.

Sibi crooned as he rolled a ball of rice and poured over it some ghee and cane juice.

"Here, O Rama!" he said. "Take this. To-morrow I will groom thee and attend to your nails. After the rice are chupatties."

Rama opened his mouth for the dainties. Sibi turned and saw Cartwright.

"He eats not with *kionki* cows, Cartwright Sahib," he said. "They are naught but *durasalas* and *meergas*. Rama is a *koomerich*. There are none like him. Make salaam and salute to Cartwright Sahib, Rama."

Eying the food on the mat, but obedient, Rama curved his trunk and made his bow. Cartwright saluted him in return, picked up a rice ball and, as Rama showed the red-lined triangle of his lower jaw, he tossed it in.

"Take good care of him, Sibi," he said idly.

"Sahib! He is the fruit of my eye, the core of my heart! I, Sibi, sleep between his feet. There is none so mighty, yet so gentle, as Rama, whose tread is thunder, and whose glance is lightning. Did he not slay the must bull? Hath he not—"

He was still sounding the praises of Rama while he fed him as Cartwright walked back to his own meal.

OFF-TRAIL PUBLICATIONS
Specializing in the era of American pulp fiction

THE WEIRD DETECTIVE ADVENTURES OF WADE HAMMOND
By Paul Chadwick
Volume 1: 10 stories, 180 pages, $18
Volume 2: 10 stories, 172 pages, $18
Volume 3: 10 stories, 202 pages, $18
Volume 4: 9 stories, 232 pages, $18

The Wade Hammond stories complete in four volumes. In these chilling adventures, all from the classic 1930's pulps, Detective-Dragnet *and* Ten Detective Aces, *freelance investigator Wade Hammond battles a series of weird enemies. Some of the best of '30s pulp fiction.*

DOCTOR COFFIN: The Living Dead Man
By Perley Poore Sheehan • Introduction by John Wooley
8 novelettes, 178 pages, $16

Weird stories from Thrilling Detective, *1932-33. A former character actor who faked his own death, Doctor Coffin runs a string of mortuaries by night and fights crime at night. One of the strangest detective series.*

SUPER-DETECTIVE FLIP BOOK: Two Complete Novels
From the pulp *Super-Detective*:
"Legion of Robots" (November 1940) by Victor Rousseau • Introduction by John McMahan •• "Murder's Migrants" (March 1943) by Robert Leslie Bellem and W.T. Ballard • Introduction by John Wooley
2 short novels, 174 pages, $18

Super-Detective *started as a Doc Savage-like adventure pulp, then changed format to hardboiled detective. The* Flip Book *features a novel from each of the two phases with intros exploring the historical background. Exciting!*

PULPWOOD DAYS: Volume 1: Editors You Want To Know
Edited by John Locke • 180 pages, $16

> *Numerous articles from the writers' magazines by and about pulp editors, with ample biographical profiles. Editors include: Frank E. Blackwell (*Detective Story, Western Story*), Ray Palmer (*Amazing Stories, Fantastic Adventures*), Edwin Baird (*Weird Tales, Detective Tales*), and many more.*

GANG PULP
Edited by John Locke • 19 stories, 294 pages, $24

> *Hardboiled stories of the criminal underworld from the first year (1929-30) of the gang pulps:* Gangster Stories, Racketeer Stories, *etc. These violent tales came under immediate censorship pressure; the history is explored in an in-depth essay. "A remarkable work of popular-culture scholarship"*—MYSTERY SCENE, *Fall 2008.*

THE GANGLAND SAGAS OF BIG NOSE SERRANO
Volume 1: Dames, Dice and the Devil
Volume 2: Horses, Hoboes and Heroes
Volume 3: Hell's Gangster
By Anatole Feldman • Introductions by Will Murray
Each: 4 novels • **Volumes 1-2**: 266 pages, $20 • **Volume 3**: 224 pages, $18

> *The complete Big Nose Serrano novels from* Gangster Stories, Greater Gangster Stories, *and* The Gang Magazine, *1930-35. Feldman was the best of the gang pulp authors, and Big Nose was his most inspired creation, the berserking king of Chicago gangsters.*

CITY OF NUMBERED MEN: The Best of Prison Stories
Introduction by John Locke
12 stories, 278 pages, $20

> *During Prohibition, famed publisher Harold Hersey turned America's disintegrating prison system into the hardboiled* Prison Stories *(1930-31). Included are stories from all six issues of this ultra-rare pulp, the startling history of* Prison Stories, *complete cover gallery, and "Harold Hersey: Tales of an Ink-Stained Wretch," the first comprehensive biography of pulp publishing's most colorful character.*

THE MAGICIAN DETECTIVE: And Other Weird Mysteries
By Fulton Oursler
Introduction by John Locke
7 stories, 210 pages, $18

> *Fulton Oursler was one of the great editors of his time, ruling over the Macfadden publishing empire for two decades. But stage magic was his first love, and, in his heart, he remained a conjurer in a black cape and top hat. In this collection of early fiction, Oursler's bewitching imagination takes flight in tales of magic, murder and mesmerizing mystery. Also featured is an in-depth exploration of the astonishing career of Fulton Oursler.*

GHOST STORIES: The Magazine and Its Makers
Edited by John Locke
Vol 1: 19 stories, 256 pages, $24 • **Vol 2**: 15 stories, 272 pages, $24

> *Macfadden's* Ghost Stories *(1926-31) presented haunted tales in every exciting arena: the Western Front, gangland, aviation, the Klondike, the circus, etc. The personnel behind* Ghost Stories *were a fascinating group: poets and scholars, war heroes and war correspondents, adventurers and Bohemians; a few became prolific pulpsters; a few became bestselling authors. And a few led haunted lives. Vol 1 includes the history of* Ghost Stories, *bios of every editor, and every Vol 1 author. Vol 2 includes bios of every Vol 2 author, every cover artist, and a gallery of all 64* Ghost Stories *covers.*

HOBO STORIES

By Patrick & Terence Casey • Introduction by John Locke
6 stories, 332 pages, $20

The Caseys were two brothers from San Francisco who broke into the pulps while still teenagers. Within a few years, they had conned their way into the prestigious pages of Adventure. Hobo Stories *reprints their series of exploits of a teenage hobo and his dog from* The Saturday Evening Post *(1914) and* Adventure *(1916-21). Included is their story of a teenage pulp writer from* Romance *(1920); and a lengthy introduction which explores the lives of the Caseys and the origins of their hobo stories.*